ALSO BY ALYXANDRA HARVEY

◆ ◆ ◆ ◆ ◆ ◆ ◆ ◆ ◆ ◆ ◆ ◆ ◆ ◆ ◆ ◆ ◆ ◆

The Drake Chronicles: Hearts at Stake
The Drake Chronicles: Blood Feud

Out for Blood

THE
DRAKE
CHRONICLES

ALYXANDRA HARVEY

Walker & Company ✸ New York

First published in the United States of America in December 2010
by Walker Publishing Company, Inc., a division of Bloomsbury Publishing, Inc.
www.bloomsburyteens.com

For information about permission to reproduce selections from this book, write to
Permissions, Walker BFYR, 175 Fifth Avenue, New York, New York 10010

Library of Congress Cataloging-in-Publication Data
Harvey, Alyxandra.
Out for blood / Alyxandra Harvey.
        p.   cm.   — (The Drake chronicles)
Summary: As a senior at the secretive Helios-Ra Academy, eighteen-year-old vampire
hunter Hunter Wild just wants to make it through her last year of school, but in order to
do so she might have to betray her grandfather and date a vampire.
ISBN 978-0-8027-2168-6 (paperback) • ISBN 978-0-8027-2169-3 (hardcover)
[1. Vampires—Fiction.   2. Schools—Fiction.   3. Grandfathers—Fiction.
4. Dating (Social customs)—Fiction.]   I. Title.
PZ7.H267448Ou 2011   [Fic]—dc22   2010008658

Book design by Danielle Delaney
Typeset by Westchester Book Composition
Printed in the U.S.A. by Quad/Graphics, Fairfield, Pennsylvania
2 4 6 8 10 9 7 5 3 1 (paperback)
2 4 6 8 10 9 7 5 3 1 (hardcover)

All papers used by Bloomsbury Publishing, Inc., are natural, recyclable products
made from wood grown in well-managed forests. The manufacturing processes
conform to the environmental regulations of the country of origin.

For Anne, from my inner ferret to yours!

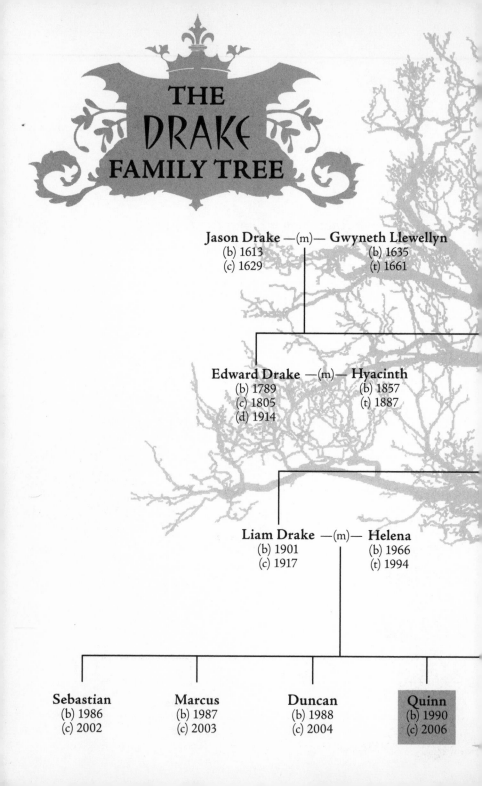

THE DRAKE FAMILY TREE

Jason Drake —(m)— **Gwyneth Llewellyn**
(b) 1613   (b) 1635
(c) 1629   (t) 1661

Edward Drake —(m)— **Hyacinth**
(b) 1789   (b) 1857
(c) 1805   (t) 1887
(d) 1914

Liam Drake —(m)— **Helena**
(b) 1901   (b) 1966
(c) 1917   (t) 1994

Sebastian
(b) 1986
(c) 2002

Marcus
(b) 1987
(c) 2003

Duncan
(b) 1988
(c) 2004

Quinn
(b) 1990
(c) 2006

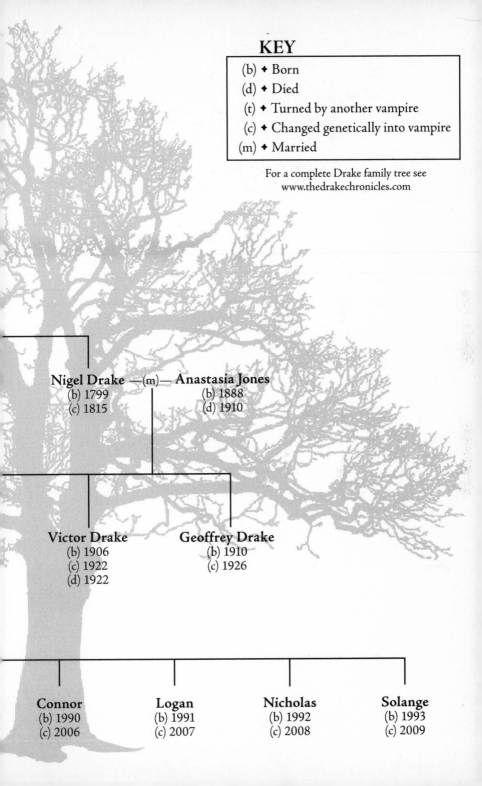

KEY

(b) ✦ Born
(d) ✦ Died
(t) ✦ Turned by another vampire
(c) ✦ Changed genetically into vampire
(m) ✦ Married

For a complete Drake family tree see
www.thedrakechronicles.com

Nigel Drake —(m)— **Anastasia Jones**
(b) 1799   (b) 1888
(c) 1815   (d) 1910

Victor Drake
(b) 1906
(c) 1922
(d) 1922

Geoffrey Drake
(b) 1910
(c) 1926

Connor
(b) 1990
(c) 2006

Logan
(b) 1991
(c) 2007

Nicholas
(b) 1992
(c) 2008

Solange
(b) 1993
(c) 2009

Out for Blood

CHAPTER I

◆

Hunter

Tuesday evening

Shakespeare said, "What's in a name?"

Well, my name's Hunter Wild, so I say: *a lot*.

For instance, you can tell by my name that our family takes our status as vampire hunters very seriously. Good thing I'm an only child—if I'd had brothers or sisters, they might have been named Slayer or Killer. We'd sound like a heavy metal band.

Hard to believe, in reality, we're one of the oldest and most esteemed families in the Helios-Ra. When you're born into the Wild family, no one asks you what you want to be when you grow up. The answer is obvious: a vampire hunter.

Period.

No ifs, ands, or buts. No deviations of any kind.

One size fits all.

"I hate these stupid cargo pants," my roommate Chloe muttered, as she did at the start of every single school year. Classes didn't start for another week, but most of us moved into the dorm early so we could spend that extra time working out and getting ready. Chloe and I have been friends since our first day at the academy, when we were both terrified. Now we're eighteen, about to start our last year, and, frankly, just as terrified. But at least we finally get to be roommates. You only get to make rooming requests in twelfth grade, otherwise they throw you in with people as badly matched as they can find, just to see how you deal with the stress.

Have I mentioned I'm really glad this is our last year?

Even if the room will probably smell like nail polish and vanilla perfume all year. Chloe already had her bare feet propped up on her desk, applying a second coat of silver glitter over the purple polish on her toenails. She was, most emphatically, not wearing her regulation cargos.

I was, but only because my grandfather dropped me off this morning, and he's nothing if not old-school. He's still muttering about our friend Spencer, who has long blond dreads and wears hemp necklaces with turquoise beads. Grandpa can't fathom how Spencer's allowed to get away with it, why there's a newfangled (his word) paranormal division, or why a boy wouldn't want a buzz cut. Truth is, Spencer is such a genius when it comes to occult history, the teachers are perfectly willing to turn a blind eye. Besides, cargos are technically regulation wear only for drills and training and actual fieldwork. And Grandpa still doesn't understand why I won't cut off my hair like any warrior worth her salt.

I totally earned this long hair.

I had to pass several combat scenarios without anyone being able to grab it as a handhold to use against me. Nothing else would extract a promise from Grandpa not to shave my head in my sleep. I think he forgets that I'm not G.I. Joe.

Or that I like looking like a normal girl sometimes, with long blond hair and lip gloss, and not just a hunter who kills vampires every night. Under my steel-toe combat boots my nails are pink. But I'd never tell him that. It would give him a heart attack.

He'd still be out there on patrols if the Helios-Ra doctors hadn't banned him from active duty last year because of the arthritis in his neck and shoulder. He might be built like a bull but he just doesn't have the same flexibility and strength that he used to. He is, however, perfectly capable of being a guest expert at some of the academy fight-training classes. He just loves beating down sixteen-year-old boys who think they're faster and better than he is. Nothing makes him happier, not even my very-nearly straight As last year. The first time Spencer met him, he told me Grandpa was Wild-West-gunslinger scary. It's a pretty good description actually—he even has the squint lines from shooting long-range UV guns and crossbows. And the recent treaty negotiations with certain ancient vampire families are giving him palpitations. In his day, blah blah blah. He still doesn't know Kieran took me into the royal caves last week to meet with the new ruling vampire family, the Drakes. And I'm so totally not telling him until I have to.

Grandpa might be old-school, but I'm not.

I like archery and martial arts, don't get me wrong, and I definitely feel good about fighting the Hel-Blar. They are the worst of the worst kind of vampire: mindless, feral, and always looking for blood. The more violently procured the better. They're faintly blue, which is creepier than it sounds, and they smell like rotting mushrooms.

Needless to say, mushrooms don't get served a lot in the caf.

But I like all the history stuff too, and the research and working with vampire families. I don't think it should be a kill-them-all-and-let-God-sort-it-out situation. I love Grandpa—he took care of me when my parents both died during a botched takedown of a *Hel-Blar* nest—but sometimes he sounds like a bigot. It can be a little embarrassing. Vampires are vampires are vampires to him. If he found out Kieran was dating the sixteen-year-old Drake vampire daughter, he'd freak right out. He thinks of Kieran as an honorary grandson and would totally marry us off to each other if we showed the slightest inclination. Hell, he tries to pair us up anyway, and he's about as subtle as a brick. Kieran's like a brother to me though, and I know he feels the same way about me. I might be willing to sacrifice a lot for the Helios-Ra, but who I date is not one of those things.

Unfortunately Grandpa's not exactly known for giving up. The thing is, neither am I. The infamous goat-stubborn streak runs strong in every Wild, and I'm no exception.

"Would you please change into something decent? Just looking at those cargos is giving me hives." Chloe grimaced at me before going back to blowing on her wet nail polish. She was wearing a short sundress with lace-up sandals and earrings that swung down practically to her shoulders. Her dark hair was a wild mass of curls as usual, her brown eyes carefully lined with purple to match her clothes. She'd already unpacked every stitch of her wardrobe and hung it all neatly in our miniscule closet. It was the only spot of neatness I'd see all year. I'd bug her about her stuff everywhere, and she'd make fun of me for making my bed every morning. I couldn't wait. I'd missed her over the summer. E-mails and texting just aren't the same, no matter what she says.

"I don't mind the cargos," I told her, shrugging.

"Please, I've seen what few clothes you have and they're all pretty and lacy."

"Not a lot of call for lace camisoles in survivalist training and drills," I pointed out.

"Well, since I don't intend to set foot in that smelly old gym until I absolutely have to, I demand you wear something pretty." She grinned at me. "I took you to dinner, didn't I?"

"We went to the caf for mac and cheese," I shot back, also grinning. "And you're not my type."

"Please, you should be so lucky."

A knock at the door interrupted us. Spencer poked his head in. His dreads were even longer and more blond, nearly white. He'd spent most of the summer at the beach, as usual. "I am so stoked to finally be on the ground floor," he said by way of a greeting. "I'm never climbing those stairs again."

"Tell me about it," Chloe agreed.

The dorm was an old Victorian five-story mansion. Ninth graders lived in the converted attic and had to climb the narrow,

steep servant stairs several times a day. Every year we were pro-
moted, we descended a floor. Our window now overlooked the
pond behind the house and the single cranky swan that lived
there.

"That bird's looking at me again," I said. He'd nearly taken a
finger my very first day at the academy when I tried to feed him
the bagel I'd saved from lunch.

Spencer sat on the edge of my bed, rolling his eyes. "It's dark
out, genius."

"I know he's out there," I insisted. "Just waiting for me."

"You can take out a vampire, you can take out a pretty white
bird."

"I guess. You don't know how shifty those swans are." I wrinkled my nose and sat on the end of my bed, resting against the
pillow. "But speaking of vampires—"

"Aren't we always?" Chloe said. "Just once I'd like to talk about
boys and fashion and Hugh Jackman's abs."

"Hello? Like you ever talk about anything else?" Spencer
groaned. "I need more guy friends."

I nudged him with my boot. "Guys would never have been able
to put in a good word for you with Francesca last year," I told him.

"Yeah, but she broke my heart."

"Give me a break. *You* dumped *her.*"

"Because there's only room in my heart for you two lunatics."

I threw a pillow at his head.

"What she said," Chloe agreed, since she couldn't reach her
own pillow.

"And anyway, if you were hanging out burping and scratching

with other guys you wouldn't hear about my visit to the vampire royal caves last week."

"We don't burp and scratch," he turned to eye me balefully. "And *what*?"

Even Chloe put down her nail polish. "Seriously?"

"Kieran took me," I said, a little smugly. It was rare that I was the one with the story to tell. Usually I was too busy trying to get Chloe and Spencer out of trouble to get into any of my own.

"Dude," Spencer whistled appreciatively. "How did you get that past your grandfather?"

"I didn't exactly tell him," I admitted. "I said I was going out for extra credit."

"Finally." Chloe pretended to wipe away a tear of pride. "She's sneaking around and flat-out lying. Our little girl."

Spencer and I both ignored her.

"So what was it like?" he asked eagerly. "Tell me everything. Any rituals? Secret vampire magic?"

"Sorry, nothing for your thesis," I told him. "But a princess from the Hounds tribe was there."

"Get out," Spencer stared at me. "You are the luckiest. What was she like?"

"Quiet, intense, French." Like the other Hounds, she'd had two sets of fangs. "She had amulets around her neck."

"Can you draw them for me?" he asked immediately.

"I could try."

"You two are *boring*." Chloe huffed out a sigh. "Quit studying— we haven't even started classes yet. Tell me about the Drake brothers. Are they as yummy as everyone says?"

"Totally." I didn't even have to think about that one. "It was like being in a room full of Johnny Depps. One of them even kind of dressed like a pirate."

Chloe gave a trembling, reverent sigh. Then she narrowed her eyes at me. "Don't you dare leave me behind next time."

"I think it was a one-time thing. Hart was there and everything." Hart was the new leader of the Helios-Ra and Kieran's uncle. "It was mostly treaty talk. I still don't know why I was invited."

"Because you're good at that stuff," Chloe declared loyally. "Idiot," she added, less loyally.

I hadn't felt particularly skilled, more like the bumbling teenager at a table full of adults. I'd had to remind myself more than once that I'd been invited, that I wasn't obviously useless or an outsider.

Especially when Quinn Drake smirked at me.

All the Drake brothers were ridiculously gorgeous, but he had that smoldering charm down to an art. The kind you only read about in books. I'd always thought it would be annoying in real life.

So not.

Although the fact that he called me "Buffy" all night was less fun.

"You have a funny look on your face," Chloe said.

"I do not." I jerked my errant thoughts away from Quinn. "This is just my face."

"Please, you never turn that color. You're blushing, Hunter Wild."

"Am not." Quinn wasn't my type anyway. Not that I knew what

my type was. Still. I was sure pretty boys who knew they were pretty weren't it.

I was spared further prodding and poking when the lights suddenly went out.

The emergency blue floor light by the door and under the window blinked on. Spencer and I jumped to our feet. The windows locked themselves automatically. Iron bars lowered and clanged shut.

"No! Not now!" Chloe exclaimed, blowing harder on her toes. "They're going to smear."

"Isn't it too early for a drill?" I frowned, trying to see out to the pond and the fields leading to the forest all around us. It was dark enough that only the glimmer of water showed and the half-moon over the main house where Headmistress Bellwood lived. "I mean, half the students aren't even here yet."

"Chloe's the one who's supposed to know this stuff," Spencer said pointedly.

"I haven't had time! I just got here!" She swung her feet to the floor and balanced on her heels, wriggling her toes. Usually she hacked into the schedules and found out when the drills were happening so we'd have some warning. She was disgruntled, scowling fiercely. "This sucks."

"Maybe it's not a drill?" Spencer asked. "Maybe this one's real?"

"It's totally a drill. And I'm registering a complaint," Chloe grumbled, slinging her pack over her shoulder. She didn't go anywhere without her laptop or some kind of high-tech device. "I'm still on summer vacation, damn it. This is so unfair."

"Glad I didn't change out of these," I told her, pulling a flashlight out of one of my cargo pants' many pockets.

"If you spout some 'be prepared' school motto shit, I am so going to kick you."

"Like you'd risk your nail polish," I said with a snort, pushing the door open. "Let's just go."

CHAPTER 2

◆

Hunter

There were students in the hallway, grumbling as they tried the front door.

"Locked." Jason sighed, turning to face us. He'd had a crush on Spencer for two years but Spencer had a crush on Francesca. Or had, anyway, but I seriously doubted he'd switch teams entirely.

"Everything's locked," Jason said. He was wearing flannel pajama bottoms and a white T-shirt. Chloe nearly purred at him even though it was a lost cause.

"Blue light over here," someone called out from the other side of the common room.

Spencer groaned. "So it's a speed drill?"

"Looks like," I agreed.

We followed the rest of the students heading down the hall to the basement door. Good thing it wasn't a stealth test, since it sounded like a herd of elephants thundering down the stairs.

"I hate this hole," Chloe said as we reached the damp basement. She shook her phone. "Nothing ever works down here."

"I think that's the point."

"Well, it's stupid. This whole school's stupid."

Spencer and I just rolled our eyes at each other. Being deprived of Internet access always set Chloe into a snit. It was her forte, after all, and she hated not coming in first.

The trapdoor leading into the secret tunnel was already open. There were sounds of fighting up ahead and very little light. The objective was to get through the tunnel, up a ladder, and onto the lawn. No one elbowed or tripped each other; it was too early in the year. Come midterms and exams there'd be insurrections and mutinies down here.

I heard a squeak from behind us and whirled toward the sound, reaching for the stake at my belt. There was always a stake at my belt. Grandpa never asked me the usual questions growing up like, "Did you brush your teeth?" and "Have you eaten any vegetables today?" It was always, "Got your stake?"

But I wasn't dealing with a vampire or a training dummy. Just a ninth-grade student who was pressed against the wall, crying. She looked about thirteen and there was blood on her nose.

"Hunter, are you coming or what?" Spencer asked.

"I'll catch up," I waved them ahead and ducked under one of the rigged dummies that swung from the ceiling, shrieking. The girl cried harder, trembling.

"Hey, it's okay," I said as she stared at me. "I'm Hunter. What's your name?"

"L-Lia," she stuttered. Her glasses were foggy from the combination of tears and damp underground air.

"Is this your first day?"

She nodded mutely.

"Well, don't worry, Lia, it gets better. Where's your floor monitor?" I asked her. She was way too young to be dealing with this. I couldn't believe her floor monitor hadn't bothered to keep an eye on her. When I found out who she was, I was so going to give her an earful.

"I don't know." Her stake was lying useless at her feet. "I want to go home."

"I know. Let's just get out of here first, okay?"

"Okay." She pushed away from the wall and then jumped a foot in the air when a bloodcurdling shriek ululated down the hall, followed by eerie hissing.

"Never mind that," I told her. "They add all the sound effects to train you not to get distracted. You read about it in the handbook, right?"

She swallowed. "Yeah. It's worse than I thought."

"You get used to it. Look, we need to run down this hall toward the ladder and climb up to get outside. There's going to be dummies swinging at you with red lights over their hearts. Just aim your stake at the light, okay? Think of it like one of those Halloween haunted houses."

"I hate those," she said, but sounded annoyed now, not nearly as scared. She scooped up her stake, holding it so tightly her knuckles must have hurt.

"Ready?"

She nodded.

"Go!"

I took the lead so she wouldn't panic again. The first "vampire" came at me from the left and I aimed for the red light. The second came from the right; the third and fourth dropped from the ceiling together. I let one get away to give Lia a chance to stab at it. It was nothing if not a good way to release frustration. It caught her in the shoulder but she managed to jab the red light.

"I got one!" She squealed. "Did you see?"

"Behind you," I yelled, throwing my stake to catch the one swinging from behind her. The red light blinked out and the dummy came to a sudden stop, inches away from Lia's already sore nose.

"Okay, that was cool," she squeaked, apparently over her little meltdown. The adrenaline was doing its work—I could see it in the tremble of her fingers and the slightly manic gleam in her eyes. It was better than panic.

"Nearly there," I told her over another recording of a grating shriek. "Go, go, go!"

We ran as fast as we could.

"Jump that one." I leaped over a dummy crawling out of a trapdoor. The tunnel was empty of other students but I could see a faint light up ahead. "Nearly there."

When we reached the ladder I pushed her in front of me. She scrambled up like a monkey. She had good balance if nothing else.

I was the last one out.

Two teachers and all of the students waited in a clump, watching for us. Lia's face was streaked with dirt and dried tears and her lip was swollen, but at least she was smiling.

"Well, well, Miss Wild." Mr. York held up his stopwatch with the most condescending sneer he could muster. "Apparently you've gotten rusty over the summer. What will your grandfather say to hear a Wild came in dead last?" He was enjoying this way too much. It was no secret that Mr. York hated my family, and Grandpa in particular. He'd been on my case since my first day at the academy. Chloe pulled a hideous grimace behind his back.

"It's my f-fault, sir," Lia stammered. "Hunter stopped to help me out."

"Did she now? Well, admirable as that may be, this is a speed test." He made a mark on his clipboard.

I really wanted to stake that clipboard.

"I hardly think Hunter should be penalized for showing group loyalty," Ms. Dailey interrupted. "We are teaching them loyalty and courage, aren't we? As well as speed?"

"Be that as it may, this test is timed. Rules are rules."

"Her floor monitor should have been looking out for her," I muttered.

"What was that, Miss Wild?" Mr. York asked.

"Nothing, sir."

"I distinctly heard *something*, Miss Wild. Students, quiet down please. Miss Wild is having trouble being heard."

God, he was a pain in my ass.

"I was only wondering where her floor monitor was." First day and I was getting reamed out for helping someone. This just sucked.

He frowned at his clipboard. "Courtney Jones."

I had to stifle a groan. Of course it would be Courtney. We'd been roommates in tenth grade and frankly, I don't think either of us was over it yet. To say we didn't get along and had nothing in common was a gross understatement. She was so in league with the nasty swan.

Courtney stepped forward, smiling winningly. "Yes, Mr. York?"

Kiss-ass.

"Is this student on your floor?"

"Yes, Mr. York."

"And did you leave her behind?"

"*No*, Mr. York." She sounded stunned and deeply grieved. Mr. York, of course, totally fell for it. At least Ms. Dailey pursed her lips. It was a small victory but the only one I was probably going to get. "Lia was right behind me, sir. She told me she was fine."

Lia was blinking like a fish suddenly hauled out of a lake. "I—"

"I see," Mr. York said, tapping his lips with his pen as if he was deep in thought. I shifted from foot to foot. Spencer shot me a commiserating wince. I winced back.

"Seeing as you are so concerned with the ninth graders' welfare, you will be Courtney's assistant. You can be in charge of all their delicate sensibilities and making sure they get through drills." Which, loosely translated, meant Courtney would get her big single room on the fourth floor and "floor monitor" on her transcripts but I would be doing all the actual work. And she'd get to boss me around. She smirked at me.

"Do you have a problem with that, Miss Wild?" Mr. York snapped.

"No, sir." I sighed. I refused to slump, even though I really wanted to. I was so not going to let him see how much he'd just screwed up my last year for me. I didn't know anything about taking care of ninth graders—or Niners, as we called them. And my course load was already approximately the size of an Egyptian pyramid. The big one.

"Good. You're dismissed," he barked at everyone before stalking across the lawn toward the teachers' apartments. Ms. Dailey patted my shoulder before following him. Courtney sneered at me and flounced away.

"I'm sorry, Hunter," Lia said, looking like she was about to burst into tears again.

"Don't worry about it," I told her.

"I didn't mean to get you in trouble," she said. "But I'm really glad you're one of our floor monitors now." She lowered her voice. "Courtney's a bitch."

I laughed despite myself. "Yes. Yes, she is."

Chloe and Spencer descended, all inflamed with righteous indignation on my behalf. Chloe shook her head. "I guess York still has it in for you. Jerk."

"That was totally unfair," Spencer agreed. "You should see the headmistress."

"No way," I said. The only teacher worse than Mr. York was Headmistress Bellwood. "She'd only tell me I was whining anyway."

"I guess. She's not exactly big with the warm and fuzzy."

Chloe slung her arm through mine. "Come on, we'll go drink hot chocolate and watch some old *Supernatural* episodes on DVD. Dean Winchester always cheers you up."

"I thought our last year was supposed to be fun," I said, kicking at dandelions as we skirted the gardens toward the now-unlocked front door.

From the direction of the pond, the swan honked mockingly.

◆

No one felt like staying up very late after that. We watched a couple of episodes and then went to our rooms. The halls were quiet. Chloe marched to her desk and turned on her computer with a determined click and set her laptop next to it. The screens flickered to life, pooling pale light over the carpet.

"I thought you were tired," I told her.

"I'm already behind," she said. "They got us by surprise. And York smirked at me like he knew. I'm so going to get him for that. And for ragging on you all the time." She cracked her knuckles. "And it starts now."

"You were the one complaining that it was too early to study."

"I changed my mind. I'm going to ace this year and then shove it up his nose." Mr. York, along with being the proverbial thorn in my side, was also one of the combat teachers. Chloe was quick and fierce on a computer but she wasn't quite as good in hand-to-hand fights. He'd only barely passed her last year.

I left her to stew. I didn't want to talk about York. It would make me grind my teeth. I didn't know anything about being a floor monitor. My jaw clenched. If I was going to relax at all, I was going to need what was in the trunk under my bed. Watching TV had helped settled my mood some, and so had Chloe's stash of chocolate macaroons, but this required the big guns. No matter how much Chloe was going to make fun of me. I pulled it out, hoping she was too buried in her work.

No such luck.

"Are those romance novels?"

I shot her a look through my hair, which was falling over my face. "Yes. And shut up."

"I didn't know you read romance novels."

"Shut up."

She turned on her wheeled desk chair. "You told me last year that you kept your stakes and stuff in there."

I pulled a book out, wondering if I should even bother trying to hide the cheesy cover. Chloe was a pitbull. "I also told my grandfather I kept my tampons in here."

"I am totally digging this new side of you."

Since she wasn't making as much fun of me as I'd thought, I stopped scowling. "I know it's silly, but I like them. They don't make me think too hard and there's always a happy ending."

"Lend me one."

"Seriously?" I asked.

"Totally. That one with the cleavage and the guy with the mullet."

I snorted. "That's all of them. The hair is rather unfortunate."

"How about that one?"

"Can't go wrong with a duke." I tossed it to her.

"Are there naughty parts?"

"Not in that one."

She tossed it back. I laughed and handed her a new one. It was five hundred pages of Victorian historical intrigue. She stared at it. "This is bigger than half the stuff on our lit class syllabus."

"Probably better researched too."

She put it next to her laptop and went back to the mysterious things she did on the Internet. I could check my e-mail and navigate some basic blog sites but that was about it. She could probably hack into government sites if we gave her enough time.

I read until she finally went to asleep and my cell phone vibrated. It was two in the morning. I flipped it open and read the text waiting for me from Kieran.

Get dressed and meet me outside.

CHAPTER 3

♦

QUINN

Connor didn't bother knocking, just opened the door and stuck his head into my room. He was pale, and not because he spent most of his time at his computer. Vampires didn't tan well and the Drakes were no exception. "Quinn, it's time."

I wiped blood off my lower lip and tossed the glass bottle in the blue recycling box sitting under a poster of Megan Fox. Connor and I were both turned three years ago on our sixteenth birthday. As twins, we shared the same blue eyes and dark brown hair and the same uncanny ability to know what the other was thinking. We'd also shared the sickness, the struggle to survive, and the searing bloodlust when we woke that first day as vampires.

Now we shared the same bloodlust every time the sun set, but it was starting to get a little better, just as Dad had promised it would. He didn't lock my bedroom door from the outside anymore.

"Better hurry, Dad's got that look on his face," Connor warned me as we ran down the stairs from the top floor of the house that we shared with our five brothers. Our sister, Solange, had a room on the second floor, which was most definitely locked—from the inside and outside—when she went to bed every single morning. She'd only turned a couple of weeks ago and our delicate, serene baby sister turned feral at the last ray of sunlight. Her best friend, Lucy, was staying in one of the guest rooms, as far away from Solange's bedroom as physically possible. We made her promise to engage the dead bolt, and Mom set two of the farm dogs to guard her every night at dusk. Just in case.

She shouldn't have been living in our house at all while Solange was so volatile. It was dangerous and, frankly, stupid. All of us could smell the sweet hot rush of the blood in her veins. It was like living inside a bakery, constantly surrounded by tempting pastries and cakes with chocolate frosting. Nicholas had a will of iron. I don't know how he did it, resisting the tender flesh on her neck every time she hugged him or he smelled her hair. My fangs poked out of my gums just a little whenever she was nearby.

I was not good at resisting girls.

Still, Lucy had practically grown up here, and since she was dating my brother she was thoroughly off-limits. And she was stuck with us for at least another week since her parents were out of town, even though vampire politics, which were messy at best, had just exploded all over us.

"Mom deserves a little pomp and circumstance, don't you think?" I asked, keeping my voice low as we passed Aunt Hyacinth's room. I wondered if she'd finally venture out of the house for the coronation. "I mean, it's not every day a vampire queen gets crowned."

"You know Mom prefers it low-key. And anyway, I like to think we're too smart to attempt a *third* elaborate ceremony."

Connor was right. Mom was pronounced queen after killing the last self-proclaimed queen Lady Natasha—to stop her from killing Solange over an ancient prophecy that foretold Solange's birth and her own rise to the throne. Now everyone was trying to kill both Mom *and* Solange. Not exactly an improvement. No one holds a grudge like a centuries-old vampire. You'd think they'd learn to lighten up eventually.

"Hell of a lot of fuss over a thankless job," I said. "Controlling vampire tribes is like herding cats. Into a bathtub. Blindfolded." I tossed my hair off my shoulder and winked at Solange, who was sitting on the bottom step, looking miserable. "Maybe we just need a king. Someone charming and handsome like me."

She flashed me a grin. "Your head's too fat for a crown."

Connor snorted and continued down the hall into the living room. I sat next to Solange. "What's up? Sitting alone in the dark is too gothic for you. Leave that sort of thing to Logan."

"I just hate this whole stupid thing," she muttered. "If one more person tries to kill someone I love over that damn prophecy, I swear I'll go postal."

I put an arm over her tense shoulders. "It'll be fine. Mont-martre's dead. And you know we'll protect you."

She speared me with a glare that could have fried the hair off my head. "That right there, Quinn Drake, is exactly what I mean. Protect yourself, not me."

I rolled my eyes. "Hello? Big brother. Occupational hazard."

"Well, get over it," she grumbled. "I seriously can't take much more. I won't have your blood on my hands. It's bad enough Aunt Hyacinth nearly died."

"But she didn't die. Drakes are harder to kill than that." She'd been seriously burned by Helios-Ra holy water, though. It ate away at her face like acid and now she refused to lift the heavy black veils she wore hanging from her little Victorian hats. "Why aren't you in there with everyone else?"

She shrugged. "No reason."

"Liar."

She shrugged again.

I frowned. "Spill it, Solange."

"I'm fine, Quinn." She sent me an ironic grin. "I can protect *you* too, you know. Annoying, isn't it?"

"Very."

She hugged me briefly. "I don't mean to sound ungrateful. I'm just worried."

I noticed the dark smudges under her eyes. Her fangs were out and her gums looked a little raw, as if she'd been clenching her jaw. "And you're hungry," I said quietly.

She looked away. "I'm okay."

"Solange, are you drinking enough? You're looking kinda skinny."

"I'm drinking plenty. I just woke up and I'm ..." She swallowed, fists clenching. "How do you get used to it? It's like this itch crawling inside me and there's no way to scratch it. You guys made this look easy. I think it's worse than the bloodchange. At least

I was unconscious through most of that. But now the lights hurt, everyone sounds like they're yelling. And Lucy." She looked like she might cry.

"What about her?"

"Lucy smells like food." She nearly gagged saying it.

I kept my smile light and didn't let her see anything but her reckless big brother who loved a good fight and a pretty girl and not necessarily in that order.

"Sol, all that's normal. Lucy smelled good before I turned and now she smells even better. But I haven't tried to eat her face and neither will you."

"She's not safe in this house."

"Safer than out there," I argued, even though I agreed with her. "Look, you used to eat hamburgers."

She blinked, confused. "So?"

"So, did you ever walk through one of the farms at a field party and suddenly try to eat a cow?"

"Um, no." Her chuckle was watery but it was better than nothing. "And, ew."

"Exactly. You can crave blood and not eat your best friend."

"You make it sound so normal. And I'm totally telling Lucy you compared her to a cow." She jerked a hand through her hair. "Between Lucy and Kieran I feel . . . dangerous."

I shrugged, trying not to scowl at the thought of Kieran and my little sister. "You should talk to Nicholas. He's looking as squigee as you are."

"Squigee? I'm squigee?" She poked me. "I don't know what that is but I am prepared to feel insulted."

"Nah, no need to be insulted. You got the Drake cheekbones like me. Saves you every time."

"Okay, no more whining," she announced decisively, faking a bright smile. "I'm getting on my own nerves. Let's go make Mom a queen."

"Yeah, because her self-esteem's so fragile otherwise," I said drily as we pushed to our feet. "She needs the boost of a crown."

"I heard that, Quinn Drake."

I winced. Vampire mothers had unfair advantages. "Love you, Mom!"

She stalked out of the living room trailing the rest of the family like the train of a dress. Her hair was in a severe braid as usual, her mouth stern. But her eyes were bright. "That's how you used to try to get out of trouble when you were little."

I grinned. "Does it still work?" She sighed, giving in to a smile. I winked at Solange. "See? Don't underestimate the cheekbones."

"Let's go." Bruno, the head of Drake security, opened the front door. The porch light made his neck tattoos look faded. He had so many weapons stashed under his coat it was a wonder he could move at all.

Dad stood very close to Mom, eyeing each of us. "We're going the long way. The rest of you go east and circle around to meet us there. Protect your sister."

Solange went red. Lucy squeezed her hand sympathetically. Solange swallowed hard and shifted a step away. Lucy frowned, looking confused and hurt. The door shut behind our parents, Uncle Geoffrey, and Bruno.

"Where's Aunt Hyacinth?" I asked.

"She's not in her rooms," Lucy said. "I knocked. I wanted to borrow one of her lace shawls."

"She will be there," Isabeau murmured in her heavy French accent. She was a Hounds princess and the reason Logan looked extra fancy in a new velvet frock coat. He couldn't stop looking at her, as if he was afraid she might drift away. There were scars on her arms and she had her dog with her as usual. He was a huge Irish wolfhound, the top of his shaggy head reaching nearly to her waist.

"Everyone ready?" Sebastian asked calmly. He was the eldest and usually traveled with our parents. It was a mark of how worried they were that he was with us instead. We got into formation, circling Solange and Lucy, guiding them outside and across the driveway to the fields leading to the woods.

"I feel like I'm in the witness protection program," Lucy whispered. "You guys need suits and dark glasses."

"I'm not wearing a suit even for you, sweetheart," I whispered back.

"You're no fun."

As the silence stretched uncomfortably, she started to hum the theme song to *Mission: Impossible* under her breath.

Solange smothered a startled laugh. "Are you nuts?"

"Your brothers need to meditate. They're all stressed out and their chi is bunching up. That can't be comfortable."

"I don't even know what that means," Nicholas hissed at her. "But there's this whole stealth thing we're going for. You're not helping."

Lucy grinned at Solange. "He's so cute when he tries to be all Alpha male."

"This is serious, Lucy."

She reached and pulled a piece of his hair. "I know that. But we're barely off the driveway."

"If you don't stop talking I will hide all of your chocolate," Nicholas promised. Lucy stuck her tongue out but she stopped chattering.

The forest was heavy with the sounds of scurrying animals and insects boring through trees and the ever-present wind slinking through the pine boughs. We crossed the narrow river, using a fallen oak trunk covered in moss. Everyone but Lucy moved so fast that we seemed to blur a little around the edges. She was panting for breath by the time we stopped in a meadow. "I'm going to need to take up jogging or something," she gasped. "For that alone, I hate you."

We let her rest for a few minutes and then continued toward the meeting spot. We didn't expect trouble since the ceremony had only been announced to a very few select individuals soon after sunset. No advance warning made it harder for our enemies to find us and disrupt the ceremony. Isabeau found the guiding mark in a tree and pointed to her left. We followed her into another meadow, ringed with pine trees. The crickets stopped singing.

We were the first ones to arrive. It took another half hour before the other council members showed up with their atten- dants. The Raktapa Council was secretive to the extreme and they didn't travel light, not even to a clandestine coronation. There were family banners and bodyguards and a lot of suspicious regal glares. The Amrita family favored caftans and saris. The Joiik were descendants of some ancient Viking vampire and were blond, pale as sunlight on armor. And we often looked like we belonged in some bizarre medieval-Victorian costume party. Of all of us there that night, only my brothers and Solange and I wore clothes from this century. Except for Logan, of course. He wore his usual eighteenth-century frock coat. And Lucy just looked like a confused time traveler, as always. Or like a little girl who'd just gone through her mother's dress-up trunk.

Mom and Dad would be here soon. Hart wasn't far either; I could hear the growl of his motorcycle on the other side of the grove. It was unprecedented for the leader of the Helios-Ra to be invited to a vampire coronation. We were making history in more ways than one tonight. The best part was that Aunt Hyacinth had joined us. She came out of the pine trees, still swathed in black lace veils, but at least she was here.

Lucy leaned into Nicholas, holding his hand. Logan and Isabeau were quiet but standing very close.

My brothers had the right idea.

We had time to kill, might as well have a little fun.

I caught the eye of a vampire girl from the Joiik entourage. She had long red hair and she smiled at me, flashing a provocative peek of fang. And a lot of cleavage. I grinned.

"Call me when it's about to start," I told Connor, following her into the woods.

CHAPTER 4

◆

Hunter

Tuesday night

Kieran was waiting for me behind the oak tree by the lane.

"What's going on?" I asked, yawning. I'd pulled my hair back in a messy ponytail and threw my cargo pants back on with the tank top I slept in.

"We're going on a field trip," he said smugly.

I blinked. "What, *now?*"

"Yeah, so hurry up." The teachers' main house was dark except for one of the upper bedrooms. The dining hall was deserted. Headmistress Bellwood's house was farther down the driveway and dark as well. "It's a long walk."

"Why can't we take one of the bikes? There's dozens of them in the garage." The forest was so thick and there were so many fields that motorbikes were the easiest mode of transportation most of the time. On our own two feet, we'd never outrun a vampire in a million years. Bikes gave us a fighting chance.

"Kinda hard with this," he lifted his arm, wrapped in a soft cast. He'd hurt it last week helping to take down the old vampire queen, Lady Natasha. He had all the fun. "And you know they monitor the fuel gauges in those things."

I raised my eyebrows. "So the teachers don't know about this little side trip."

"No."

"Kieran, I'm already in trouble."

He snorted. "You're never in trouble."

"York."

He winced. "Bummer. Well, forget him. Hart himself gave permission to have you there."

"Seriously?"

"Yeah, so let's go already," he said impatiently. "It's at least an hour's walk from here."

"Where the hell are we going?" I muttered as we cut through the field and into the woods. The mosquitoes swarmed almost instantly. I slapped them away. This had better be worth it.

"Vampire coronation," he answered.

Totally worth it.

"What? Really? How did you get me clearance?"

"Hart asked for you. You shouldn't sound so shocked; you were at the meeting last week. You did good, kid."

"Kid? You're barely a year older than me."

"But I'm wise, little sister."

"Just get us there, Obi-Wan."

The moon poured out enough light to make the grass silver. The mosquitoes got worse the farther in we hiked and I didn't care one bit. We were going to a vampire coronation.

Grandpa would have been horrified.

I was thrilled.

There hadn't been one for over a hundred years. The last "queen," Lady Natasha, had been tolerated, not officially crowned. When her lover, Montmartre, discarded her and set his sights on Solange Drake, Lady Natasha had gone crazy and tried to kill Solange. Everyone knew she was the first girl born to the Drake family in eight hundred years and prophesied to be the next queen. Only, she didn't want to be queen—though that was hardly enough to stop Montmartre. He'd tried to abduct and marry her to take her power, but he'd been foiled by the Drakes and Isabeau St. Croix, the Hound princess I'd met at the treaty talks. And Kieran, of course, who was Solange's boyfriend now and wore his broken arm proudly. With Montmartre finally dead, the Host, minions who had acted as his personal army, had scattered. It gave the Helios-Ra an advantage.

The hundreds of *Hel-Blar* that Greyhaven, Montmartre's lieutenant, had created and left to run savage took that advantage away again.

There were so many of them that they were starting to close in on Violet Hill and other small towns in the area. The school now required twelfth-grade students to help on patrols until the problem was dealt with.

We walked for almost an hour until we reached a clearing with several parked motorcycles, all black. Helios-Ra agents. Hart and his group must have arrived already.

"Are we late?" I wished I was wearing proper clothes. I looked completely rumpled. I wasn't sure what one wore to a vampire coronation, but I had a feeling cargos and a tank top weren't it. I didn't even have my jacket with the vials of Hypnos set in the sleeves. Hypnos was a fairly new drug we carried in powdered form in little pen-shaped devices. Anyone who inhaled it, vampires included, were hypnotized for a short time into doing whatever they were told. It helped balance the odds since humans were susceptible to vampire glamour. Chloe's mom was a biochemist and had helped develop the newest version of Hypnos.

Of which I had none tonight.

"I'm not prepared." I showed him my bare wrists. No Hypnos, no daggers, nothing.

"You won't need anything," he assured me. "Besides, I know for a fact that you have no less than three stakes on you right now, and those boots have blades in the soles."

"Still."

"We don't have time to go back." He nudged me gently into a jog, flipping open his cell phone to use the GPS. "We're not far. The coordinates came in just before I got you."

"It's not at the caves with all the pomp and ceremony?"

"No way. After two botched assassination attempts in a single week, the Drakes decided on a secret coronation."

"That is so cool." And I still couldn't believe I'd been invited. "Will the council be there?"

"Representatives from each ancient family, yeah."

The Raktapa Council were formed of the three most ancient and powerful vampire families. The Helios-Ra had a similar council.

"Who else? The Hounds?"

"Yeah, Isabeau, the princess you met last week."

"That is so cool." I nearly bounced on my toes. "Thanks for coming to get me."

"Just don't tell Caleb it was me."

"As if I'm telling Grandpa at all."

"Good plan."

The concept of treaties between the peaceful vampire families, the Helios-Ra, and the Hounds was exciting to me. As exciting as firearms and surprise nest-takedowns was to Grandpa. And we'd almost lost the chance at an alliance entirely when Hope, one of the higher-ups, had sent her own rogue unit to attack the Drakes. She'd nearly taken down the entire society with her, putting any future hope of diplomacy in serious danger. I really admired Hart and what he was trying to do. Especially since Hope had killed his brother and partner, Kieran's father, in order to rule with Hart. Grandpa, of course, wasn't exactly full of admiration for the treaty. Big surprise. I hated to disobey him even when I knew he was wrong. So if he didn't know about it, he couldn't forbid me to be a part of it and I wouldn't have to lie and do it anyway.

"Can't we go any faster?" I urged, nearly plucking the GPS out of Kieran's hand. This was better than prom.

He swatted me away. "Cut it out."

"Can you believe we're doing this?" I shook my head. "I thought you were usually on Grandpa's side with this stuff."

"Yeah, then I met a girl."

I smirked. "I totally love that."

"Yeah, yeah. It also helped to learn that vampires didn't kill my father."

We stepped around a copse of elm trees and came face-to-face with a vampire, armed to his pointy fang-teeth. Instinct had me reach for my stake. He was wrestler-huge and bone-pale.

"We got the call," Kieran said, stepping in front of me. He stomped on my foot while he was at it. I fell back, but only a little. I might be thrilled to be here but I was still in training. I didn't smile prettily at vampires in the middle of the night in the middle of the woods. I was no Little Red Riding Hood.

"Password?"

Kieran glanced down at his phone's display and read off a word in a language I'd never heard before. It sounded old.

The guard nodded. "Go ahead. Turn right at the cedars and go straight through into the pine forest."

"Thanks."

It felt weird to turn my back on a vampire. I must have more of Grandpa in me than I thought.

The red pines towered above us, the ground a carpet of fallen needles and not much else. In the center, Helena Drake and her husband, Liam, waited, along with most of their sons, Isabeau, Lucy, and a bald human bodyguard. Hart was on Liam's left, with three more hunters. The Raktapa families were there, each with a guard holding up a banner painted with their family insignia. The Drake banner was a dragon entwined with ivy and Latin words I couldn't read. There were other vampires as well, nearly a dozen of them.

I didn't see Quinn.

Not that I was looking for him.

And not that his twin, Connor, wasn't standing right next to Solange, looking exactly like him. Except that Connor's hair was shorter.

Still.

I followed Kieran to Hart's side. He kept sending Solange sidelong glances. She smiled, pale as a pearl. Her fangs were very sharp but delicate. Treaties were all well and good in theory but something else entirely when a vampire was flashing fangs at someone you considered to be your brother. I wondered if I should worry about him.

"Hunter." Hart smiled at me. "Glad you could make it."

"Thank you, sir." I tried not to flutter and went overboard into formal cadet stance. He was the head of the entire society and he knew my name and he'd asked for me specifically.

"At ease," he said. "You're here to witness history, not do battle," he added.

"Yes, sir."

"We're nearly ready," Liam called out pointedly.

Quinn sauntered out of the woods, a vampire girl on his arm. They were both grinning and it was totally obvious what they'd been doing. He was just as gorgeous as I remembered, his long hair falling nearly to his shoulders, his eyes so blue they didn't seem real. The girl giggled.

I refused to stare. Mostly.

It wasn't my fault if I could still see him out of my peripheral vision. It was a hunter's duty to be aware of her surroundings.

Even if those surroundings included a beautiful vampire with a charming smile who liked to flirt with anything that had boobs.

Except for me, apparently.

I did *not* just think that.

Luckily the ceremony began before I embarrassed myself completely. I was also exceedingly grateful that vampires couldn't read minds.

Quinn was only smirking at me because he smirked at everybody.

Helena stepped forward, flanked in a semicircle by Liam and Hart on one side, the Council representatives and Isabeau on the other. The rest of us stepped back to form a loose clump of bystanders who eyed each other cautiously. We'd all lost family members to each other at some point in our history. You didn't automatically forget that.

"Weapons down," Helena said grimly.

The reaction was equally grim. No one wanted to be the first to relinquish any weapon, not in this crowd. Glances flickered back and forth, mouths tightened, hands curled into fists. No one moved.

Until Solange lifted her chin and pulled three stakes from her belt, holding them up so that everyone could see. Then she dropped them in the grass.

Silence. The kind you can only get when you're surrounded by vampires. It made my shoulders tense.

Helena was the next to disarm herself. She had a small arsenal on the ground by the time she was done. Everyone else followed their lead until we stood in a circle of discarded stakes, swords, daggers, crossbows, and Helios-Ra UV guns.

The coronation was simple and quick; there were too many *Hel-Blar* in the area and too many unproven loyalties. I imagined the more traditional version was longer and full of grand speeches and costumes. This one was as impressive in its own way. At least, I thought so. The pine trees were solemn, silent witnesses and the wind was warm and smelled of wet earth, tossing the boughs aside to show us glimpses of the stars. A wolf howled in the distance. Fireflies glimmered all around us.

Liam's voice was warm as whiskey and just as strong. "Do you acknowledge Helena Drake as the queen of the vampire tribes by right of conquest?"

One by one the representatives knelt, saying "aye." The council members wore elaborate gowns and suits. Isabeau didn't kneel, but she inclined her head respectfully. The Hounds offered fealty to no one but their Shamanka. Spencer would have given his left arm to meet that Shamanka but she wasn't here. Apparently she never left her caves. Hart nodded as well.

I tried not to look as awed as I felt. Helena stepped forward. Her hair was in a long black braid down her back and she wore a sleeveless black dress with a wide belt that normally hung with daggers and stakes. Her boots made me drool. I was sure she could have concealed at least four different kinds of knives in them. I *so* had to get myself a pair.

"I promise to stand between the tribes and danger, to foster autonomy and respect between the families, the councils, and the society. I promise to be your queen until such time as my daughter might choose to relieve me."

"Oh, Mom, not you too," I distinctly heard Solange mutter. Kieran reached for her hand. She leaned into him. A few of the vampires stared at them. Someone hissed and was elbowed into silence.

Helena dropped to one knee after everyone else had risen again. "I serve the tribes."

Liam unwrapped a velvet bundle, producing a slender silver circlet. It was set with three huge rubies and smaller pearls. Liam crowned his wife, looking proud. Isabeau tilted her head faintly, frowning thoughtfully at the crown.

There was a round of applause and silver pendants were handed out to the assembled group. They looked kind of like Catholic saint medallions, only they were imprinted with the Drake insignia on one side and the royal symbol on the other—a ruby-encrusted crown and sword. I slipped mine into my pocket. I couldn't wait to get back to the dorm where I could properly admire it.

The way another vampire, a different girl this time, was admiring Quinn.

There was no doubt he was a player, and there was no doubt none of his girlfriends minded. I turned away, waiting for Kieran and Solange to finish their discreet snuggling. The council was already leaving, to spread the word of the coronation. I shivered lightly in my tank top as the night cooled.

"Hey, Buffy."

I froze.

Quinn.

I turned slowly on my heel. "My name's Hunter."

"I know." He grinned. He was wearing his medallion around his neck on a silver chain. "But you've got the whole Buffy thing going. Though I think you might be cuter."

I was *not* going to giggle. I wasn't that kind of girl.

And hunters didn't giggle at vampires.

It was an unspoken rule.

"You're cold," he murmured when goosebumps lifted on my arms. I was really glad I *was* cold and didn't have to wonder if his presence was making me shivery and ridiculous. He stepped closer to me, blocking the wind. Pretty much blocking everything. "Better?" he asked casually, the way Spencer talked to me. Still, he was really close.

"Oh my God, Quinn," Lucy interrupted, causing us both to jump. "Could you stop flirting for three seconds and come *on?*"

CHAPTER 5

◆

Hunter

Wednesday Morning

Chloe was far too cheerful.

"Am not," she insisted, sipping root beer out of a straw as loudly as she could to annoy me. "You're just grumpy."

It was possible she was right. I hadn't even realized I'd spoken out loud.

I hadn't gotten back until four o'clock in the morning and it was only eight thirty now. We didn't get up this early even when we had classes, because they ran from 1:00 to 4:00 P.M. and again from 8:00 P.M. to midnight. We had to be used to late hours in our line of work. And Chloe was usually the last one out of bed, grumbling the entire time. I didn't know how or why she'd become a morning person over the summer but I suspected it was just to bug me.

I pulled my pillow over my head. "Too early."

"Just taking my vitamins," she said.

"You don't take vitamins."

"I do now. Mom gave them to me after my last report card. And these gross protein shakes, which I conveniently forgot to pack." She slurped more root beer. Loudly.

"Don't make me stake you." I revealed just enough of one eyeball to glare at her menacingly.

She grinned. "Morning to you too, sunshine. Want a vitamin?"

"Who are you, evil pod person, and what have you done with Chloe?" I was too tired even to yawn. My eyes felt glued shut. I snuggled deeper into my warm blankets. Chloe finally finished her root beer and went back to her computers. The tapping of the keyboard lulled me to sleep.

For about five minutes. Until the phone rang.

I threw a stake at it.

The receiver clattered to the ground and Chloe jumped, knocking her chair over. She whirled around, pointing at me accusingly. "You scared the crap out of me."

I wasn't too tired to grin. "Sorry."

"You will be, Wild." She tossed the receiver back into the cradle. The academy was too cheap to spring for cordless phones like every other modern facility on the face of the planet. My cell phone trilled, vibrating across the surface of my night table. I grabbed it, frowning at the display.

I sat straight up in my bed, swearing.

"Who is it?" Chloe asked.

"Bellwood."

Chloe's eyes widened. "About last night? York already nailed you for being a good person."

I swallowed, flicking my phone on.

"Hello?" I sounded hesitant, even to my own ears.

"Ms. Wild?"

"Yes."

"This is Headmistress Bellwood. You will come to my office, please."

"I . . . what's this about?"

"Don't play games, Miss Wild, I haven't the time. You left school property last night, after the drill."

"Uh . . ." I just stared helplessly at Chloe while the headmistress continued to lecture me in that stern, dry voice of hers.

"I will expect you in five minutes."

"Yes, ma'am."

I hung up and closed my eyes briefly. Grandpa was going to kill me.

"What happened?" Chloe asked.

"She wants to see me."

"That's never good."

"Tell me about it." I kicked free of my blankets, grabbing for my cargos and a T-shirt with the Helios-Ra High School logo printed on the front.

"You can't be getting busted that hard for helping a Niner? Before school even starts?"

"No. For sneaking off campus last night."

"For sneaking—*what*? Hunter Wild, you went and had fun without me?" She sounded both stunned and hurt.

"Of course not." I hastily tied my hair back. "I'll tell you all about it later. I gotta go."

"*You* snuck out." She shook her head as I hurried out the door. "And *I'm* the pod person?"

◆

I ran all the way to the main building where classes were held. Headmistress Bellwood's office was on the ground floor overlooking a rose garden she rarely stopped to enjoy. The school felt hollow and eerie without the usual scuffle of shoes or locker doors slamming.

And almost as creepy was the headmistress, who belonged in a Victorian gothic novel, scaring the children in an orphanage. Her hair was pulled back tightly, without a single strand daring to escape. She wore the same black suit she always wore and the same pearl earrings. If she'd had glasses, she would have been glaring at me over their rims. At least I was in proper school attire, but I hadn't had time to brush my teeth or wash my face.

"Ms. Wild, have a seat," she said when she saw me hovering in the doorway.

I swallowed and stepped inside her office, which was scrupulously neat, as expected. There were no mementos on her oak desk, no family photographs—even though I knew she had two daughters.

But she did have York cluttering up her office.

He'd been standing in the corner by the window and file cabinet, no doubt hiding to take me by surprise. I stopped in the middle of the room, standing at attention. Mostly so I wouldn't give in to the temptation to throw something at his head.

"The headmistress asked you to sit down," he said.

I sat down.

She put her pen down and looked at me, abandoning her paperwork. "I should tell you, Ms. Wild, that we installed new surveillance cameras on campus over the summer."

I was so totally busted.

And it was worth it. I'd been to a vampire coronation. Surely that was worth a lecture and some detention. I schooled my expression so that I looked properly chastised. If York thought for one second that I wasn't suffering enough, he'd try harder to have me punished.

"You were caught on video sneaking off school property in the middle of the night. I hardly need to tell you this kind of behavior is inappropriate. What do you have to say for yourself?"

"Uh . . ." *Hart, who is technically your boss, invited me to see Helena Drake get crowned in the woods?* Headmistress Bellwood would never believe me. And I wasn't entirely sure if it had been a clandestine assignment. I hadn't thought to ask, and no one had said. I'd have to call Kieran. "I—"

"You're not going to tell me that you were running laps or practicing drills, are you?" she interrupted drily. "Because I can assure you, there isn't a single excuse you could give me that I haven't heard before or that would exonerate you."

Damn it, and I totally had one.

"Yes, ma'am."

"Ms. Wild, I am very disappointed in you. You have been a model student these last three years. I would hate for that to change," she added pointedly. If her tone had been a weapon, it would have been a fencing rapier that drew blood with barely a scratch. York's would have been a cudgel.

"Yes, ma'am." I tried not to squirm or fidget.

She leaned back in her chair. "Two months' detention, one month of kitchen duty, and three demerits."

Crap.

"Three?" I gaped. We were allowed five per year; the sixth got us expelled. I'd never even had one. York looked smug.

"And we'll have to call your grandfather, of course," he added.

Double crap.

"But . . ." I had no idea how to talk my way out of this one. I wasn't prepared. Another rule broken. I was *always* prepared.

So not fair.

"You may go."

I stood up and went to the door, avoiding eye contact with York. It would just piss me off even more to see him looking so pleased. He really did hate me. Weren't teachers supposed to like everyone? Or at least fake it?

"Oh, Ms. Wild," the headmistress stopped me at the door, one step away from freedom.

"Yes, ma'am?"

"I don't want to see you here again."

"No, ma'am."

I dialed Kieran's cell the minute I was outside. The last of August's sweltering heat pressed all around me. I was sweating by the time I reached the barn, which had been converted into the school gym. I got his voice mail. I swore for a good long minute before adding, "Was last night a covert op? Because I want my demerit points wiped. And you suck as an undercover agent. Didn't you know there were new cameras?" And then I swore some more.

I stomped through the locker room, pulling on my workout clothes with enough force to stretch the fabric. The locker door had a satisfying slam and metallic reverberation when I kicked it shut. I was going to kick the stuffing right out of my favorite punching bag. Twice.

Except that Chloe was already using it.

"Okay, now you're just freaking me out," I said, stopping to watch her roundhouse kick. It was still a little sloppy, lacking power. Her thick curls were damp and tied back in a messy knot. Her gym shorts and sneakers were brand new.

"If you're on York's radar, then so am I," she grunted. "And if I fail his class this year my mom will kill me. Over and over again."

I went to the bag next to hers. I stretched for a few minutes and then taped my hands.

"So are you doing time or what?" she asked, trying an uppercut. The bag swung back and nearly batted her across the room.

"Two months' detention, kitchen cleanup, and demerits."

She paused. "You got demerits?" The bag swung again, hitting her in the hip and shoulder. She stumbled. "You've never gotten a demerit."

"I know," I said grimly. "If you let your hip pivot just a little when you do that punch, it'll be stronger. And use your first two knuckles for your jab."

I flicked on the ancient stereo in the corner with the toe of my shoe and turned up the volume until the windows rattled slightly. We stood side by side and punched and kicked the punching bags for a good half hour without talking. My lungs were burning and my face felt red and sweaty when I finally stopped. Chloe was bent over, panting and gagging. I handed her a bottle of water.

"Thanks," she croaked.

"You're overdoing it," I croaked back. "I've never seen you work out that hard."

She wiped her face with a towel and shrugged. "Then I guess I'm due. I can't fail the year, Hunter."

"You're not going to," I assured her. I'd never heard her this worried. She did so well in all of her computer classes and was already assigned to the Tech department. Her combat skills wouldn't hold her back from any of that.

She sighed. "You know I'm not very good at this stuff."

I finished my water and threw the bottle into the recycling bin. "Well, I am, so no worries. Listen, we can practice together. It'll be fine."

"Yeah?" she asked hopefully.

"Of course."

She grinned, looking slightly less panicked. Then she hiccuped and grimaced. "Good, 'cause that protein powder tastes like crap. Mom sent me a new tub." She scowled. "And if it makes me fat, I'm wiping her hard drive."

CHAPTER 6

◆

QUINN

Thursday evening

"God, Quinn, how many freaking girls' phone numbers do you have on this thing?" Connor shook his head, scrolling through my cell phone address book.

I shrugged, grinning. "I can't help it if I'm irresistible." Sitting on the edge of his bed, I leaned back against the wall. Moonlight filtered through the open window. The wind tasted like pine needles and smoke. "You'd get more girls if you ever actually left your computer."

He didn't even look up. "If I didn't spend so much time on that computer, you'd never get your phone working again. Or your laptop. I keep telling you not to open e-mail attachments from people you don't know."

"She was really hot."

"And now your computer's down."

I grimaced. "And my phone. Is that a virus too?"

"No, genius. It's just so crammed full of texts from girls sending you smiley faces and x's and o's that it's clogged up and buggy."

"Can you unbug it?"

Now he did look at me, all affronted techie. "Of course I can debug it. Question is, can you stop getting girls' phone numbers?"

"Hell, no. And why would I want to?"

He did whatever it was he did, hitting buttons, muttering curses, taking the innards of any technological implement personally until it bowed to his will. And then he grinned smugly, reaching for one of the bottles of blood in the bar fridge by his bed. He opened one for himself and then tossed me one, along with my phone.

"There. It'll work but it won't be completely reliable until you delete some of those contacts."

I scrolled through the names regretfully. "You're cruel, man."

"I prefer Evil Genius." He turned back to his computer.

"You should have more fun, twin of mine," I suggested.

"Or you could have *less* fun and leave some for the rest of us."

"There's no such thing." I left him to his machinations and went downstairs, trying to remember who Karin was and why she'd sent me a sonnet about my hair. The lamps were dim, the dogs snoring in the foyer. The front door opened and Logan and Isabeau came in, Isabeau's wolfhound trotting at her side.

I waved at them but didn't stop. I could hear someone's heartbeat in the back corner where the library joined the living room and the kitchen. It was going a little too fast for my liking.

I went straight into the living room, narrowing my eyes at Solange's back. Her arms were twined around Kieran's neck. His hands were a little too clever.

"Black, don't make me kill you," I told him pleasantly. He jumped and pulled back, his ears going red. Solange sighed.

"Thanks, Quinn," she said. "Way to ruin the moment."

"I try," I said, unrepentant.

"Someday, I'll actually get to kiss you without one of my nosy annoying brothers barging in," she whispered to Kieran.

"Don't count on it," Logan said as he and Isabeau followed me. Kieran's phone rang inside his jacket. He looked relieved to answer it.

"You kiss girls all the time," Solange pointed out to me. Lately the only girl Logan kissed was Isabeau.

"Flattery will get you nowhere." I made myself more comfortable.

"You're not going away, are you?"

"Nope."

Solange folded her arms. "Lucy and Nicholas are making out in the solarium. Go bug them."

"But I like bugging *you*."

"*Quinn.*"

"Solange, look at your eyes," I said softly, too softly for Kieran to hear me. She frowned, then glanced into the art nouveau mirror on one of the shelves. A bronze woman in a flowing dress held up the reflection of Solange's pupils, ringed in red. The dark pupils all but swallowed up her usually blue irises. She froze, shooting me a horrified look. Her fingers trembled slightly when she reached up to touch the tips of her fangs. They were completely extended, in full hunger mode.

She tilted her head down and stepped into the shadows.

"I have to go," she told Kieran abruptly, and then bolted upstairs before he could answer. He flicked his phone off and frowned at me.

"Is she okay?"

"She'll be fine." She just needed more blood and less human temptation. The hunger wasn't easily explained, or easily controlled. Kieran would know that as a vampire hunter. But as her boyfriend, I wasn't sure how much he really got it. He took a step, as if he was about to follow her. "Just leave her be," I advised him quietly as Isabeau moved up the stairs, light as smoke.

He didn't look convinced but he nodded once. "I have to go anyway. Duty calls."

"Yeah? Who are we staking?" There was only a faint sarcastic edge to my voice. He was a vampire hunter, after all. And I was a vampire.

"*Hel-Blar,*" he replied, heading toward the front door. "Got an all-call alarm. They're getting a little too close to town tonight."

"Yeah?" I grabbed my coat, even though I rarely felt the cold. I had stakes and various supplies in the inside pocket. There was a dagger strapped around my ankle, under the ragged bottom of my jeans. "Sounds like fun," I said, showing my fangs. "Let's go."

◆

We were in the woods when the smell hit: mushrooms and mildew and wet, ancient decay.

Hel-Blar.

"Incoming," I warned Kieran. He flipped a UV gun out of its hidden holster. I filled my hands with stakes, nostrils flaring as I tried to pinpoint which direction the stench was coming from. It was so thick and gag-inducing that it seemed to be everywhere. Kieran slipped on a pair of nose plugs. I knew what that meant and it had nothing to do with the miasma of rotting mushrooms and stagnant pond water.

"If you hit me with any of that Hypnos, I really will kill you," I said darkly.

He didn't have time to answer.

We were surrounded.

I didn't know what they looked like to Kieran's human eyes, but to me, even in the dark, they were bruise-blue and gangrene-black and utterly unnatural. Their teeth were all fangs, all contagious saliva, all feral, savage hunger. They even fed off other vampires, which no other vamp did. It wasn't nutritious like straight human or animal blood. It was about the kill, not the feeding.

And it was just rude.

I staked the first one after he swung down from a tree and knocked Kieran off his feet. He howled, jarring his wounded arm. The *Hel-Blar* burst into a cloud of blue-tinged dust that made us both gag. Kieran rolled to his feet. I was already leaping for another *Hel-Blar.*

There were four more that I could see, or hear, scuttling through the undergrowth. There was a pop from Kieran's gun and the bullet capsule of UV-injected water dug into a *Hel-Blar* chest and exploded. He screamed, smoked as if there was fire burning him from the inside out, and then he disintegrated.

I ducked a stake, then a fist. I kicked my boot into a chin, threw a stake with hard-won accuracy. We trained for years to be able to do that. I was grinning as I came out of a lightning spin. I was covered in ashes—I even had to shake them out of my hair. And the air stank, positively putrid with rot.

But at least this was simple.

I knew who the bad guys were and I knew how to dispatch them. It wasn't politics or assassination attempts or abductions.

In short, it was the best night I'd had all bloody month.

The fight was short and brutal. One of them got away but since neither Kieran nor I were bitten or dead, I counted it a success.

Kieran cradled his injured arm gingerly. "Bastard nearly broke it again," he said.

"Bastard's under your boots now," I told him cheerfully. I'd learned long ago you had to block out the rush of regrets that followed the adrenaline dip after a fight. Otherwise the loop of thoughts could pull you under. Did you just kill someone? Or was it a monster, plain and simple? Did that make you a monster? Was it murder if you were defending yourself? Was it a war and were we just soldiers trying to survive?

I preferred the adrenaline rush.

Kieran frowned, looking around. Then he checked the GPS on his phone. "We're near the school."

"Yeah?" I was grateful for the distraction. "I don't suppose they wear uniforms? Mini kilts? Knee-high socks?"

Kieran half smiled. "Is that all you think about?"

"If I'm lucky," I answered grimly as we started to walk. The wind off the mountains was cold and fresh, cleaning out the stench of *Hel-Blar* from my nostrils. I inhaled deeply. I didn't breathe exactly. My body didn't require it, but it was an ingrained habit. And inhaling helped us recognize and catalog scents. I still wasn't sure how the whole vampirism thing worked. Uncle Geoffrey called it biology, Isabeau called it magic. I just knew I was faster, stronger, and virtually immortal.

It didn't suck.

Well, so to speak.

Just around the time I could smell the warmth of many human bodies gathered in close quarters, I smelled something else.

The first was seductive and actually made my stomach growl, the way humans might feel after smelling a grilled cheese sandwich. The second made my head spin.

Blood.

So much blood, my fangs elongated past their usual battle-length. My gums ached. My throat ached. My veins ached. Hunger slid through me, weakening me like poison. And there was only one antidote.

Blood.

Kieran grimaced. "Do you smell that?"

I nodded and tried not to drool on myself. I had to clear my throat before I could speak properly. "Animal," I said. "And . . . something else."

"What, like hunters?"

I tracked the aroma, licking my lips only slightly.

Then we saw them.

"Not exactly," I said, hunger fading. The bloodlust still had my nostrils twitching but I wasn't thinking about a liquid supper anymore.

Animals hung from the trees and lay in a pool of clotting blood on the edge of the woods, their scent leaking into the field. There were three rabbits, a badger, two raccoons, and a small heap of mice.

"What the hell?" Kieran asked, disgusted and confused. "Who did this? And why? They're not drained."

"Not a vampire then," I said through my clenched teeth. "We don't waste blood." Because you never knew when your next meal might be. "Give me those nose plugs."

He handed a pair over. I shoved them in and waited for the red haze to stop licking at my every sense.

"Whoever did that added human blood to the mix." The lights of the school were gold, glimmering like honey. "Which means there'll be more *Hel-Blar* around here before you know it."

Kieran went pale, paler than any vampire.

"I have to check on Hunter," he said, breaking into a run.

I didn't want to admit how cold I got, or how fast I followed him, until the trees were a blur of green around me and I left him behind altogether.

CHAPTER 7

♦

Hunter

Jenna found me after dinner. I was crossing the lawn, wondering where Chloe was. She hadn't been in the dining room and she was already up and out by the time I woke up. She'd also been awake way later than me, tapping away at her computers. She was determined to break the school Web codes that controlled schedules, private files, and surveillance cameras. The latter might be useful actually. But she also wanted to be a martial arts expert, crack shot sniper, and kickboxing queen.

"Wild! Hey, Wild!"

I turned to see Jenna jogging my way, cutting across the grass from the track field. Her red hair was bright as ever, as if she were about to catch fire. We'd been friends since crossbow practice in tenth grade.

"Hey," I said. "Have a good summer?"

"Yeah, pretty good." She grinned at me. "Heard you got busted already."

"York." York liked her though, so she didn't have the same issues I had.

"And you snuck out," she continued. "I'm so proud."

"Why does everyone keep saying that?" I wondered out loud.

"Because you're unfairly gorgeous, blond, smart, athletic, and a straight-A student." She grimaced. "Wait. Why am I friends with you again?"

"Give me a break," I said, then smirked. "And by the way, all my demerits were wiped." I couldn't help but gloat just a little even if I couldn't elaborate that Hart himself had called the head-mistress to absolve me. "York was speechless for fully three whole minutes and then he looked like he'd bitten into a rotten egg."

"Man, I wish I could have seen that." York might treat her well, but she was still a loyal friend and didn't like the way he singled me out all the time.

"It was pretty sweet," I admitted. "I should have taken a pic-ture." I had a miniature camera located in the school pin on my shirt. All graduating students had them. Actually, even Niners had them, but they were expected to acquire them on their own, usually through outright theft. I guess it wasn't technically theft since the teachers hid them around. In our last year they handed us the newest and highest-quality cameras in our orientation packets.

"Speaking of your hotness and athleticism," Jenna said.

I paused, raised my eyebrows. "What, already?"

"Come on," she nudged me, the freckles on her nose and cheeks incongruous against the bloodthirsty gleam in her eye. "You can't tell me you haven't missed it."

I shrugged. "Maybe a little. But why am I always the bait?"

"Because of all those disgusting good qualities of yours I just listed."

"Uh-huh."

"It's true," she insisted.

"Please, *you* could be the bait." She was just as good a combat student as I was.

"And deny you the chance to wear something pretty?"

I couldn't deny it was an incentive. Grandpa encouraged civilian clothes only for practical, don't-be-obvious reasons, and he didn't exactly endorse cute dresses and strappy sandals. And I was better at hand-to-hand combat. Jenna's expertise was her aim, both with a crossbow and a handgun. We didn't use regular bullets, of course, since they didn't do much against a vampire. We used bullet-shaped vials of what we called holy water, basically UV-infused bullets.

"When?" I asked, giving in just like she knew I would.

"Saturday night, meet at the van at eleven."

"Wait," I stopped her before she could jog away. It was vaguely inhuman how much she loved to jog. "Did you clear it? York's just dying for an excuse to bust me again."

"Yeah, I got Dailey's signature." She waved and picked up her pace, heading back to the track. I continued across the lawns to the dorms. Hart might have gotten me out of detention and demerits, but there was one thing he couldn't save me from.

Floor monitor duties. And being Courtney's assistant.

I think I preferred demerits.

I couldn't put it off any longer. Well, just a little bit longer but only because I wanted to swing by my room and grab an elastic band. It was so muggy and hot, my hair was sticking to the back of my neck.

When I opened the door, a rubber ball full of pink glitter hurtled toward my head.

I ducked and it missed my nose, but not by much.

"What the hell, Chloe?" I said just as she yelled, "Get the hell out!"

She looked up from her computer, paused. "Oops. Didn't know it was you."

"Who else would it be?" I kicked the ball back inside. It rolled toward her, bumping against her foot. I grabbed an elastic band from my desk and tied my hair back.

"Your little Niners have been coming by all morning," she said grimly.

I winced. "Seriously?"

"Yes." She speared me with a look. "It's annoying. I didn't like Niners when I *was* one. They're either needy or macho or both."

"I'll fix it," I promised, holding up a hand to curtail a long rant. She had that look on her face. She got her temper from her father, who was one of those temperamental chefs who threw pasta and entire chickens when a meal didn't go as planned. His assistants quit on a regular basis. I'd seen grizzly old vampire hunters with fewer battle scars.

"I'm staking the next pimply faced thirteen-year-old who knocks on that door," she told me.

"I'll go right now," I said. "Have another vitamin."

"Ha-ha," she grumbled, turning her attention back to her keyboard. I hurried out before she remembered I was there. Spencer was coming out of the small kitchen, a cup of coffee in his hand. He wore a chunk of turquoise on a braided hemp necklace.

"Did she throw stuff at you?" he asked, nodding toward my door.

"Rubber ball. You?"

"Xena action figure."

"That's never a good sign."

"I know. She loves that thing." He frowned. "She's all stressed out. I've never seen her like this."

"She'll calm down. York spooked her with that drill. She's afraid she's going to fail the year."

"Like she couldn't break into his computer and change her grades if she wanted to."

"Yeah, but her mom's on her case too."

"That woman is terrifyingly efficient. I like your grandpa better, even if he could snap my neck without breaking a sweat."

"Yeah, he's the best," I said proudly.

Spencer snorted noncommittally, then threw his arm across my torso to stop me so abruptly that I stumbled.

"*Ooof*. What is *wrong* with you?"

"Sorry," he said sheepishly.

"And why are you staring at my boobs, perv?"

"Is that the medallion you told us about? From the coronation."

I glanced down. The silver pendant on its long chain had fallen out of my shirt.

Spencer looked positively greedy. "Can I see it?"

For some reason I didn't want to take it off. I held it up but kept it around my neck. "It's not magic, Spencer, just a symbol."

"That's half of what magic is," he said. "Symbology." He ran his finger over the insignias. "I'd love to do some tests on this."

I batted his hand away. "Forget it. It'll come back melted or smelling like cheese."

"One time," he muttered. "One time I misread a spell and I'll never live it down."

"You smelled like cheese for a month."

"Believe me, I remember. I still can't eat grilled cheese sandwiches."

Satisfied that he was distracted from trying to steal my necklace, I looked up the long staircase and squared my shoulders. "Here goes nothing."

"You'll do fine." He snorted. "And pretty much no matter what you'll do, you'll be better than Courtney."

That was comforting, at least.

Still, there seemed to be fewer stairs than usual. I reached the top floor distressingly fast. It smelled like popcorn. The common room looked the same, but there were plants in the windows. That was new. Homey.

"Courtney put those there," Lia said, when she saw me looking at them. She looked more cheerful today, less like she was about to have a panic attack. She still looked really young though. "Hi."

"Hi," I said back. "You okay?"

She looked embarrassed. "Yeah. Sorry about that. I totally lost it yesterday."

"It happens to all of us," I assured her.

"I bet it's never happened to you."

She was right. But that was only because I'd been five years old when Grandpa had started my training. When I'd thought there were monsters under the bed, he taught me how to do a proper sweep to get rid of them.

"So are you settled in?" I asked, changing the subject.

"Pretty much."

"And you know not to use the last shower stall in the back?"

Her eyes widened. "Why not? It's the cleanest one."

"Let me put it this way: magic gone wonky plus a cranky ghost makes for ice-cold water. Or sometimes blood instead of water."

"Okay. Gross."

"Yeah, that's why no one ever uses it. But they never put that stuff in the orientation manual."

She shivered.

"Don't let it get to you." I smiled. "By this time next month you'll know every corner of this place." I went toward the bulletin board, smiling at the two girls sprawled on the couch watching television. "Also, don't eat the meatloaf."

"I'm thirteen, I'm not an idiot."

I laughed. "Okay, then." I scrawled a note on a piece of paper and tacked it to the board. "Can you do me a favor and spread the word for me? Ask the girls not to bug my roommate or she'll send viruses to their computers."

Lia blanched. "She can do that?"

"Yup."

"Cool."

"She's just as likely to throw something at you though. Anyway, I'll come up here once a week . . . say Thursdays after dinner, if anyone needs to talk to me." Not that I expected they would, since they had Courtney, who was actually supposed to be doing this, and what did I know about this stuff?

"Are you the new monitor?" one of the girls asked.

I nodded. "I guess so."

"She's my *assistant*." Courtney sneered from the doorway to her room, which was decorated from floor to ceiling in purple. Her hair was in perfect hazel-brown waves to her shoulders, her eyes expertly lined and smudged with silver eye shadow. Her dress was really pretty, with lace layered over silk. I coveted it instantly.

Which just made me cranky.

"Courtney," I said evenly, counting to ten.

"You're not the floor monitor," she said defensively. "You're my lackey. Your job is to do what I tell you to."

"You wouldn't need an assistant if you'd done your job properly in the first place," I shot back. Like hell I was going to let her make me her minion.

She narrowed her eyes at me. "Excuse me, but it's not my fault one of them was too slow. She had to pass the entrance exams like everyone else. She should've been fine."

"She's thirteen," I said softly, since I knew everyone around us was eavesdropping.

Courtney blinked. "She is?" She frowned and flipped her hair over her shoulder. "Whatever," she added, her cheeks pink. "York says I'm in charge."

"He would," I said under my breath.

"And if you don't do your job, I'm supposed to tell him about it."

"Fine," I said through my teeth. "I already posted my hours so chill, already."

"My family's just as good as yours," she snapped suddenly.

It was my turn to blink at her. "Okay." I didn't know what else to say to that.

"I mean it."

"I'm sure you do."

I was so glad we weren't roommates anymore. I'd rather have Chloe throwing stuff at my head any day. I heard one of the doors creak open. "You, in room 403!" I snapped. "Always check for creaky hinges before you try to listen in on someone. It's a dead giveaway." There was a gasp and the door slammed shut, followed by stifled giggles. I rolled my eyes. "So's that," I muttered.

"Look, I don't need your help," Courtney insisted hotly.

"You need some kind of help," I said, turning on my heel and going back downstairs. I was on the landing when my phone vibrated in my pocket as a text message came through.

Hel-Blar attack. All 12th-grade students
to town line rendezvous.

I took the rest of the steps at a dead run.

Spencer was already in my room when I got there. Chloe was shoving a stake through one of her belt loops. She looked excited. She never looked excited about drills and outright runs.

"You got the message?" Spencer flicked me a glance.

I nodded, reaching for my jacket. I secured the tear-gas pen, altered to hold Hypnos powder, in my cuff. "*Hel-Blar* on the out-skirts of town again?" I asked. "That's twice in one week."

"And enough of them this time to call us all in," Spencer added grimly as we thundered down the hall. The front door was already open. A cluster of Niners stood on the stairs watching the dorms empty of twelfth-grade students, armed to the teeth.

Courtney shoved past them, stakes lined up on her designer leather belt. "Hunter," she smirked at me. "Someone has to stay behind and babysit the girls, as you so kindly pointed out."

I did not like where this was going.

"So you stay," I replied tersely. "You're the floor monitor."

"You're my assistant," she strode past me. "So assist."

I grabbed her elbow. "You said you didn't need help, remember?"

She shrugged me off. "Let go. You're the one who was all worried about them." She jerked her head toward the lane, visible through the open door. "There goes York. Should we ask him?"

Crap.

"Why do you have to be such a bitch, Courtney?" Chloe snapped. "Is it your superpower or something?"

"Shut up." She flounced out, hurrying to catch up with York.

"Sucks," Spencer said. "Want me to stay?"

I shook my head. "Sounds like they need you." My teeth were clenched so tight it was hard to speak.

Chloe made a face. "Sorry," she said, shutting the door behind them.

I was left standing in the foyer under the dusty chandelier, covered in stakes, with night-vision goggles pushed up on my head like a headband.

Talk about being all dressed up with no place to go.

The Niners were whispering excitedly to themselves, a few brave ones coming down to press their noses to the windows. Jason, who was the boys' ninth-grade monitor, turned to me sympathetically. "You're having a hell of a year so far, aren't you?"

I had to grin, even if it was only faintly. "Maybe I should have Spencer check me for curses."

"Wouldn't hurt," he said before turning to the nervous students. "Everyone back upstairs. Now."

They went reluctantly, but they went.

"Did you tell them their common room windows have a better view of the vans leaving campus?" I asked, remembering how we used to sneak out of bed and cram ourselves into the window seats, jockeying for the best position to watch the official runs and middle-of-the-night drills in the woods.

"No way," Jason said. "I might lose my spot." He slung an arm over my tight shoulders. "Come on, Wild, let's go watch reruns of *Warriors* on the History Channel and wait up like little old ladies left out of all the fun."

I let him lead me up the creaky old staircase, dragging my feet a little.

"I can't believe I'm missing the first real vamp takedown of the semester," I said glumly.

The chandelier flickered once and then all the lights went out.

I whirled just in time to see a shadow pass by one of the front windows.

"Or not," I amended.

CHAPTER 8

◆

Hunter

Jason was already upstairs when the first *Hel-Blar* crashed into the foyer, shattering the glass. I was still on the landing and the only one properly armed.

"Go!" I yelled up to Jason. "Trip the alarms."

He hesitated.

"Just go!" I insisted before leaping off the landing. I grabbed the chandelier and used it to swing forward, gaining enough momentum to catch the *Hel-Blar* in the chest with my heels. He was swept off his feet just as the chandelier chain snapped and dumped me in the center of the foyer. The crystal beads rained down on our heads, skittering into the broken glass from the window. The *Hel-Blar* didn't stay sprawled on the ground for long. The smell of wet mushrooms was overpowering. He snapped his teeth at me, all pointed and needle-sharp. I shoved a stake through his chest and he crumbled into ash, leaving behind an empty pile of clothes.

I didn't exactly have time to pat myself on the back.

Several more *Hel-Blar* came racing out of the woods, like blue beetles. There were thumps upstairs, a shouted curse. They must be on the roof as well. The tenth and eleventh graders would have already barricaded themselves in their rooms or else gone for the secret passageways leading outside when Jason turned on their silent alarms. I should get back upstairs and help him corral the Niners. I kicked the ash off my boots and took the stairs two at a time, slipping in a pair of nose plugs.

It didn't make sense. Vampires didn't attack the academy as a rule, at least not in the last few decades, and the *Hel-Blar* never had even before then; why would they bother now? They didn't have a leader or political aims, just an overwhelming hunger that usually chose the path of least resistance.

Another beast came through the broken window and raced up the stairs behind me. I barely heard him, only felt the press of air full of rotting vegetation and copper. There was blood on his chin.

I went low because he expected me to jump and leap out of his way. Instead, I dropped and swept my leg out, catching him in the ankles with the steel toe of my boots. I activated the tear-gas pen in my sleeve because he was moving too fast for the blade in my boot to be useful. Hypnos wafted out in a puff of white powder, like confectioners' sugar. He was already leaning over me, his saliva dripping onto my shoulder, by the time I could bark out an order and be relatively confident there was enough Hypnos in his face to do the trick.

"Drop!"

He collapsed on top of me like a load of bricks.

I wiggled out from beneath him before his teeth could accidentally graze my neck. There was nothing more contagious than the kiss of a *Hel-Blar*, no matter how doped up he was. His pupils were dilated, ringed with a tiny sliver of pale gray. His skin was tattoo-blue and mottled.

Grandpa would have told me to stake him then and there. He was *Hel-Blar*, after all, the most vicious of the vicious. But I couldn't just take out a will-less, unarmed opponent, even if he was dangerous, even if it was tactically sound. It just felt wrong.

I shoved him away, making sure to use enough force to crack a few ribs. I might have more scruples than my grandfather, but I wasn't soft. And I didn't want him staying here to jump back into the fight after the Hypnos wore off.

"Go back to your nest," I snapped. "And stay there. Don't hurt anyone on the way."

"I will kill you, little girl—"

"And shut up," I added.

He stumbled down the steps, making weird growling sounds in the back of his throat.

I knew the precise moment Jason reached the main alarm switch. The altered tanning-bed bulbs set all around the dormitory, from windowsills to garden landscaping lights, seared through the darkness. It was high-powered UV light with the same toxic effect on vampires as sunlight. It wouldn't make them burst into flames like movie vampires, which would have been a hell of a tactical advantage. But it would at least weaken them considerably. And it should convince any other vampires coming this way to turn back.

I met Jason on the third floor, trailing students heading for the secret passageway door.

"You all right?" he asked.

I nodded. "Two down."

"This is unbelievable," he snarled. "They're coming down from the roof too. There are at least three upstairs."

"I saw that many coming in through the back," an eleventh-grade girl, still in her pink pajamas, offered. "From the gardens."

"What the hell is going on?" I shoved my hair back into its ponytail.

"It does seem rather sophisticated for the *Hel-Blar*," Jason muttered as we rounded the corner and came up against the wooden panel door. "Let's go," he called out to the other students. "I'll take point."

"But they're outside too," one of the ninth-grade boys said.

"We can't stay here," I told him. "Anyway, the tunnel leads far enough away, near the road and the van parked under the willow trees."

"That broken-down, rusted old thing?"

"It only looks broken down," I said grimly. "And there are two more vans hidden deeper in the woods. Now move."

"Don't argue, Joshua," Lia said, shoving him to get him going. Her hands were trembling and her hairline was damp with sweat, but she was keeping it together. I turned my back to them, watching for *Hel-Blar*. We could hear their footsteps creaking through the ceiling. The old wooden floorboards were meant to be creaky like that, to teach us how to move quietly and give us fair warning if someone was sneaking around.

The light pouring through the windows was almost blinding. It should weaken them, but if they were in a battle frenzy they could still do a considerable amount of damage before they realized they should retreat. The secret passageway door slammed open. I was still guarding the rear so I had to look over my shoulder when I heard Kieran's terse voice.

"Exit's blocked," he said.

"Crap," I muttered. "Sophie, take my position," I said, turning to stare at Kieran. He was in regulation cargos, a strap of stakes over his good shoulder. "What are you doing here?"

"Talk later."

"Bet your ass," I muttered. "And what do you mean the exit's blocked?"

"Dead end, Buffy," Quinn said, coming out of the passageway behind Kieran. He looked just as gorgeous as ever, even covered in dust. His hair was loose, his eyes blue as fire.

I gaped at him. "What the hell are you doing here?"

"We came to rescue you." He grinned at me as if we were alone at a candlelit dinner, his fangs gleaming like ivory daggers.

"You do realize you're in a *vampire hunter* school, right?"

"He's a vampire!" The eleventh-grade floor monitor flung a stake at Quinn. Quinn snarled, leaning to the right until his torso was practically parallel to the floor. The stake thudded into the wall.

"Stand down!" I yelled as Kieran stepped in front of Quinn. "He's a Drake! And an ally."

There was a startled pause, then grumbling and frantic whispers.

"You know him?" Jason stared at me as if I'd just grown an extra head.

"Kieran, you're fraternizing with the enemy now?" Sophie snapped.

"He's a vampire," Simon muttered. He was in eleventh grade now and already covered in scars. And he was built like a big blond Viking. "What are we waiting for?"

"He's a Drake," I repeated. "And Hart's signed a treaty with them so stand the hell down or I will put you down."

"It's not right, is all I'm saying. In case you two haven't noticed, we kill vampires. Kind of under attack right now."

Kieran snorted. "I'm not going to let you kill my girlfriend's brother, so get over it."

"You really *are* dating a vampire?" Sophie goggled at him. "Dude."

I stood very pointedly next to Kieran, blocking Quinn. He was close enough that I could feel the coolness of his body, the noticeable absence of his breath on the back of my neck. It should have creeped me out. I was kind of surprised that it didn't.

"Look, could we debate the bigotry of this organization at some other time?" I bit out. "Quinn's not our problem right now. As Simon pointed out, the *Hel-Blar* are." I lifted my chin, glaring down at everyone. "And Kieran outranks us all, so shut up and follow orders or I'm handing out demerits."

"Can you do that now?" Kieran whispered at me.

"I have no idea," I hissed back.

"Okay, listen up, people," Kieran raised his voice so that it was all gravelly and impressive. I wasn't particularly impressed since we'd grown up together and I'd force-fed him mud pies when we were little, but it seemed to work on everyone else. Lia actually sighed.

Only a thirteen-year-old vampire hunter would get a crush in the middle of a vampire attack.

I was a little bit proud of her actually.

"The tunnel exit is no good," Kieran continued. "We had to barricade it behind us and set fires to keep the *Hel-Blar* from using it. Someone's tipped them off about it. That's not our concern right now. Our only goal is to take as many out as possible and stay alive in the process. Don't be a hero or I'll have Hunter take you down. That said, the lights should keep the worst of them away. In the meantime, I want everyone bunkered in the tenth-grade common room. It's the easiest one to defend and the windows are barred." That had less to do with protection and more to do with a prank Kieran and his friends had apparently pulled in tenth grade.

"What are you waiting for?" Kieran shouted as the *Hel-Blar* came down the stairs. "Go! Monitors on perimeter," he added, though they were well trained enough to do it anyway. I stayed where I was.

"Hunter, go," Kieran said, drawing a stake.

"Give me a break." I took out my own stake and stepped aside just enough to keep Quinn out of my way and vice versa. "Your arm's busted. You need me."

Kieran didn't have the time to argue with me. He couldn't have changed my mind anyway. He was the closest thing to a brother I had and I wasn't about to leave him behind. Not when the other students were plenty well protected now. And while I trusted that Quinn was a good fighter, he was dangerously cocky too.

Three *Hel-Blar* came from the top floor and another two from our right. Quinn laughed before throwing himself at them. He actually laughed.

"Is he insane?" I asked, flinging a stake at one of the *Hel-Blar* on the right.

"Pretty much. Duck!"

I ducked. Kieran's stake whizzed over my head and pinned the second vampire to the wall. Another stake finished him off. I held my breath until the ash settled. Breathing in dead vampire dust is just as gross as it sounds.

We'd dispatched them all when Quinn turned back to us, grinning. "That was fun."

"You're—" I cut myself off as the shadow of a smaller, more cunningly hidden *Hel-Blar* dropped from the ceiling ledge. She landed behind Quinn, every fang exposed. "Quinn, down!"

Quinn dropped into a crouch, revealing a stake in each hand. Before he could spin and jab up with his weapons, I threw a pepper egg. He blinked at it with the kind of astonishment that would have been funny in any other circumstance. The black-painted egg-shaped container was thin and made to break on impact. When it struck the last *Hel-Blar* in the face, it splashed a combination of ground glass, cayenne pepper, and Hypnos into her face. She recoiled, screeching and clawing at her red, watering eyes. One of Quinn's stakes pierced her heart and finished the job.

We joined Kieran on the next landing and stood there for a long moment. The only sound was Kieran and I panting. The house was quiet.

"I think that was the last of them," Kieran said finally. "I'll go up and do a sweep. You guys watch the front and back doors."

I led Quinn down to the end of the staircase. I stood on the last step, able to see not only the front door but right through the broken windows to the lawn. He stood next to me on the ground, facing the other direction, toward the back door. My one step advantage made us almost the same height. Our shoulders touched, the banister between our bodies. Adrenaline was still flooding through me, making me feel inexplicably like giggling.

"You guys throw eggs now?" Quinn asked, raising an eyebrow. "What the hell's that about?"

"It's a ninja thing," I shrugged. "We've only started using it recently. One of our history teachers is into that stuff."

"You're kinda scary, Buffy." He winked, then looked suddenly thoughtful.

"What?" I asked.

"I was just wondering if you'd consider teaching Lucy some moves."

"Lucy? Your sister's best friend?"

He nodded. "She needs some extra tricks up her sleeve. Our family is proving to be a bit of a liability and she's only human." He flicked me a glance. "No offense."

"None taken," I returned drily.

"You know what I mean. She's vulnerable. And her parents will be back soon and she'll go home. We're just a little worried."

He smelled like smoke and incense. I probably shouldn't be noticing that. What was wrong with me? I wasn't usually the type to get all flustered over a good-looking guy. Even a *really* good-looking guy who kind of resembled Orlando Bloom. Plus, he saw me as a fellow soldier. I'd been fighting next to guys long enough to know the look. I tried not to sigh. It would have been a totally inappropriate reaction. I was a hunter. I was supposed to be cool under pressure.

"So, would you?" he asked again.

"What?" I gave myself a mental shake. "I guess it would be okay, if the headmistress approves."

"Do you always do what you're told?" he drawled.

I snorted. Flustered or not, I was still me. "That's what storybook villains always say to the girls to get them to do something stupid."

There was a pause before he chuckled, as if the sound surprised him. "I'll just take that as a yes."

"I'm sure you usually do."

His grin widened and he nudged my shoulder companionably. "I like you, kid."

I tried not to groan out loud. I was as bad as Lia.

I had totally developed a crush during a vampire raid.

And he saw me the same way Kieran saw me—as a little sister.

I didn't exactly have time to analyze the fact that I was crushing on a vampire.

Besides, anyone with eyeballs would crush on Quinn Drake.

Right now I was far too busy running up the stairs toward the screaming. Quinn was at my heels, cursing. "Hunter, wait. Let me go ahead."

"Not a chance." I ran faster. He was quicker, of course, being a vampire and all. In fact, he was practically a blur of color streaking past me. It didn't seem fair. I worked my ass off to be as fast as I could, I ran, I practically lived at the gym most mornings, and I had to put up with York. All Quinn had to do was die.

Not exactly a viable option for me.

CHAPTER 9

♦

QUINN

When I got to the common room, where the screaming had originated, it was quiet again. I waited for Hunter to catch up.

"So not fair," she muttered, gasping for breath.

Kieran stepped into the hallway, grim-mouthed. "Man down. Well, boy, anyway."

"Is it bad? What happened?" Hunter brushed past him to see for herself.

The room was bright considering all the light reflecting through the windows. It was getting warm, too. Definite drawback to those UV bulbs; the students might be sunburned by morning. While they'd no doubt trade a peeling nose and heat blisters over getting eaten by a *Hel-Blar*, I, however, was feeling like I might cook right through. Sunlight wasn't good for us. I wouldn't burst into flame or anything dramatic like that, but I'd get weak and pass out.

In a school full of vampire hunters.

No thanks.

I put on my sunglasses and flicked up the collar of my shirt. The back of my neck already felt tender. In the center of the room, the students were huddled around a couch where a very skinny student was moaning. There was blood soaking his white T-shirt. I tried not to lick my lips. I didn't think it would go over well.

"Will," Hunter said. "Shit. Was he . . . ?" She trailed off, wincing. His shoulder looked bad, his shirt torn.

"He wasn't bitten," Kieran went to stand beside her.

I stayed by the door, watching the shadows in the hall and trying not to be distracted by the scent of so many humans in one room. If my stomach growled they'd probably stake me before I could explain it was an involuntarily reaction. They craved donuts, I craved blood. It was just one of those things.

"The screaming came from the girl who found him. The blood's from when he tripped and fell on his own knife."

I snorted. They were shish kebabing themselves for us now. They may as well offer themselves up on silver platters. Hunter shot me a look, as if she knew what I was thinking. I just shot her back a crooked grin. She wasn't likely to apologize for accessorizing with stakes and I wasn't going to apologize for my fangs.

"*Hel-Blar* tried to drink from him," Kieran continued tersely. "Apparently got a mouthful before Will got away."

Her eyes widened. "Crap. Will he turn? Are there marks?"

"I don't think so. But no one can tell me for sure if there was any saliva or blood exchange. It was just a convenience feeding."

"So he needs the infirmary," Hunter said.

"There are some teachers on campus," Kieran assured us. "But they've got their hands full."

"I'll take him," she offered right away.

Kieran frowned. "Hunter, campus is crawling with *Hel-Blar*."

"Duh. And you have to stay here. You're the one with the actual rank; the rest of us are just students. Plus, you've only got one good arm."

"Shit," he grumbled. He knew she was right. "I don't like it. It's dangerous."

I didn't like it either.

"Blah, blah, blah," Hunter cut him off. "Are you going to hold my hand every time we're out in the field?"

"There's gratitude for you," Kieran said.

She kissed his cheek. I was oddly glad it looked like the kind of kiss Solange might give me. Sister to brother. "I love you, stupid."

"You too, idiot."

"So get out of my way already." She had to shove him. "Give him some space," she told the others, trying to get through the clump of horrified students. "You'll be fine, Will."

"That's a lot of blood," someone said dubiously.

"Which is why I'm taking him to the infirmary." She hooked her arm under his shoulder and helped him up. He was clammy and pale and looked surprisingly heavy for someone so lanky. And he was about a foot taller than she was, which didn't help matters.

"I've got him," I murmured, coming up to support his other

side. Will jerked away wild-eyed, and then gagged on a sound of pain when his shoulder bled more profusely at the sudden movement.

"Easy," Hunter said gently. "He's just helping."

I couldn't stop my fangs from biting through my gums. I clamped my lips together. I was glad my eyes were hidden behind sunglasses. I knew they'd look too blue and too pale in this weird light.

"Vampire," Will croaked.

"Want to lose your arm?" Hunter asked him sharply. He shook his head, gulping. "Then shut up and let him help you."

"Yes, ma'am." He nearly saluted.

Kieran moved aside to let us out the door. "Watch her back," he told me.

I snorted. "I let you grope my little sister and I haven't broken your other arm for it yet. You can trust *your* little sister with me."

Hunter paused. She skewered each of us with a stare. Someone in the room started to sweat, she was that good. I could have kissed her right then and there.

"First—*ew*. Second—I can look after myself. If you guys want to do the macho knight-in-shining-armor thing, do it on your own time. And find yourself another damsel in distress, because I'm not her."

We exchanged a glance, then looked at her. Kieran sighed. "Just be careful, Hunter."

"I'm always careful."

"Uh-huh."

She stumbled a little. "Look, Will's leaving a puddle of blood on the floor and he's not getting any lighter. Stop worrying and let's do this already."

At that moment the phone in the common room, all of the phones in the dorm, and every cell phone in every pocket rang.

The sound was sudden and shrill enough to make everyone jump. I jerked back slightly as it pierced my sensitive hearing. Hunter nearly dropped Will. I caught him and hefted him easily over my shoulder in a fireman's hold.

"What the hell is that?" I snapped as Hunter checked her phone. The text and voice mail icons flashed.

"It's the first all-clear," Hunter explained as she read the message. "We're still in lockdown but the immediate attack should be over."

Kieran nodded. "Go on then. And try not to accidentally stake a prof making the rounds."

She made a face. It was cute as hell. "How was I supposed to know she wasn't a vampire? And that was four years ago. I'd barely been here a month," she grumbled.

I carried Will down the stairs. Hunter went ahead. She pushed the front door open and slipped out first to make sure it was safe. I could have told her not to bother. I couldn't smell a fresh waft of mildew and mushrooms so I knew there was no *Hel-Blar* in the immediate vicinity.

The lights outlined everything in pale yellow, like a movie special effect. Every leaf was delineated, every blade of grass. On the edge of the gardens there was a blackness soothing to my eyes. They were actually watering under the force of so many UV bulbs.

She led me down the path from the dorm to one of the main

buildings. The lower floor was the infirmary—I could tell by the sheer blinding force of the white paint on the walls and the faint underlying odor of antiseptic.

Will moaned again.

"Nearly there," Hunter promised. "Theo'll fix you up in no time. You know he's really good with stitches."

"That *Hel-Blar* bitch stank. And she had white spiky hair. D-Don't want to turn into that," he stammered. "Gran would . . . kill . . . me."

We exchanged a grim look over his head. It was hard to know if he'd been speaking metaphorically or not. You never could tell in hunter families. Or vampire families for that matter.

"You won't," Hunter said with a confidence I could tell she didn't really feel. "They have meds now, to stop the change. If they catch it early enough, it has a pretty good success rate."

"How good?" I asked softly.

"Fifty-six percent success rate, according to the files Chloe hacked into last year," she replied, barely above a whisper. I wouldn't have heard her at all if it wasn't for my excellent hearing.

"More pills," Will babbled, delirious with pain and fear. "Those new vitamins taste like ass."

Hunter chuckled. "That's what Chloe says. You must be taking the same kind."

He didn't answer, having passed out on us. Luckily we were on the walkway to the infirmary door. A nurse met us halfway. His black eyes were curious and concerned and they didn't change, not even when they landed on my fangs. I was impressed.

"Uh . . . vampire?" he asked.

Hunter nodded. "He's a Drake."

"Well, I'm not going to bow to His Fangness, if that's what you're implying." His scrubs were the color of seaweed and he wore them like armor.

"Like I'm that stupid, Theo," Hunter shot back, half grinning. Theo was obviously someone she liked. I decided I wasn't jealous. I didn't do jealous, not with girls.

"Will here needs stitches and antibiotics or whatever," she said as they wrestled Will through the door and onto the nearest cot. The fluorescent lights made me squint.

Theo took one look at Will and forgot about me entirely. He pried Will's eyelids open and shone a light into them, frowning at the messy wound.

"Knife?" he asked.

"Yeah," Hunter replied.

"You guys stab yourselves a lot?" I asked.

Theo's mouth quirked. "You'd be surprised."

"*Hel-Blar* got him too," Hunter added.

Theo didn't stop his ministrations, not even for a moment. But I heard his heart accelerate. "Explain."

"He got the wound before a *Hel-Blar* found him but she apparently lapped at the blood."

"Shit. Not good." He called out for another nurse. "Bite too?" He looked for teeth marks.

Hunter shrugged apologetically. "No one's sure."

"All right, let us do our work," he turned away, shouting orders at his assistants even as he cut through the rest of Will's shirt. Needles slid under skin. Hunter looked away, swallowing.

"Don't tell me blood makes you nauseous," I said, amused. I moved closer, ready to catch her if she fainted.

"Not blood," she shuddered. "Needles."

"Then why don't we get out of here?" I suggested. "You can't do anything else for him but Kieran could probably use you. And I'm feeling a little exposed here with all these lights."

She nodded, following me back outside. "I wonder how the others are doing in town."

"Montmartre and Greyhaven sure left a mess behind," I agreed. "Bastards."

"Who's Greyhaven?" Hunter asked.

"One of Montmartre's lackeys. His first lieutenant, actually. He made his own *Hel-Blar* on the sly, trying to create his own personal army, like Montmartre's Host."

"Oh, great, 'cause that's just what we need," she said drily.

"One of the Hounds staked him," I assured her. "One of Isabeau's friends."

The Hounds were a superstitious and solitary tribe of vampires, many of them having been turned by Montmartre but rescued from the grave before he could recruit them. They had old magic the rest of the world had forgotten about centuries ago.

We walked in an easy companionable silence, even though she still held a stake in her hand and I still had my fangs out. I was the first to hear the faint hiss. I stopped suddenly, turning my head slowly.

"There," I murmured before vaulting into the lilac bushes bordering the dirt path. Hunter caught up to me just as I was snarling over a lump in the grass on the other side of the bushes. The

Hel-Blar was female, lying on her back, hissing weakly. There was blood on her mouth, and her bloodshot eyes were wild. Her skin was mottled blue, nearly gray. Her hair was in short bleached-white spikes.

"She's the one who attacked Will!" Hunter exclaimed. She stepped closer, stake raised.

The *Hel-Blar* started to convulse, blood and saliva frothing at the corner of her lips. She flailed and hissed. I stepped partly in front of Hunter. We both stared at her, speechless, when she screeched and then disintegrated.

We didn't say anything for a long moment.

"What in the hell was that?" I finally broke the silence.

"I have no idea," she answered. "I didn't even touch her!"

"Vampires don't just disintegrate like that—not without a pointy stick or lots of sunlight." And we hadn't been close enough to hurt her. If I didn't know better, I'd have sworn she'd been sick in some way, or poisoned.

But that was impossible.

Before we could decide what to do, flashlights sliced across us. Hunters and two professors ran at us from either direction.

"Stand down," one of them ordered. "We'll take it from here."

"She's gone." Hunter blinked as one of them crouched to gather the ashes. "We didn't touch her. She just . . . fell apart. Like she was sick or something." She shook her head. "I know that sounds crazy."

I didn't say anything but I bent my knees slightly, in case I needed to leap out of the path of a crossbow bolt or a stake. You never could tell with hunters. Some of them were jumpy.

"Back to your room, Wild," one of the profs snapped at Hunter. "And Agent Black is waiting to escort you off the premises, Mr. Drake," she said to me, clearly not pleased to even acknowledge my presence. I could smell the fear on her skin, like a perfume.

"He helped us," Hunter pointed out, frowning, "while the rest of you were elsewhere."

I admit I got a charge out of watching her defend me. I hadn't expected that. Kieran had told me enough about her family that it was frankly surprising she hadn't tried to stake me yet, out of principle.

The professor stood to block our view of what they were doing. "*Now*, Miss Wild. That's an order."

Hunter looked like she wanted to argue but she just nodded sharply, turned on her heel, and walked away, tugging my hand so I'd follow.

"Something's not right," I said when we were out of earshot.

"I know," she agreed grimly as we stepped onto a lawn bustling with students, teachers, and the occasional hunter in full gear. The predator in me rose to the surface. It was a struggle not to growl out loud. Kieran came to get me, nodding at Hunter to move toward the dorm before she could say anything else.

"What the hell, Kieran?" I barked.

"Not here," he barked back.

CHAPTER 10

◆

Hunter

Friday afternoon

No one would tell us anything, even the next day.

The most information I could get was out of Theo, and he would tell me only that Will was critical but hadn't turned or died as of yet. It wasn't much to go on.

It didn't help that Chloe wouldn't stop complaining.

"It's so not fair," she said again as I wiped the sweat off my face and began my cool-down stretches. We were in the gym, which was nearly full. The attacks last night had all the students eager to train again, even though those of us left behind at the school had seen the most action. Which was what had Chloe in a snit. Her face was nearly purple.

"Take it easy," I told her. "You're going to give yourself a heart attack if you keep pushing like that."

She drained her water bottle and wiped her mouth. "I feel fine, and I had my checkup yesterday to prove it. So there." Students had to get a physical exam at the beginning of each school year.

"Well, you're the very flattering color of raw hamburger," I corrected. "Not a good look for you."

"I just need to take another vitamin," she panted, shaking out what looked like a yellow horse pill from a bottle she pulled out of her bag. It had her mother's name printed on it: Dr. Cheng.

"How do those not make you gag?" I asked her.

She shrugged. "You get used to it. Not that you'd need to."

"Not this again."

"Well, it's true," she insisted. "You're a natural athlete. *And* you get straight As."

"So do you!"

"I suck at the combat stuff."

"You don't suck," I said, pulling the elastic out of my hair. I was getting tired of defending myself when I hadn't done anything wrong. She was so prickly this year. I couldn't imagine how stressed she was going to be when classes actually started. It was kind of making me wish we weren't sharing a room. "But you are getting on my nerves."

"Not all of us are getting commendations for saving lives," she said. It sounded suspiciously like whining. "You kicked ass last night and all I saw was the back of a *Hel-Blar* head as it turned to ash. And I wasn't even the one who staked him."

"You're pouting because you didn't get to kill anything?" I asked her, astounded. "Seriously?"

"You don't get it."

"Got that right."

She shoved her stuff into her bag. "Everything's easy for you."

I blinked at her. "Are you high? Have you not been paying attention the last couple of days?"

"You came out smelling like roses every time."

"And that's a bad thing?" I couldn't believe her. "Shit, Chloe. What's *wrong* with you? You're my friend. You should be glad I didn't get slammed with all those demerits York tried to give me."

"I *am* glad."

"No, you're not. You're ragging on me because I got attacked by vampires and you didn't."

"I'm just tired. *God.*"

"Then get some sleep," I shot back, annoyed. "And get a grip."

"You're not perfect, you know."

I stared at her. "When did I ever say I was?"

She scowled. "You act it."

"I do not."

"Yes, you do. You're good at everything."

"You're nuts." I slung my gym bag over my shoulder and stalked away before I said something I might not be able to take back. I couldn't believe the way she'd talked to me, the way she'd looked at me—like I was making her life miserable. I'd never seen her like that. She was still muttering to herself when I slammed the door behind me. I didn't even bother changing, just went outside in my gym shorts and tank top. I didn't want to be near her for a second longer than I had to right now. We never fought, not like this. We bickered over stupid stuff during exams, but so did everyone. This was something else. I knew her mother was being even harder on her than usual, but how was that my fault?

"Hunter! Did you want to—whoa." Jenna raised her eyebrows when I swung around. She was coming from the cafeteria with a basket and Spencer and Jason behind her. "Scary face."

"Sorry." I sighed, trying to shake off my mood. It wasn't fair to take it out on them, especially after getting mad at Chloe for doing the very same thing to me.

"You okay?" Spencer asked.

"I'm fine," I grumbled. "Chloe needs therapy though."

He snorted. "Tell me something I don't know."

Jenna held up her basket. "Picnic time. You in?"

"Always," I answered, following them off the path toward one of the back fields bordering the woods. We did this every time we needed a little privacy from possible surveillance cameras, bugged phones, and teachers in general. It wasn't easy to hide in a school that trained you in spy maneuvers and combat. Campus was full of bugs and hidden cameras. Sitting in the middle of a field was our favorite way to trade information. The potato salad wasn't a bad incentive either.

We spread out a blanket and dug into the food right away. We sat shoulder to shoulder, angled out so that we could see in all directions and no one could sneak up on us.

"So what's the scoop?" I asked, wiping mayo off my top lip. "Any word on Will?"

"Nothing new," Jason said. "He's stable enough but they're still waiting to see which way he goes."

"It was weird." I frowned. "Really weird, the way that *Hel-Blar* just disintegrated."

"Something's up," Jenna agreed, her red hair caught back in a messy braid. Her sneakers had little stars all over them.

"The Niner boys are whispering about some kind of pill that will make them stronger," Jason said, shaking his head. "I totally don't want to narc but, man, I'm going to have to if I can't figure out where they're getting it from."

I went cold.

"Wait. What?"

"They're saying it's some kind of vitamin that makes you stronger."

"Will mentioned something about taking vitamins," I said quietly. I looked at Spencer pointedly. "And Chloe's taking all these vitamins and protein powders."

He frowned. "But her mom gave her those. She's a doctor and a biochemist."

"True."

Jenna tilted her head. "If they really are vitamins, who cares? I mean, I'm taking vitamin C right now. My roommate's got that flu and I really don't want to catch it. If they need to think it makes them better fighters, where's the harm? It's not like they're on steroids."

"I guess." I wasn't sure why, but I wasn't convinced.

"But we all agree we need to find out what's going on, right?" Jason asked. "I mean, with the *Hel-Blar* and all the secrecy and some of the teachers being all weird?"

Spencer lay on his back, soaking in the sun and abandoning

his watch. No one was paying attention to us anyway. It was too nice a day.

"We'll figure it out," he said yawning. His dreads spread out around him like honey-pale snakes. "We always do."

◆

I didn't see Chloe for the rest of the day. But when I went back to our room Friday evening after dinner there was a note on my pillow. It was in her handwriting and read, *Sorry. I think I have a wicked case of PMS.* She'd left a chocolate bar and a new romance novel as a peace offering. I wasn't mad anymore, but I was still worried.

So I did what any vampire hunter would do.

I snooped.

I felt bad going through her stuff but I couldn't help myself. It was no use booting up her computer and going through her files; some of that encryption stuff may as well have been in ancient Babylonian for all that I understood it. Her gym bag was by her bed though, the zipper half open. I could see the white plastic cap on the bottle with the prescription sticker poking out. I plucked it out of the bag, along with the second bottle I found underneath it. That one was a popular brand of protein powder. I looked inside and sniffed it but it seemed innocuous enough. Not that I really knew what I was looking for.

The second label described the contents as a multivitamin and it had Chloe's name on it and her mom's. They looked normal and even had the regular gross vitamin smell.

I should let this go. I was being ridiculous.

But it didn't stop me from pocketing one of the vitamins in case I needed to get it analyzed later.

I was probably just being paranoid. It happened sometimes to hunters. And PMS could totally account for Chloe's weird mood swings and sudden obsession with working out and combat practice. Still, I kept searching.

I didn't find anything, though—just her normal assortment of nail polishes and data sticks and computer parts, and her secret bottle of peach schnapps in the back of her closet in her left rain boot. She hid a bottle there every year.

I was being a paranoid idiot.

I closed the closet door with a determined snap. I had enough to worry about with Courtney and the Niners and Will to be rifling through my friend's stuff.

Like the fact that Quinn was waiting for me in the clearing in the woods right this very moment.

The sun had fully set while I was rummaging through Chloe's things, which meant Quinn was out there with Kieran and Lucy. Kieran had gotten permission for me to train Lucy as long as we did it out of sight of the school and kept it quiet. It wasn't a precedent they wanted to set, and there was something about insurance as well. Whatever. I didn't want an audience. I felt self-conscious enough knowing Quinn would be there.

I took the bag of supplies I'd packed earlier and ducked out of the dormitory, cutting through the gardens to the woods. I avoided the squares of light falling over the grass from the infirmary. The woods were quiet and warm, thick with the smell of pines and the yellow lilies from the edge of the pond. I followed the glow of light on the other side of the pine grove to the clearing where Kieran had already set up a perimeter of lanterns.

I paused at the sound of a footfall behind me. "You're not supposed to be here."

"You're not the boss of me," Spencer returned good naturedly. "And we're not getting left out of another night of your stealthy fun."

Chloe was beside him, smiling hesitantly. "Okay?"

I wrinkled my nose. "Okay. As long as I can kick your ass in the name of training."

"Deal," Chloe slung her arm through mine. "I want to get a look at one of the famous Drake brothers." She lowered her voice. "I really am sorry I snapped at you."

"I know." *And I'm sorry I went through your stuff*, I thought. But I didn't say it.

Quinn, Lucy, and Kieran were waiting for us in the meadow. Quinn was leaning against a tree, looking dangerous and hot.

"Yummy," Chloe murmured to me. Quinn flashed us a grin. I fought a blush.

"Vampire hearing, remember?" I murmured back.

She shrugged, grinning back. I tried not to feel jealous of the way he winked at her. I turned my attention deliberately to Lucy. She was wearing an embroidered peasant top with jean shorts and Doc Marten boots. Her hair was in a straight bob, her glasses dark-rimmed.

"I'm so going to learn to kick your ass." She smirked at Quinn. "And your brother's."

"Where is Nicholas?" Kieran asked.

"He's locked in a closet," Lucy said with grim satisfaction. After a moment of stunned silence, Quinn snorted out a laugh.

"You locked your boyfriend in a closet?" I asked.

"Cool," Chloe approved. The rhinestones on her earrings caught the blue lantern light.

Lucy shrugged. "Serves him right. He locked me in there last week."

Kieran rolled his eyes. "He was trying to save your life."

"Whatever. Don't make me lock you in there too." She rubbed her hands together excitedly. "Come on, Hunter. Show me some stuff."

"Yeah, Buffy," Quinn grinned amiably at me, pushing away from the tree as we stepped farther into the clearing. "Show us your moves."

Lucy shoved him gently toward me. "Use him as your vampire dummy."

"Hey now."

"This was your idea," she told him. "You're the one who wanted me armed and dangerous."

"What the hell was I thinking?"

She kissed his cheek, as if he really was her big brother, then turned to me expectantly.

"First, I need to see your style," I said.

"Steamroller," Kieran said blandly.

She narrowed her eyes at him. "Can I practice on him?"

I swept my arm out in invitation, grinning. "Be my guest."

She danced back and forth like a boxer, but she was all grace and little technique.

"Just run at him," I suggested.

She lowered her head and charged him like a demented bull. Kieran waited until the last possible second before stepping out of the way, smirking. Lucy stopped herself, but only barely. Another step and she would have brained herself on a tree. She whirled.

"Damn it!" She pointed at Kieran and Quinn. "Don't you dare laugh."

Quinn pressed his lips shut with exaggerated care.

"It's okay," I said. "Take a swing at him now."

Kieran backed up so fast he nearly tripped over his own feet. "No way. She already punched me in the face once."

"Me too," Quinn said. "She has really good aim."

"Good. I can work with that," I replied. "Kieran, pretend to attack her."

He looked dubious but complied. When he grabbed Lucy's shoulder, she turned into a wildcat. She flared, kicked, bit. I was pretty sure I even heard her hiss. After a few minutes, Kieran was scratched and bruised and she was panting and red-faced.

"Not bad," I told her. "But you'll wear yourself out long before you do any actual damage."

She thumped her chest. "I'm starting to get that," she huffed. "I think my heart just exploded."

"We should probably stick to stealth and escape. I can show you how to inflict the maximum amount of damage with minimum force, which will buy you time to run away."

Quinn pinned Lucy with a fierce and knowing glance. "But you actually have to run away, brat."

She made a face. "Yeah, yeah."

"Show me your aim." I handed her three rocks and pointed to

a slim birch. She tossed her hair back off her face, took a deep breath, and launched them. She hit the trunk dead center every time. Spencer whistled through his teeth, impressed. Chloe looked like she was ready to start taking notes.

"Is it true Hope tried to recruit you?" she asked.

"Yeah," Lucy grumbled. "As if I would turncoat for some cheesy comic-book league." She paused, winced. "Oops. Sorry."

I shrugged. "Hope wasn't true Helios-Ra." Never mind that Grandpa had been rather sympathetic to her ultimate goals. Since Lucy had proven herself with her aim and the turn in conversation was making everyone uncomfortable, I showed her our altered ninja eggs.

She blinked. "I'm going to throw Silly Putty at vampires?"

When I explained what was in them, her eyes shone.

"Okay, these I officially love." She proved her point by juggling them, ending with a bow and a flourish. "Let's see you do that, 007," she teased Kieran.

"You should get yourself some Hypnos," I suggested. "I can't give you any because it's against school rules. But if you get some, I can give you an old tear-gas pen you can fill up and tuck in your sleeve. And I have a bunch of eggs without the Hypnos."

"Uncle Geoffrey probably has a stash of the stuff by now," Quinn told her. "Not that I approve," he said to me.

I wasn't the least bit apologetic. "You have pheromones, we have Hypnos. Call it even."

"We're not the ones selling our weapon on the black market and taking unfair advantage. We only use our glamour to protect ourselves."

"First, we don't sell it." I raised an eyebrow. "And second, are you really trying to tell me you've never used your pheromones to steal a kiss?"

"I steal them the old-fashioned way," he said. "With charm."

"Lucy, aim for the big swelled head when you throw those eggs," I said.

"I usually do." She grinned.

"You should also get a staff or a walking stick, something you can attach a blade to or sharpen to a point. It'll keep your attacker out of biting range."

Quinn kicked up a long stick with his boot, throwing it to me.

"Show me," he said as I caught it. I twirled it once. I admit I was showing off a little. If he was going to insist on seeing me as one of the guys and a fellow soldier, I was damn well going to out-soldier him.

"Come on, Buffy," he urged, pale eyes twinkling.

"Any time, Lestat," I shot back.

We circled each other in a slow, predatory dance. It was easy to forget we had an audience. His blue eyes were sharp and hot, like the heart of a candle's flame. It could warm me or burn me clean through.

"No Hypnos," he murmured.

"No pheromones," I countered, though I didn't know how much actual control he had over that sort of thing.

He was quick, of course. Vampires always were. But we'd been trained to focus on that blur of movement, on the displacement of air, on the tiny meticulous details that might just save our lives.

When he came at me I had to convince my reflexes that I

wasn't actually allowed to stake him. The first part of him that was close enough to un-blur was his fangs. They were mesmerizing, but not so mesmerizing that I didn't swing out and catch him in the sternum with the end of my stick. I could tell by the flare of his grin that he felt the impact. I'd never met anyone who enjoyed a skirmish quite so much. Even Grandpa saw it as duty before pleasure. With Quinn, it was almost like he was flirting with me.

I couldn't be sure if he was going to lean in to tear out my jugular or kiss me senseless.

Instead, he kicked out and tripped me, but when I fell backward his hand was at my back to catch me. My left arm crossed between us, fist pressed over his heart to prove my point. I might have staked him in that moment, if the situation were different.

But I might not have been alive to do it.

His fangs rested tenderly on the inside of my throat. The length of our bodies pressed close together. I felt the coolness of his skin and wondered if the heat of mine felt like a burn to him. It was the first time I could actually understand the seduction and the allure of baring your throat to a predator. It had always seemed like madness to me, or the result of reading too many novels. It still did. But there was the barest sway of my body toward him.

His hair swung out to briefly curtain our faces. There was something in his expression that I couldn't entirely decipher.

And then he stepped back abruptly, his familiar smirk erasing that mysterious warmth I'd glimpsed.

Chloe was the first break the silence. She let out a shaky breath.

"Is it suddenly hot out here, or what?"

CHAPTER II

♦

Hunter

Saturday morning

When I woke up the next morning, Chloe was still sitting at her desk and frowning at her computer. I couldn't imagine how she couldn't have a wicked headache. Her shoulders were hunched, the monitor's glare was annoyingly bright, and there were three empty cans of a sugary energy drink on the floor by her chair. Her usually perfect hair was decidedly frizzy, pinned in a knot on top of her head. This was not the Chloe I was used to, perfectly polished and fashionable even in her pajamas. She was also tapping her foot incessantly, like a woodpecker too frantic to realize it was hitting metal, not wood.

I sat up, blinking blearily. The light was pale at the windows, barely light at all. The forest was still dark, as if it was as sleepy as I was. "Chloe?"

"Just a minute." Her fingers clattered over the keyboard. She didn't look up. Something about her, the frenetic energy or the slightly manic way she was chewing her lip, made my stomach nervous. When she suddenly shoved away from her desk, cursing, I jumped.

"Damn it," she seethed. "I really thought I cracked it that time." She glanced at me, at the window. "What time is it?"

I turned the clock radio around so its bright numbers could glow red judgment at her. "5:34."

"Ew."

Now that was more like the Chloe I knew.

"Why'd you pull an all-nighter?" I asked, trying not to sound worried. "It's not like you have homework due. School hasn't even started yet. And it's way too early for classes anyway. Or for normal humans to function."

"I didn't mean to. I just got on a roll with the security codes. Well, I thought I was on a roll, anyway. I'm so handing this in as my independent study." She rubbed her red-rimmed eyes. "I feel like shit."

"They have this new cure for that," I said drily. "It's called sleep."

"Ha-ha."

"Are you gonna crash now or what?" I insisted. I could pull the plug on her computer but she'd probably scratch my eyes out. And it was too early for a catfight. She yawned and crawled into her bed. She was asleep before she'd even answered me.

I decided to take advantage of the early hour and the still dormitory. It was so rarely quiet and today was Saturday. All the students who weren't already here would start arriving after breakfast. Courtney would almost certainly pawn off some of her less glamorous duties on me, and then tonight we were going into town for vampire bait night.

So if I was going to follow through on the possibly illegal idea I'd had last night before falling asleep, now was my best chance.

I grabbed my knapsack and stuffed it with supplies as Chloe began to snore. I didn't bother changing out of my pajamas since I planned to go right back to sleep as soon as humanly possible, but I did stop by the bathroom. There was just enough light from the windows to make the hall gray instead of black. I stayed on the edge of the staircase so it wouldn't creak, skipping the third and eleventh steps altogether.

As much as my grandfather was strict and full of hunter pride, he'd given me awesome toys over the years—mostly old weapons, crossbows, and surveillance equipment.

It was the latter I was planning to put to good use.

I didn't have Chloe's knack, and I could hardly ask for her help. After that *Hel-Blar* woman died and Will mentioned vitamins, I knew something was up—I just had no idea what. We needed more information on this so-called vitamin, but I didn't know anyone in the science department I trusted enough to test the pills I'd pocketed. Chloe's mom helped devise Hypnos, and apparently she had a hand in the vitamins too, but that kind of chemistry or biology or whatever was way beyond my scope.

But I did know someone who might able to help me.

Quinn.

If Kieran trusted him, surely that meant I could too.

Even if he was a vampire.

And I was a hunter.

When had life become so freaking complicated?

For the part of this mess where I was essentially accusing higher-ups in the league and my friend's mother besides, I was on my own. I wouldn't even tell Kieran about that right now. He was already walking a thin line by dating Solange and allying himself with the Drakes. Not only would they have him under some kind of surveillance, but he didn't need extra flack for my unproven theories.

And anyway, it was far more likely that if the vitamin was making Chloe act weird, it was because she was taking it too often. Maybe she was even allergic to it.

There were too many questions that didn't make sense and not nearly enough answers.

So I was bugging the eleventh-grade common room.

Also, I was going to have to steal a sample of Will's blood from the infirmary.

I had no idea if this sort of thing could get me expelled or if I could plead extra credit. I hoped I never had to find out. It was worth the risk, though. This is where Will would hang out when they finally released him from the infirmary.

I only had three reliable microphones and just one of them had a motion sensor. I hid one under the couch, tucked behind the ugly brown fringe and a gross lump of gum no one was likely to want to breach. Another one I slid inside the removable drawer handle on the bottom left of the dresser under the bulletin board. I figured those would be the two most likely places students would gather to talk. There was no point in tapping the communal phone; they only used it to call home when they were out of minutes on their cell phones.

I could hear the faint sounds of someone padding down the hall toward the bathrooms. I had just enough time to duck behind the coat tree, still thick with discarded and lost clothes from last year. The student ambled past, scratching parts of his anatomy I didn't need to know about.

I unscrewed the knob on the top of the coat rack and dropped my last microphone into the pole. Luckily the microphone was an old-fashioned one from WWII and fit into a ballpoint pen–like casing. Unluckily, it dropped straight to the bottom, where I might never get to fish it out again. I couldn't risk trying to shake it loose now either. Cursing, I ran all the way back to my room.

I slipped under the sheets, the muggy August morning already too humid for blankets. Chloe was still snoring. I rubbed the coronation medallion I wore around my neck and hoped I knew what the hell I was doing.

This had every indication of going horribly wrong.

Into the breach, then.

I lay there, staring at the ceiling, and wondered what exactly I was going to say to Quinn.

◆

"You're late," Courtney snapped at me later that morning.

"I'm not late because I didn't have an appointment," I replied.

And I was late because I'd been at the infirmary, stealing a test tube of blood. Theo wouldn't let me in to visit Will, but he left me alone in the waiting room after wheeling the cart of blood samples into one of the examination rooms to await pick-up. All I'd had to do was reach around the curtain. The only difficult part was making sure I had the right sample. Apparently there were a lot of students with the weird flu that was going around because there were a lot of tubes in the tray. The thought of that many needles had me cringing.

So did the fact that I'd stolen a vial of Chloe's blood as well. But at least they hadn't reached the end of the alphabet yet for the yearly checkups, so I was off the hook with needles for another week at least.

"Just stand over here." She actually snapped her fingers and pointed behind her.

I stared at her. "Woof." I was glad I'd worn my favorite pair of pink cargos. She'd coveted them since we'd roomed together last year. Small, petty revenges were all I was likely to get.

And about a hundred demerits for poking her eyes out if she kept glaring at me like I was some disgusting substance she'd just stepped in.

She sniffed and ignored me. Fine by me.

The staircase was packed full of wide-eyed students and parents lugging suitcases. The dorm felt like a beehive, vibrating with sound and energy. There'd be stings by the end of the day, no doubt. Lia was hovering in the common room, trying to get a look at her roommate before having to introduce herself. Courtney smiled at all the parents and introduced herself politely and pretended I didn't exist. She wiped her hands with alcohol sanitizer after every hand she shook. Another student had been carted off to the infirmary with a high fever this morning.

I slipped my cell phone out of my pocket and texted Kieran to get Quinn's phone number. I texted him quickly and tried not to obsess over every word.

> Need to ask you a favor. Can you come by the school Sunday night? Meadow, midnight. Don't tell Kieran. Hunter.

It wasn't like I was asking him out or anything. I was only asking for a professional courtesy. I shouldn't worry about whether or not I sounded too formal or curt or if he'd think I had a crush on him.

Because I didn't.

Mostly.

It was only natural to be curious about Quinn. He was a vampire, for crying out loud, and a Drake. He was becoming a friend of Kieran's too, so that made him a friend of mine.

And so what if he was gorgeous.

Lots of guys were gorgeous.

Of course, he was the first one to make me feel like blushing when I so much as thought his name. Like right now. Damn it.

"Oh, hello, Hunter." One of Grandpa's friends smiled at me, effectively distracting me from my mental freak-out.

"Mr. Sagasaki." I smiled back. His hair had a lot more white in it than the last time I'd seen him. He hadn't made it to our family barbecue this year, which is when I usually saw him and his son, who was standing beside him, a full foot taller than last year.

"Oh, call me Louis, honey. You're practically family." Mr. Sagasaki grinned. "I used to change your diapers, after all."

At the sound of his name, several heads turned. Courtney's eyes widened and she stood straighter, smoothing her hair back. Louis was a hunter with the kind of reputation it took decades to build. He had a record seventy-two vampire kills and had once taken out a *Hel-Blar* nest all by himself, two doors down from a grade-school ballet recital. I wasn't sure about that part of the rumor but I knew he was good. He had the scars and the faded tattoo on his upper arm to prove it.

"Mr. Sagasaki. It's a pleasure to meet you," Courtney held out her hand. "My name is Courtney and I'm the girls' ninth-grade floor monitor."

He shook her hand. "This here's my son, Martin."

"Hey, Hunter," Martin said, trying to hide his relief at seeing a familiar face. It probably wasn't cool for a fourteen-year-old boy to appear the least bit nervous about his first day at the academy. It hadn't been cool for me as a thirteen-year-old girl either, but Grandpa got me into classes a year early out of sheer stubborn pride that I could do better than anyone else.

"Hey," I said. "Still a mean shot with that crossbow?"

He nodded proudly. Over his head, his dad winked at me.

"Glad he's in good hands, Hunter," he said, urging his son forward so they could unclog the traffic jam of people trying to move around them. "You too, Kelly."

"It's Courtney," she corrected, but he was already out of earshot. She glowered at me. "I'm the floor monitor. You shouldn't hog people like that. It's rude."

I rolled my eyes. "I'm not going to ignore a family friend because you're insecure."

This was possibly part of the reason why she hated me so much. I just couldn't let her weird bragging and overcompensating go by unremarked. I went back to checking my phone before I could say anything else.

No reply text from Quinn.

Maybe he wouldn't answer. Maybe he was busy with his tongue in some girl's mouth.

Maybe I was an idiot.

It was noon, the hottest, brightest part of the day. He was a vampire. Duh.

I slipped my phone back into my pocket and vowed never to mention to anyone that a straight-A vampire-hunter student had momentarily forgotten that vampires didn't waltz about in broad daylight.

Talk about being off my game.

I went back to standing at attention and tried to look like someone you'd trust your thirteen-year-old kid's safety to, someone my grandfather would be proud of.

Not like someone daydreaming about a vampire.

CHAPTER 12

•

QUINN

Saturday evening

I couldn't stop thinking about Hunter.

If I'd been any one of my brothers, I would have mocked myself mercilessly.

Because she wasn't just human, she was a hunter. I suddenly had way more sympathy for what Solange was going through. Although, at least Hunter didn't smell like food to me. Mostly.

But she did smell damn good regardless.

I wondered if she'd gotten into trouble for wandering around campus with a vampire. Or if that boy we'd taken to the infirmary had turned and now there was one more *Hel-Blar* that needed to be put down. If they kept attacking like this, it wouldn't be long before the residents of Violet Hill began to wonder what kind of creatures lived in the mountains and the forests on the edge of town. Soon it wouldn't be safe for anyone to go out at night—but try telling that to the college students and the wilderness freaks.

There were stories already, and stories were never good. We relied on secrecy, and the common belief that vampires don't exist, to keep us safe. But the current pop culture obsession with all things vampire wasn't helping us any. We really had to get a handle on this *Hel-Blar* infestation, and fast. Mom was sending out patrols, and Kieran said the Helios-Ra were scouting as well.

I couldn't help but wonder if Hunter would be recruited for one of those patrols. She was good enough. I'd seen that for myself. And Hart had called her into the meeting at the caves last week and to the coronation. That said something.

I hadn't quite been able to ask Kieran if she had a boyfriend.

The question throbbed like a broken tooth, impossible to ignore, impossible not to poke, just to see if it still hurt.

I never did this.

I liked girls—human or vampire. I liked them a lot, but I never wondered what they were doing or if I'd hear from them. Because I always heard from them, usually more than I liked. I treated them all well, don't get me wrong. You couldn't be raised by my mother and not treat girls with a hell of a lot of respect. But they knew up front that I wasn't looking for strings, just a good time for everyone involved.

And none of the humans knew I was a vampire. I wasn't stupid.

Well, except for that one time.

But that was a long time ago. It wasn't even worth mentioning.

Besides, Hunter was different. She was strong and brave and sexy. I loved the way she looked at me, just slightly suspicious, as if she was thinking about kicking my ass. That shouldn't be hot, but it was. And I was just itching to convince her to unbraid all that blonde hair. She'd look killer with it down.

Damn it, I was thinking about her again. About her *hair*.

"Shit," I muttered. If I wasn't careful I'd start writing sonnets too, like Karin had written for me. "I have to get out of here."

◆

The royal caves were a good distraction, because if you lowered your guard for a moment, you could get your head chopped off.

Right now that sounded perfect.

I nodded at the guards at the main entrance and strolled into the caverns. They were lit with torches, the tunnel opening into several larger chambers. The largest one was the Great Hall, which suited the Drake family's very medieval tendencies. Just look at our only surviving matriarch, Veronique Dubois. She was even scarier than Mom was, and she could embroider your funeral shroud by hand. It was easy to accept Mom as a queen, or Veronique. Dad had that monarch thing going for him too. I had a harder time picturing the rest of us as royal princes. Connor didn't like people, vampire or otherwise. He just wanted to be left alone with his computers. Logan dressed like a pirate. And I knew more about pick-up lines than I did vampire politics—and I didn't have any great desire to learn more about it.

But I did have a great desire to stop vampire assassins from attacking my mom and my sister. So I'd man up and study vampire politics and show my face in court and pretend I knew what the hell was going on.

Anyway, it was better than mooning over Hunter Wild.

The Great Hall was drafty, the oil lamp lights flickering. It was saved from being damp and unwelcoming by the piles of thick rugs underfoot and the tapestries hanging from iron rods. Veronique had sent a huge banner embroidered with the Drake family crest and the royal vampire crest, which now hung behind a wooden table ringed with chairs. The chairs each had thick wooden backs, to protect against stakes, arrows, and daggers. Dad was all about treaties and diplomacy. Mom was all about the attack. Between the two of them they might actually be able to control the chaotic vampire tribes, at least for a little while.

Vampire tribes tended to be independent at best and belligerently autonomous at worst. Ruling them was mostly about making sure no one wiped each other out in such a public manner that we'd all be discovered. Prosaic but true.

"Quinn." Sebastian raised his eyebrows. "You walked right by that girl. What's wrong?"

"I did?" I looked over my shoulder. A vampire with short brown hair and beauty mark at the side of her mouth winked at me. I winked back. Then I turned back to Sebastian, horrified. "I didn't even see her."

"You're off your game."

"Shh, keep it down, will you?" I straightened my shirt. "I have a reputation. I'm going back. She's cute."

"Forget it. She flirts with everyone."

"So?" I grinned.

"Just come on. Mom and Dad are in the back room. And we can't handle any more disgruntled exes."

"My exes are never disgruntled." That was a point of pride actually. "Any more packages for Solange?" Solange's bloodchange pheromones, coupled with the old prophecy, had sent more vampires than we could count into a frenzy. They sent her gifts, stalked her, and generally acted like asses.

"Twelve letters, three packages, and a box of puppies."

I winced. "Puppies?"

"They're fine. Isabeau took them all."

"Good. Who eats puppies?" I shook my head.

"Yeah, Isabeau swore in French. A lot."

"Hot."

"Yeah, Logan nearly went cross-eyed."

"So where are they now?"

"Isabeau's gone back to the Hounds and Logan's studying up."

"He's studying?" I shuddered. "For what? Girlfriends give exams now?"

"He's an honorary Hound, remember," Sebastian reminded me as we passed two more guards and entered the private family room. Logan had gone through the ritual initiation of the Hounds, something that was rarely offered to anyone not already connected to the reclusive tribe. "So he wants to know more about them. Connor downloaded stuff from some ancient library in Rome."

"Do they know he hacked their system yet?"

"Hell no," Connor replied from where he was trying to fix Mom's laptop. "I'm just that good. Though even I can't get wireless down here."

"So what's going on?" I asked. "Dad looks like he's about to break into song. It's kind of scary actually." A grown man shouldn't wear that kind of goofy grin. Especially when he was my father.

"We just got word that a Blood Moon is being called for November."

"Seriously?" No wonder Dad looked so happy. Blood Moons were only very rarely called, and no one knew who exactly called them. It was essentially a week-long festival with the main night reserved for tribal leaders to talk treaties and various vampire issues. The last one had been nearly a hundred years ago. "Why now? 'Cause of Mom?"

Sebastian nodded. "And the *Hel-Blar*. They're becoming a real problem, and not just here in Violet Hill."

"Any word on why they swarmed the Helios-Ra school?" I asked.

Connor shook his head. "Nothing yet."

"Well, it sure as hell wasn't an accident. And you didn't see that *Hel-Blar* disintegrate. It was weird."

"We're looking into it," Dad called over to us. "And I mentioned it to Hart."

"Good. There are a lot of kids in that school."

Sebastian raised an eyebrow. "Not every day I hear you worrying about hunters."

I shrugged.

Connor snorted.

"Shut up," I told him. Sometimes the twin connection was a pain in the ass. I hadn't said a word to him about Hunter, but he already knew I was into her.

If the royal courts and all their melodrama weren't enough to stop me from thinking about her, I'd just have to think of something else.

"I'll check out the scene in town."

"Hot date?"

"Working on it."

CHAPTER 13

◆

Hunter

Saturday night

I know it's not very secret agent of me, but I really, *really* love dressing up.

Even if it's just to flitter around like dumb horror-movie vampire bait.

I love choosing a dress, shaving my legs, and painting my toes. I love pretty sandals with little heels, though I couldn't exactly wear them tonight. I'd never get a good kick in with those, and I wouldn't be able to outrun a raccoon. So I wore a pair of low-top Converse sneakers with my sundress. It was blue, with lace at the hem and spaghetti straps, which Grandpa thought were trampy because my shoulders were bare. I added a matching chunky turquoise necklace and pink lipstick.

Chloe grinned at me from where she sat on the edge of her bed. Against all odds, she was ready before me. And she wasn't wearing any jewelry or makeup. Just jeans and a tight T-shirt. Her hair was in a simple braid. I barely recognized her.

"You look great."

I twirled once. "If a vampire muddies this dress, I'm kicking ass."

"I'll help." Her eyes shone. I'd never seen her so happy to fight before. She usually preferred flirting with locals at the club over the actual work of bait-nights. Maybe she'd just changed over the summer and I was being paranoid. I really hoped so.

"Where are your weapons?" She tilted her head curiously.

I held up my purse. "In here. And I've got a stake strapped to my thigh."

"Ooh." She waggled her eyebrows. "Sexy."

"Yeah, yeah."

At the bottom of the stairs outside our room were clusters of whispering Niners. They stared at us like we were movie stars.

"Creepy much?" Chloe muttered at them.

Lia was the only one brave enough to step out of the pack. "Is it true you guys go to town and lure vampires out of clubs?"

I nodded.

"That is so *cool*," she breathed. "Can we do that?"

"You're not allowed off campus at night until you're sixteen," I said as we shut the front door behind us. We hurried down the lane to the garages, passing students out for a walk or a jog on the track and others lying in the grass by the pond and catching up with each other. Night had just barely settled over the school, making the old buildings look somehow quaint and old-fashioned. I wouldn't have been surprised to see the ghost of a Victorian gentleman or a pioneer woman churning butter on the porch of the headmistress's house. Jenna, Spencer, and Jason were waiting by the old van we'd booked for the night. It was unassumingly gray, clunky, and hideous. And it beat walking to town, hands down.

"Get in," Jenna said, sliding into the front seat before anyone else could. She loved driving almost as much as she loved shooting stuff.

"Shotgun!" Chloe yelled. She always got shotgun because she made mixes for the half-hour drive to town. I climbed in the back with Spencer and Jason.

"So where are we going?" Spencer asked as Jenna pulled out, scattering gravel. "The Blue Cat?"

"The Blue Cat shut down last month," Jason told him, raising his voice over the loud music that filled the van.

"What about Conspiracy Theory?" Jenna asked. Everyone nodded. Conspiracy wasn't a dance club like the Blue Cat had been, but it was a funky cafe in an old three-story house with live bands on the weekends. It'd be the most popular spot now— mostly because none of the other clubs let in minors as easily as Conspiracy Theory did.

I rolled my window down, enjoying the cool breeze that smelled like cedar and grass, flatly refusing to check my phone one more time. I had a life; I was busy taking out bloodthirsty vampires to make the neighborhood safe again. I didn't have time to wait around for Quinn Drake to deign to honor me with a reply.

The forest and mountains gave way to fields and farms and then the tiny town of Violet Hill, tucked into the edge of the lake. It was mostly art galleries and old bookstores and organic cafes. There were probably more crystal shops in the village than in all of San Francisco. Every July there was an art festival and people drew on the streets with chalk. There were farmers' markets and a pioneer museum. I loved it, even though Grandpa thought it was run by a bunch of, and I quote, "pot-smoking hippies." He could overlook that though, since it was a convenient crossroads for several vampire tribes, both civilized and *Hel-Blar*.

There were other creatures too, according to Spencer, but I'd never seen any of them. He was convinced there were werewolves, but even his professors in the Paranormal Department wouldn't give him a straight answer. I kept telling him that probably meant one of *them* was a werewolf. You never could tell at our school.

Jenna drove too fast, as always, so we made it to the main street in twenty minutes. Violet Lake looked like a dark blob of ink on the edge of the paper-white stones. We parked down the street from the coffeehouse and walked up through the abandoned factory district. All half a block of it. Violet Hill was nothing if not quaint.

"That's the one," Chloe said confidently, nodding to the old glass factory. Broken shards still glittered on the pavement, even though it had closed ten years ago. It was wide enough to maneuver in with some cover, so we wouldn't draw the attention of any late-night pedestrians. They mostly went in the other direction toward the taxi stand or the bus stop.

The lawn outside the cafe was littered with smokers, the music from the jazz-rock band pouring out of the open door. We eased through the crowds and claimed the torn velvet couch in the very back where the light was dim and the floors were sticky with spilled drinks. Candles burned everywhere in jam jars, and twinkly lights were wrapped around the bar counter. The buzz of the espresso machine was a constant vibration under the music.

I took everyone's drink orders since I was the bait. I was the one who had to prance around being all obvious and dumb. I giggled.

"Better," Spencer approved. "You sound less like you ate an angry helium balloon."

I made a face at him before making my way through the crowd toward the counter. I eyed the patrons unobtrusively. The three guys at the pool table were trying to look like predators, all suave and cool, but they were harmless. The girl in the back corner flirting with a guy in a leather coat was on my radar. She looked hungry and I didn't know if it was for attention or blood. The two at the table under the window were underage and desperately trying not to look it. The waitstaff looked harried and didn't have time to care who was drinking illegally and who wasn't. Besides, it was Violet Hill, possibly the most liberal, free-thinking town on the planet. Drinking was no big deal. Fur coats and pesticides on the other hand . . .

The bar was actually a series of old wooden doors hinged together. The one at the end had belonged to a saloon at the turn of the century. There were two bartenders and a press of thirsty people waving money and shouting orders over the band. I fluttered my eyelashes and leaned on the bar, making sure my cleavage, such as it was, was visible. Part 1 of the plan required I be seen.

"A shot of Kahlua, please," I ordered. I made sure my voice was a little too loud. I leaned farther over, catching the eye of two guys who were staring at me. The one on the left might possibly be vampiric. It was kind of hard to tell. I worked up an annoying giggle.

He raised his glass to me and eased out of the line, leaving a gap and a better view of the people on his other side.

I choked on the giggle.

"What the hell are you doing here?" I scowled at Quinn.

It was just my luck that he was lounging there with a pretty girl on each arm. No wonder he hadn't answered my text message.

And worse, he would catch Part 2 of the plan, in which I was soon going to make an ass of myself, and he'd miss Part 3, in which I redeemed myself by kicking actual ass.

"Buffy." He grinned, eyes flaring when he took in my short dress and daring neckline. I forced myself not to blush or fidget. I lifted my chin, daring him to make a single comment.

"Your name's Buffy?" The girl on his left sneered.

The other girl pinched her. "Don't be rude." She smiled at me apologetically.

Quinn didn't look away from me once during the whole exchange. I raised an eyebrow.

"Shouldn't you be tucked away safely in your little bed?" he asked.

"Shouldn't you be wearing a red velvet jacket and talking with a bad European accent?" I shot back.

"Are you really from Europe?" the first girl asked, misunderstanding. She ran her finger along his collar. "Do you live in a castle?"

I snorted and turned away, taking my shot glass off the sticky counter. Quinn's hand closed lightly around my wrist.

"You're not legal," he said, nodding at the Kahlua.

"My ID says differently," I assured him with a bland smile. I wasn't about to tell him that the drink was just for show. I needed to appear drunk. *Appear* being the operative word, because a drunk hunter was a dead hunter.

He leaned in, tucking my hair behind my ear and whispering so that only I could hear. His girlfriends frowned. Three guys and a girl near the band seemed suddenly interested in us.

"Where do you keep a stake in a dress like that?"

I angled my head to whisper back, half smiling. "Strapped to my thigh."

He drew back sharply, blue eyes burning. I smirked and flounced away. I could feel him watching me the entire way back to my table. The others had gotten their Cokes already and they drank them slowly, looking relaxed. Only I knew each of them had stakes inside their jackets, Hypnos in their sleeves, and blades in the soles of their boots.

I tossed back my shot with a flourish. I could hardly convince a vampire I was drunk if he couldn't smell alcohol on my breath.

Spencer frowned at me. "You know how you get when you drink," he said loudly.

I shrugged, laughed. "I'm just having fun. You should try it sometime." Under my breath I added, "The group by the stage, possibly two guys who went up to the second floor." I reached for the whiskey sour he'd left on the table, surreptitiously spilling most of it on the table.

"How many shots have you had?" Jason demanded.

"Just the one. Don't be such a spoilsport. *God.*" I stumbled, just a little. Jason opened my purse and took out the three shot glasses I'd slipped in there before leaving. He made a big production of tossing them on the table and looking disgusted. I just laughed and prayed Quinn was too far away, too distracted by the pretty girls throwing themselves at him, to notice me.

"You promised you wouldn't drink," Chloe said.

"You guys are *lame,*" I said, too loudly. A few heads turned our way. Chloe hid a gleam of satisfaction behind a fake worried scowl. I twirled away. "I'm going to dance if you're all going to be such boring old ladies."

This was the part I hated the most: dancing by myself like an idiot.

But it worked every time.

I twirled and shook my hips and giggled when I tripped into someone leaning against the amps. He caught me easily, smiling. His hands were cold, his eyes a pale hazel.

Vampire.

"I'm so sorry," I simpered at him.

"That's okay," he replied, still holding onto my arm. He was good, I'd give him that. His expression was open and guileless. He successfully avoided the silky menace that was always such a dead giveaway. With his blond hair and white T-shirt he looked like a local college student, the athletic sort with lots of interesting arm muscles and strong shoulders. Just the type a drunk underage high school student would flirt with.

I hated flirting.

"Thanks for catching me," I said, stepping closer. "My name's Amber."

"Of course it is." I pretended not to understand what he meant by that. "It's a very pretty name."

Ha.

"Your friends appear to be ditching you," he added. His own friends pressed closer. I turned my head to see Chloe and the others leaving.

I pouted. "They're no fun."

He was still holding on to my elbow. "We were just leaving too. They're shutting the doors in half an hour but there's a party down the street." He drew his hand down my arm. "Want to come with us, Amber?"

Gotcha, you undead bastards.

I bit my lip, tilted my head. "I don't even know your name."

"It's Matthew." He nodded to his friends. "That's Nigel, Paul, Sam, and Belinda."

There were a lot of teeth suddenly gleaming at me. The smiles were calculating. Amber, fictional though she might be, would have found them charming and fun. So I smiled back.

"Okay, I guess." The music pulsed between us. "Is it far?"

"Not at all." His hand moved to my lower back, pressing me forward and out the door. I had just enough time to glance at the bar. Quinn was gone.

Outside, the wind had cooled. Litter skittered along the curb.

Matthew led us down the street, toward the dark alleys, away from the pubs and restaurants, just as we'd planned. I hesitated.

"Come on," he said. "I thought you wanted to have some fun."

Nigel laughed. "Yeah, Amber, don't wimp out on us now."

I shrugged and let them convince me. The others would be positioned around the old glass factory. Jenna would likely be on a rooftop somewhere. We turned a corner, effectively shielding us from the parts of town still inhabited to the stretch of abandoned warehouses. Our footsteps echoed. The streetlights were dim.

Amber was an idiot.

But Chloe was a bigger idiot.

Chloe knew the plan.

It was her bloody idea in the first place to corner the vampires on the other side of the glass factory where there was an abandoned parking lot full of weeds, a broken-down wall for cover, and nothing else.

Not, I repeat, *not* by the road where anyone might drive by. It was unlikely, true, but still possible.

And yet there she was, hollering like a lunatic and launching herself at us.

I didn't know where the others were, beyond *not here* and not close enough to be of any immediate help. What had Spencer been thinking, to let her run off on her own?

She managed to knock Nigel off his feet, at least. She'd improved in the last week, but not enough to take on five vampires and survive, even with my help. I took advantage of the brief moment of surprise when the vampires whirled to see what crazy animal had pounced on their friend. I stepped back and liberated the stake from my thigh holster. Matthew glanced at me and licked his lips.

"Well, now, Amber," he said as his fangs protruded from his gums. "Aren't you suddenly more interesting."

I didn't waste my breath answering him. The other four circled Chloe, showing their own fangs.

If we lived through this, I was so going to kill her.

I only had the one stake. If I used it on Matthew, it left Chloe unprotected. And she was already on her knees, a hole ripped in her jeans, blood on her lip. She used her wrist harness to send a stake through Nigel's heart. He crumbled into ash. Go, Chloe.

Of course, now the rest of them were really pissed.

And I couldn't reach her.

Our teachers were always going on about how vampires would chase you if you ran away; the predator in them found it hard to resist the hunt.

I really hoped they were right about that.

As backup plans went, this one kind of sucked.

I turned and ran, pausing only to shoot Matthew the most taunting smirk I could manage. Because teasing an angry vampire is always such a good idea.

I ran fast.

Matthew, of course, was faster. Much, much faster. And so were his friends.

On the plus side, it left Chloe only one vampire to deal with, and he was fairly small.

On the minus side, it left me three.

I didn't make it to the glass factory parking lot, but I was close enough that a good yell should alert the others, if there wasn't a cold pale hand currently squeezing my trachea. I gagged on a breath, eyes burning. I clawed at the hand out of instinct, even though I knew it wouldn't do me any good. When I started to see spots, my training kicked back in.

I had a perfectly good stake.

I shoved it through Matthew's chest as hard as I could. My vision was gray and watery and lack of oxygen was becoming a serious issue. I didn't quite get his heart; I was an inch or so shy on the left. But at least it hurt him enough that he released me with a yell. Blood welled around the stake, still sticking out of his rib cage, while I heaved air into my screaming lungs. I also turned to deliver a kick to his wound with the heel of my shoe. He didn't turn to dust but he stumbled out of reach. And then Belinda had me by the hair, wrapping it around her wrist and yanking savagely.

I could all but hear Grandpa's grumble of disapproval.

Why did a certain kind of girl always go for the hair?

My neck muscles stretched near to breaking, my head angled painfully to the side, exposing my jugular. Saliva dripped on my arm and onto the ground. She was drooling. Gross.

"That wasn't very nice," Matthew said, approaching me. He plucked the stake out of his flesh as if it were a thorn off a rose-bush. Red petals of blood scattered around him. Belinda held me steady for him, giving into the temptation of my blood by nipping me once. It was no worse than a bee sting but I recoiled, going cold down to my bones. She licked at the tiny puncture marks as if I was bleeding ice cream.

"Ew," I tried to elbow her. "Get off me."

I couldn't see how Chloe was doing, couldn't even hear her. I could only see Matthew's sharp teeth and the way he twirled the bloody stake over his knuckles, like a street juggler. Even his polo shirt was suddenly menacing.

"Ever wonder how it feels to get one of these in the heart?" he asked pleasantly.

I tried to shrink back, even as Belinda forced me forward. I crushed her instep. She didn't let me go but she did swear viciously, which I enjoyed.

Where the hell was everyone?

"It seems only fair," Matthew continued. "A bit of karma, if you will." He twirled the stake again. "Shall we see how long you scream?"

"Are you ever going to shut up?" I snapped, fear and irritation filling me in equal measures. "This isn't your monologue, Hamlet. It's the battle scene, in case you've forgotten."

His eyes narrowed so fast they nearly sparked. They were the color of honey on fire. One of the others growled like an animal, low in his throat. It made all the hairs on my arms stand straight up.

I was going to die for making fun of Shakespeare.

My English Lit professor would be so proud.

And then Matthew was screaming.

The stake clattered at my feet but I couldn't reach it. I used Belinda's iron grip to secure a pivot that knocked Sam off both his feet as he came at me. Out of the corner of my eye, I saw Matthew hit the ground, broken glass grinding under his weight. There was a blur of movement and then the shadow coalesced into a dark shirt, pale skin, and blue eyes like burning gasoline.

Quinn.

I had no idea where he'd come from and I didn't have time to wonder about it. Belinda was clacking her teeth at me.

"I said"—I elbowed her in the nose, hearing bone snap—"get"—I used the side of my hand to chop at her wrist—"off!" And then I dropped, pulling her off balance so that she stumbled. I used the momentum of a roll to toss her over. I managed to stretch just enough to reach the stake. I blocked Belinda's second attack, mostly by happy accident. I twisted the stake and shoved it as hard as I could. She went to ash and drifted over the dirty pavement.

Matthew howled. He reared up furiously, slashing at Quinn with a penknife. I threw a rock at his head and kicked back to trip Paul before he could make a grab for me. Quinn leaned so far back his hair brushed the ground. He went into the turn completely and landed beside me.

"Back-to-back," he ordered, but I was already pressing my shoulder blades against his. Standard hand-to-hand combat stance.

He was grinning.

I rolled my eyes. "How is this fun for you?"

He shrugged one shoulder. "Not ash yet."

"I can fix that," Matthew hissed.

"You're right," Quinn said conversationally to me, as if we weren't currently outnumbered and fighting for our lives. "This one just won't shut up." Quinn's punch was so fast I heard the crack of one of Matthew's fangs against Quinn's knuckle. I didn't see it but the sound was unique. "Let me help you with that."

"You broke my tooth!" Matthew spat blood, the whites of his eyes going red with rage. It was just distracting enough that I missed

Paul's fist, until it caught my cheekbone. Pain bloomed over my face. I'd have a wicked bruise by morning. I stumbled back, bumping Quinn's arm. He flicked a glance over his shoulder.

"Shit," he said."Your face."

"Ow." I agreed.

"Where the hell are your friends?"

"I don't know." But at least all the vampires were attacking us, not Chloe. Right now I wanted to kill her myself. I fumbled for the silver whistle around my neck, hanging next to the Drake coronation medallion. I only wore it on bait-nights. It looked like a little silver pendant but it was much more useful. I blew into it and the shrill whistle pierced the night.

"I don't even want to know," Quinn muttered, moving so fast he was a dark shadowy blur like ink spilled in the shape of a man. He was fighting off all three vampires as best he could, circling me protectively like dark fog.

"Let me help," I shouted.

"You're hurt."

"I'm *fine*." I insisted. The day one little punch, vampiric or not, took me out of an entire fight was the night I was no longer a Wild. "Let me in," I adjusted the hold on my stake, slippery with Matthew's blood. My throat hurt from being strangled, my face hurt from being punched, and we were surrounded.

And I was kind of having fun.

Probably not a good sign.

CHAPTER 14

◆

Hunter

"On your right," Quinn barked, materializing on my other side. I jabbed the stake to my right and caught flesh and bone, but not heart. Still, Paul stumbled and slowed down enough that I could see him clearly now, even in the dim light of a single faded streetlight. I jabbed again, hit closer to the heart.

And then everyone else was there in answer to my whistle. Jenna's wicked aim took out Sam with a crossbow arrow. Jason stood back, holding Chloe, who clutched her side. I saw Spencer pop his vial of Hypnos and knew what he was about to do.

I took a deep breath, whirled, and grabbed Quinn, jerking him toward me. His eyes widened. My mouth closed over his just as Spencer tossed the Hypnos. It was everywhere, like confectioners' sugar on a cupcake.

"Vampires stop!" he yelled.

I kissed Quinn harder, making sure he wasn't inhaling any of the powder. He kissed me back, returning the favor.

His mouth was just as delicious as I'd imagined it would be. Not that I'd been thinking clearly about it. Not that I was capable of thinking right at that moment anyway.

His lips were cool, as if he'd been eating ice cream. His hands gripped my arms, holding me tight against his chest. His tongue touched mine, lightly, then deeper, until even my knees felt weak. I kissed him back. I wasn't going to pull away and be the only one feeling soft as water. He made a sound in the back of his throat, like a groan or a purr.

It made me feel stronger than if I'd been fully armed.

His eyes opened, the pupils wide and very black. It was a long hot moment before I realized the sounds of battle had faded altogether, and not just because of the kiss. I pulled away, taking a deep breath. I knew I was blushing, knew Quinn could feel the warmth of my blood rushing to the surface of my skin. I took another breath.

Everyone was staring at us.

"Dude," Spencer said.

I cleared my throat, taking a big step away from Quinn. I couldn't look at him. I didn't want to know yet if he was smirking. Matthew and Paul, the only two remaining vampires were slumped at our feet, glaring at us with furious pale eyes. Jenna stood over them, crossbow at the ready.

"Hypnos is going to wear off soon," she warned.

I pushed my hair off my face. "We need to tie them up." My voice was only a little squeaky.

"What for?" Quinn asked. "Stake them."

We all stared at him. "They're prisoners of war," I said.

"They're vampires."

"So are you."

"So I know what I'm talking about."

I shook my head. "You can't be serious."

"You haven't seen your face, Hunter," he said coldly.

No, but I could feel it. The bruise was already throbbing under my eye and across my left cheekbone.

"We can't just kill them in cold blood," I insisted as the heat of battle faded. "We're not assassins."

"Then I'll do it."

I stepped between him and the vampires. "Don't."

"He has a point," Jason said quietly.

"Hello? Killing a prisoner of war? Do you know how much detention that would be?" I swung around to stare at him. And now that they were immobilized, we'd have to stake them when they couldn't fight back. Maybe I was being stupid, but it felt wrong this way. It was different in battle.

"Whatever we do, we have to do it fast," Jenna interrupted us. "Like in the next three minutes."

"We have enough rope to tie them up and call the mobile unit. They'll come get them and lock them up."

"Your puny knots won't hold them," Quinn said as I flipped open my cell phone and hit speed dial.

"Then your vampire ones will." I gave him a dry glance, waiting for the call to go through. "So get tying."

Jenna handed him the rope hanging from her belt. Quinn sighed after a moment and took it. "This is a bad idea," he muttered, yanking hard on the rope.

"I'm with you," Jason muttered back.

"Chloe needs a medic," I said after I'd given our coordinates to the agent on the other line. I slipped the phone back in my purse. "So why don't you guys take her back and I'll stay here and wait for the unit."

"It's just a flesh wound," she tried to joke. "Ow. Stupid vampire speed. Used my own knife against me."

"You shouldn't have snuck off on us," Spencer said flatly to Chloe. "And you're not staying here alone," he told me firmly.

"I'll stay," Quinn said quietly.

I turned back to him, surprised. "You don't have to. This is what we're trained for, remember?"

"I'm staying." He raised an eyebrow. "You need me."

I opened my mouth to argue, just on principle, but Spencer cut in. "He's right." He tossed me an extra vial of Hypnos from his belt. "Just in case."

"Chloe's starting to bleed on my new shoes," Jenna interjected. "So let's go already."

I bit my lip. "Should I go with you?" I asked her. "Are you okay?"

She was a little pale but she looked more mad than in pain. "I'm fine. I'm sure I just need a couple of stitches."

"And a smack on the head," Jenna told her. "You *knew* the plan."

"Can you yell at me later?"

"Count on it. We were in position. We almost didn't get here in time."

They hurried off, still bickering. The night was silent and a hundred shades of blue and gray. The streetlight made the shattered glass look as if some of the stars had fallen from the sky, littering the pavement. It was almost pretty.

You know, except for the two vampires currently tied up and wanting to kill me, the other vampire scowling at me, and the throbbing of my face.

I shook my head. "Grandpa would just love this."

Quinn looked at me quizzically.

"The fact that a vampire is helping me babysit two other vampires," I explained.

"Not a fan of the alliance?" he mocked.

"Um, no."

"This bunch was hunting tourists all summer," he said. "The papers were full of animal attacks on hikers, but animals don't bite throats and drink blood. And now they've moved on to high school girls and college students. Not all bad vampires are conveniently blue," he added, referring to the *Hel-Blar*.

"I didn't say I wanted to buy them cake," I defended myself. "I just don't want to murder them either."

"They'd have murdered you."

"All the more reason to not do what they'd do."

His grin was crooked. "You must drive your grandfather crazy."

I half grinned back. "Probably. And, ironically, he'd agree with you. He'd want me to stake them as well."

"I like him already."

"He'd want me to stake you too."

"That's just because he's never met me. I can be very charming."

"I bet you can. The girls at the cafe seemed to think so anyway." Now *why* had I said that? He gave me his usual insufferable smirk. I was spared his reply when he tilted his head.

"Two cars, from the north."

"That'd be the unit. Maybe you should go."

"I'm not leaving you here."

"I just meant the League might have questions, might . . . you know. Vampire. Car full of vampire hunters. You do the math."

"You're worried about me," he said softly, stepping closer. I was suddenly very aware of my short sundress and my bare shoulders.

"It's only polite," I replied. "And I want something from you."

"That sounds promising." He dipped his head toward mine. "And that kiss wasn't polite."

I swallowed. "I was saving you from the Hypnos."

"Remind me to thank you later."

There was the sound of engines approaching, loudly enough that I even could hear them. "Please just go."

"Let me take you home," he murmured. "I'll hide if you tell them you've got a way home already."

I met his eyes, could see the glitter of them even in the darkness. "Why?"

His mouth brushed my ear, sending shivers over my scalp and down my neck.

"Because you want to."

The worst of it was, Quinn was right.

I did want to be alone with him.

Luckily the two vehicles stuffed with stern Helios-Ra agents screeching around the corner were rather distracting. Quinn was somewhere in the dark shadows of the warehouse district and I was standing alone with two bound vampires at my feet. I probably looked fairly impressive, especially for a student.

I just felt confused.

"Hunter Wild?" the extremely competent-looking woman asked as she slid out of the passenger seat of the first SUV. She had nose plugs loose around her neck and a phone earpiece wrapped around her left ear.

I nodded. "Yes, that's me."

"Your call came in," her companion added. He was very tall, with incredibly white teeth and a nose that had clearly been broken repeatedly and tilted drastically to the left. He would have looked scary to anyone else, especially with the scar tissue on his neck. To me, he just looked like family.

"Brandon." I grinned. "Nice to see you."

He grinned back and nodded to the vampires. "Nice job, kid."

"I had help," I hastened to explain. "There were five or six of us. The rest took Chloe back to school for stitches. I'm just the last on cleanup."

"That would be us, actually," the woman said, waving the others out to grab the vampires. "Good work, Wild. I see your family reputation isn't just hype."

"Thanks." I shrugged one shoulder. I wanted to tell them Quinn had helped us but I wasn't sure if that would just make everything more complicated. They'd definitely take me back to school themselves if they knew he was still lurking around. It was best to pass on the info to Kieran to pass on to Hart. "So what's going to happen to them?" I asked as the vampires were tossed into the back of the van.

"Don't worry about that," she said grimly. "We know Matthew. We've been trying to find his nest for weeks now."

I swallowed. I really hoped I hadn't just handed prisoners of war over to an execution squad. "Brandon?"

"Don't worry about it, kid. It'll be fine." Which wasn't exactly an answer. He held the door open. "Hop in, we'll take you home."

"That's okay," I said, lying through my teeth. "We took one of the bikes and I should get it back. It's just on Honeychurch Street." Which was around the corner, near the cafe. I really hoped Quinn hadn't been lying when he said he'd get me back. I didn't have enough cash to call a taxi and I wasn't looking forward to the hour-and-a-half walk in the dark back to school.

"Are you sure?"

I nodded, trying to smile like everything was normal. He gave me a friendly salute.

"All right, get gone then. We'll keep an eye on you until you reach the corner. Movie theater'll be letting out the late show. You should be fine." He winked. "Anyway, you got the bad guys already."

"I guess so." I walked away, casting glances out of the corner of my eye to see if I could spot Quinn. There were only squat gray buildings with broken windows and tall weeds growing between the cracks in the pavement. A raccoon waddled behind a garbage can.

The Helios-Ra SUV and the van idled until I reached the corner and waved, before turning onto Blitt Street. Sure enough, there were loads of people coming out of the theater and out of Conspiracy, which was closing its doors. I eased back into the mouth of the alley between a bookstore and an occult shop with crystals glimmering in the display window. Even closed down for the night it smelled strongly of Nag Champa incense. Spencer hung out here all the time, digging through herbs and stones and bronze statues, all in the pursuit of secret spells and magic amulets. I wondered, not for the first time, if the proprietor had any idea how many of her customers were undercover vampire hunters.

I also wondered where Quinn had gone off to.

I flicked my hair back and tapped my foot impatiently. Five more minutes and then I'd have to find my own way. I couldn't wait all night. Not when it was Quinn we were talking about. He might have seen some cute girl and would spend the next hour flirting with her and forget all about me.

"In case I haven't mentioned it yet, you clean up good, Wild."

Or not.

I turned to see him drop down off a fire escape behind me. It was at least three floors up but he landed as gracefully as a cat, looking just as smug as one.

"Show off," I said blandly.

He shrugged one shoulder. "I don't believe in hiding who I am."

"Um, isn't that kind of a requirement when you're a vampire?"

"In general, yes. But you already know I'm a vampire, so why pretend otherwise? I won't lie to you, Hunter."

Damn, he was good at that smoldering thing.

My insides quivered a little, despite myself. Maybe I'd been reading too many romance novels lately.

"Come on," he said softly. "I'll take you home."

It felt weirdly normal to cross the street with him, like all the other couples heading for their cars. We must have looked like we'd been on a date, especially when he led me to his black convertible Mustang and opened the passenger door for me. The seats were soft leather and all the chrome shone as if it had been recently polished. There wasn't a speck of dust or a single piece of trash on the floor mats.

"Nice car," I said, mostly to fill the sudden silence.

"Yeah, it was my aunt's car back in the day. She's a pack rat, thank God."

I had to laugh. "Only a Drake would pack-rat a car, like a memento."

"You should see some of the stuff she keeps." He shuddered. I couldn't help but be curious.

"Like what?"

"Finger bones."

"Um . . . ew."

"You want ew? She keeps them in an old Cadbury box. Try being seven years old and thinking you found the jackpot secret stash of chocolate. Talk about a rude awakening." He shook his head, throwing his car into reverse and backing away from the curb. "Put me off chocolate for a good year and a half."

The wind was warm on my face and lifted my hair every which way. It'd be a mess of tangles by the end of the ride but I didn't care. It felt nice to sit in a car with a boy. I could almost pretend it was that simple.

"Did you ever find out whose fingers they were?"

He shot me an incredulous look. "You don't ask Aunt Ruby questions."

"Why, is she mean or something?"

"No, just insane." He said it nonchalantly, without judgment. It was just fact.

"Oh."

"Hunters killed her family."

"Vampires killed mine," I pointed out defensively.

His voice softened. "I wasn't accusing you, Hunter."

I winced. He had saved my life tonight. I shouldn't be snapping at him. "Sorry."

He shrugged. "No big deal. It's weird, isn't it?"

"What is?"

"Treaties and all that. It's like we woke up one morning and we weren't supposed to be enemies anymore. It'll take some getting used to."

"True," I said. "I think it's really cool though."

"Unfortunately, not everyone agrees."

I thought of my grandfather and what he would do if he could see me now. "I know. But it's worth protecting."

"Yes," he said, and something about the way he was looking at me made me think he was talking specifically about me. "It is."

That was crazy though, wasn't it? I was just a hunter to him, one of the guys. But he hadn't called me Buffy since the cafe. He'd actually used my real name. Did that mean anything? *Get a grip, Wild,* I told myself. *He was also making out with at least two different girls not three hours ago.*

He slowed the car before we reached the turnoff for the school. He pulled into the undergrowth and turned the engine off, killing the lights. We were well-hidden by the grass and low-hanging tree branches. Fireflies winked at us from the field across the street. There wasn't a single other person, human or vampire, anywhere. Even the stars hid themselves behind thin clouds, as if to give us privacy.

"I got your text while I was waiting for you. You have a favor to ask me?" he said, turning to face me. Even in the darkness, his cheekbones were strong, his face pale. His teeth gleamed, looking slightly too sharp even with his fangs retracted.

"So you did get it?" I asked, suddenly babbling. "I wasn't sure. I mean, sometimes we don't get very good reception at school. But I guess you know that, living on a farm and all." *Shut up, shut up, shut up.*

He smiled slowly. "Hunter, are you nervous?"

"Shut up."

"Are you going to ask me to prom?" he teased.

"Shut up," I repeated, choking on a horrified laugh.

He grinned. "I look pretty good in a tux."

I rolled my eyes, suddenly comfortable again. "And you're so refreshingly modest."

"It's a curse," he agreed cheerfully. Then his eyes went from silver rain to stormy lake. "And you're still wearing the coronation medallion."

I felt like I'd been caught mooning over his photograph. I tucked the pendant back into my dress. I wiped my damp palms on my lap. "Can I trust you with school secrets?"

"Helios-Ra secrets? Cool." He leaned back, satisfied.

I bit my lip. "Never mind. This was a bad idea."

He touched my hand. "I'm kidding. What is it?"

I hoped I wasn't about to make a really big mistake. He felt trustworthy though, even with the charming smirks and the fangs. I pulled the vitamin I'd stolen from Chloe's bag out of my purse. It was in a little plastic bag, the kind you get when you buy jewelry. "I need to have this analyzed," I explained quietly.

"You must have labs here at school."

"We do. But I don't know anyone well enough to trust them with it."

"But you trust me."

"Yes." Even if it didn't make any sense.

He took the pill, frowned at it. "Looks like a vitamin."

"I'm really hoping that's all it is."

"But you think it's something else?"

I nodded. "Chloe's taking them and she's been weird and moody."

His eyebrows rose. "Steroids?"

"Maybe. She's obsessed with taking them and working out and getting strong, so it's possible. And that guy Will? The one we took to the infirmary? He said something about vitamins too, remember?"

"Huh. How is he anyway?"

"Nothing definitive yet. And no one will tell us anything about that *Hel-Blar* woman who disintegrated. There's definitely some weird shit going on."

"Yeah, that wasn't normal," Quinn agreed. "I'll see if my brother Marcus can analyze this. He's good with that sort of thing. I'd ask my uncle, the biology teacher, but he'd have way too many questions." He slipped my only piece of evidence into his pocket.

"Can you analyze this too?" I asked, pulling the blood samples out of my purse. I was the kind of girl who carried blood in her purse and daggers in her boots.

Maybe I should see the school counselor.

I felt nervous but relieved at the same time as he pocketed the samples. A totally uncharacteristic giggle stuck in my throat. I might finally get some answers after all. I touched his wrist and it was cool under my fingertips. "Thank you."

He paused, eyes narrowing. "You're not taking this stuff too, are you?" he asked sharply.

"No way." He leaned closer, sniffing along my collarbone and under my jaw. "What are you doing?" I whispered.

"Just checking," he answered, somewhat hoarsely.

"Checking what?" My pulse fluttered.

"We can usually smell drugs in a human's bloodstream. We can definitely taste it."

"I told you I'm not on anything."

"I know. You smell like . . . raspberries . . . and limes."

"Is that . . . good?"

I felt him smile against my skin. "Yes."

"Oh." I swallowed. It was getting difficult to form a coherent sentence. "So, you could sniff Chloe? Or Will? And know if something was wrong."

"Maybe. I'd rather breathe *you* in, though."

Yup, he was really, *really* good at this.

I actually felt like I was melting, like I was on fire, like I'd swallowed those fireflies.

He pulled back just enough to look at me, as if I was a puzzle that needed solving, or a candy he wasn't sure he was allowed to eat.

Bad analogy.

His fangs lengthened, but only a little. I wouldn't even have noticed if I wasn't used to watching for things like that. And it didn't make me nervous for some reason. I wasn't scared, and not just because I had a purse full of small sharp weapons. There was something between us suddenly, and it wasn't merely a secret unraveling.

It was something else, something more forbidden, more mysterious, more delicious.

I closed the tiny gap between us, swaying toward him as if he was a magnet. Our eyes connected, held. His pupils dilated, irises lightened. I smiled.

"You're not the only one who wants a taste," I said.

And then he was kissing me, or I was kissing him. We were just suddenly in each other's arms, like lightning—not there, then just suddenly there. Everywhere. His mouth was wicked, his tongue bold. I couldn't get enough. I tingled all over. His hand dug into my hair, cradled the back of my neck. He pulled me closer. The muscles of his arms were sinewy under my palms.

I'd never felt like this before.

He was a vampire and I didn't care.

I was a hunter and I didn't care.

I could barely catch my breath and I didn't care.

I just wanted more.

And then the car could barely contain us and his elbow accidentally hit the horn. The sudden noise cut through the warm summer night and we jumped, pulling apart. I was light-headed, disoriented. My lips felt warm, swollen.

He smiled ruefully, forcing himself to release me. "Guess that's my cue to take you home."

"I'd better walk from here," I murmured. "Surveillance cameras."

"Text me when you get in," he said. "I'll wait right here until you do."

"Okay." I was pretty dazed, surprised that I could stand up properly. I was really glad he looked just as bewildered.

"Good night, Hunter."

CHAPTER 15

◆

QUINN

I grinned all the way home.

I'd bailed on two hot girls, nearly been staked, and had to hide from a car full of vampire hunters in full battle gear.

Totally worth it.

Nicholas was on the front porch when I pulled the car up the driveway. He shielded his eyes from the glare of the headlights, fangs gleaming.

"How was your date?" he asked as I slammed the car door shut.

"Which one?"

"Show-off."

"With great hotness comes great responsibility," I answered. I was still grinning.

"Up for patrol, pretty boy?"

"Always." I was still wired from the fight and the kiss. Kicking *Hel-Blar* ass sounded like the perfect way to end the evening.

"There's a pack in the hall closet," Nicholas told me. I went in and grabbed it along with a handheld crossbow, stuffed into the sleeve of an old coat no one ever wore. It was my favorite, and I had the worst time hiding it from Lucy. I slung the pack over my shoulder and went back outside.

There were still some scorch marks at the end of the porch and a soggy plank that would rot through if we didn't replace it soon. Hope's rogue Helios-Ra unit had done some serious damage when they'd tried to blast their way through the house. We hadn't finished all the repairs yet but at least we'd patched up the big gaping hole in the wall.

I tied my hair back and loaded the crossbow. An unloaded crossbow would be about as useful as a spoon. Mom could have been an undead boy scout with all her "Be Prepared" speeches. "Let's go."

On the farm and in the thick woods around the mountains where we patrolled, we didn't have to hold back. We could move as fast as we wanted and not worry that we might appear blurry to human eyes. There was freedom in that, and exhilaration.

I hadn't been lying when I told Hunter I didn't believe in hiding who and what I was. I also didn't believe in moping about because I happened to be undead.

In my opinion, being a vampire kicked ass.

And undead was better than dead.

Okay, when I was human, the thought of drinking blood had me worried I was in for a lifetime of an eat-your-

Brussels-sprouts-they're-good-for-you diet. But once I'd changed, so had my taste buds. Why turn your nose up at what kept you alive? Or, not dead? Whatever.

The only drawback, as far as I could see, was that it was easier to score a cheeseburger than a pint of blood. And I missed the whole sunlight thing, but I got over that pretty quickly. It made me feel like crap now anyway. Duncan was the one who moaned about daylight and not being able to taste coffee anymore.

I just counted myself lucky that girls thought vamps were cool, even if they never actually realized I was a vampire. Pheromones had their uses.

The irony that I wasn't crushing on one of those girls, but on the type that *killed* vampires, wasn't lost on me.

But I wasn't going to let it ruin my night. Or the taste of her, still on my lips.

"You're actually strutting," Nicholas muttered.

"Just a little. It's good for the soul." I ducked under a low-hanging branch. The smells of damp earth and cold wind and cedar was thick as smoke. "Finally got rid of that Matthew vampire and his gang." We hadn't had a lot of time to deal with him what with Solange dying at her own birthday party. And anyway, the Drakes weren't vampire police. We just tried to take care of our own backyard. I wasn't joking when I told Hunter not all bad vampires are easily recognizable.

"Are they dust?"

"Not all of them. Hunter and her friends were there. She called in some Helios-Ra cleanup crew to take them into custody."

"And they just left you there?" he asked incredulously.

"Like I hung around to shake hands."

The forest was dark and full of shifting shadows but we could see just fine. Another perk to vampirism: really great night vision. I saw the leaves shifting, the outline of tree branches and ferns and the path glowing as if the moon were full over head. Everything seemed to glitter, just a little, around the edges. An owl called from some pine bough, searching for unwary mice. The owl would have to find new hunting grounds or go hungry tonight. Vampires tend to scare small animals into hiding.

Nicholas paused, sniffed. His expression went flat. "*Hel-Blar*," he mouthed.

I nodded, catching a whiff of boiled mushrooms and mildew. If the *Hel-Blar* ever got their shit together and figured out how to cover their stench, they'd really be a force to be reckoned with.

I took point, steadying the crossbow. Nicholas walked backward behind me, a stake in each hand. There was no one I trusted at my back more than one of my brothers.

The *Hel-Blar* came in a wave, three of them swinging down from a branch, bursting out of a thicket, and leaping out from behind a thick elm tree. A crossbow bolt hit the first one in the chest, piercing his rib cage and his heart. He screeched and crumbled into a gray dust. The next one crashed into me, knocking my crossbow into a patch of primroses. Nicholas was occupied shoving a stake, only half-stuck, into the last one.

"Drakes," my *Hel-Blar* laughed at his companion. "Even better."

His many fangs clicked at me hungrily and the sound was like bones breaking. I leaped back out of the way, avoiding the drip of his saliva. No one knew how contagious it really was. And this guy didn't look like he was about to conveniently disintegrate, like the woman at the high school. Whatever sickness she'd had clearly wasn't widespread through the *Hel-Blar*.

He followed my backward bend, clinging like a barnacle. I used momentum against him, falling into the undergrowth and flipping him over my head. He landed in a crouch, snarling over his shoulder. His veins were nearly black under his blue skin. There was fresh blood under his fingernails.

I didn't bother scrambling to my feet; I just rolled toward my discarded crossbow. The first bolt missed, biting into a birch tree and sending papery bark into the air.

"Nick, you okay?" I yelled. He grunted what I thought was a "yes." I loosed another bolt and it missed the heart again, but at least it sliced through his shoulder. He hissed in pain.

Good.

Except now he had an open bleeding wound that might contaminate Nicholas or me.

Bad.

And now my *Hel-Blar* was closing in and staying just in front of Nicholas so that if I used my crossbow I risked shooting my own brother. I was usually a pretty good shot but there were just too many variables. I exchanged my crossbow for the stake inside my coat and launched myself into the fray, hollering.

I don't care what Mom says about the advantage of surprise; a good battle yell can sometimes make the difference between winning or losing.

The *Hel-Blar* yelled back and then we were grappling again, trying to see who could cause the most damage. He didn't have a weapon. They mostly used their numerous fangs and the threat of their poisoned blood. I shoved the stake toward his chest and he blocked it, trying to shove it back. I held on with a viselike grip, my fangs burning through my gums, my fingers cramping around the stake. Out of the corner of my eye I saw a cloud of ash and heard Nicholas cough. *Hel-Blar* ashes were nasty.

I kneed the *Hel-Blar* in the groin and then used my free arm to drive my elbow into the back of his neck. Already doubled over, he staggered and folded further.

Right into my upraised stake.

The force of his flailing body drove me to my knees, and then I was alone with the ashes drifting into the grass and the blood-stained stake. I dropped it, scrubbing my palms clean in a pile of fallen leaves.

"Three down." I pushed to my feet. "Not bad." I dusted my shirt off, grimacing. "But I'm going to smell like soggy mushrooms for the rest of the night."

"Did that seem kind of easy to you?" Nicholas wondered out loud.

"Easy? Are you smelling the smell?"

"Seriously. Didn't they seem tired to you?"

I frowned. "I guess they could have fought harder. It's not like they laid down and died for us like that chick at the school though."

A flock of birds winged into the sky in the near distance, interrupting us with their excited squawking. We exchanged a knowing glance, breaking into a run. Nothing tired out the *Hel-Blar* like fighting or feasting. And both would disturb a flock of sleeping birds.

We ran harder. The wind pushed at my face with cool fingers. Our feet barely touched the ground, broke no twigs, made no sound to betray our presence.

What gave us away was the shocked sound both Nicholas and I made, abandoning all of our training in two choked curses.

It was hard to stay stealthy when you stumbled across your baby sister, ankle-deep in a mountain stream, red-pupiled, fangs flashing, and stakes flying from her fingertips.

Hel-Blar clicked their jaws at her from both banks, blue-tinged as poison beetles. She looked our way. Either she didn't have the time to recognize us or we'd really pissed her off.

One stake whistled toward us, then another.

"Solange, no!" I yelled.

Nicholas was too busy running forward, heedless of the stake aimed at his heart.

Because Lucy lay at Solange's feet, sprawled over the black river pebbles, her blood leaking like red ribbons into the water.

CHAPTER 16

◆

Hunter

Later Saturday night

I texted Quinn on my way to the infirmary to let him know I was safely on campus. Chloe was standing right inside the door, a bandage under her T-shirt and another one on her forearm. She was pale and her pupils were dilated but otherwise she seemed all right.

"I feel good," she said, weaving on her feet. Her smile went decidedly goofy. "Theo's nice."

"Theo gave you painkillers." I was relieved to see she was fine.

"Yup. Better than vitamins. Better than *candy*." She sounded shocked. And she was slurring her speech.

"Sit down before you fall on your face." I nudged her gently into a chair.

She poked her bandage. "Do I have a ghost arm now? Can't feel it."

"Stop that," I told her. "Or it'll hurt like hell tomorrow."

"'Kay."

"If you start drooling I'm taking pictures."

"'Kay."

I was grinning at her when the shouting started. I leaped forward just as the curtain to the back examination rooms swung open. Will thundered toward me. I was surprised enough just to stand there and stare at him. He was faintly blue, his eyes bloodshot. It didn't really register at first. Theo and Jenna were behind him and so was Spencer, holding a cloth to his neck. The cloth was rapidly turning red, almost as rapidly as he was turning white.

"Stake him!" Theo shouted at me. There was a long hypodermic needle in his hand. "Stake him now, Hunter!"

"What?" I had the stake in my hand. I was close enough to reach him. I was also frozen. "Are you kidding?"

"Now!" All three of them yelled in unison. It was enough to get me moving. So was Will, lunging at me, saliva dripping off his fangs. When did he grow fangs? There was mottled bruising on his neck and two festering puncture wounds. Jenna threw a tube of antibiotic ointment, hitting the alarm button on the wall. Help was coming.

But not fast enough.

"Shit!" I yelled, because I had to yell something. Will was wearing one of those hospital paper gowns, with the same tousled hair as always, the same earnest face. He was the class sweetheart for every class, even if they weren't in his year. He was nice to everyone. He wouldn't hurt a fly, which made vampire hunting problematic. But his parents wouldn't hear of him dropping out. So he did the best he could and immersed himself in the Science Department, where there was less actual fighting.

He was the one who asked the shy girls hiding in the corner to dance at school functions.

And now he was the one hissing at me.

Definitely not Will anymore.

"Shit!" I hollered again as his fist cracked against my shoulder. It didn't reach my face because I'd leaped sideways, but not quite fast enough. There was blood on his mouth. And blood on Spencer's throat and hemp T-shirt.

Every ounce of training snapped to attention inside me.

I went with my sideways lunge and then spun around so I came up behind Will. He was in the classic newborn *Hel-Blar* frenzy, which I'd read about but never actually seen in person. Their thirst for blood was primal and vicious and unstoppable. The moment I'd left his line of vision, he'd focused on Chloe, who was weaker. She was slouched in the hard plastic chair, giggling.

"You smell like old socks," she told him pleasantly, before shaking her head. "No, like mushrooms." She looked concerned. "That's bad, right? I can't remember why that's bad."

She was still babbling to herself when he lunged for her and I lunged for him. My stake went through his skin where his hospital gown gaped open. I angled it away from his shoulder blade and then pushed with as much strength as I had, still shouting profanities. Because cursing was better than thinking about what I was doing.

Staking a friend.

He yelped, tried to spin around to grab at the stake. He managed half a spin, just enough to meet my eyes before he crumbled into ashes on the shiny linoleum floor. Theo was the first to reach me. His hands were on my shoulders.

"Did he bite you? Are you hurt? Hunter?"

I didn't drop my stake, because I'd been taught never to drop my weapon, but my fingers felt weak, my palms sweaty. I thought I might throw up.

"Hunter, are you hurt?"

I shook my head, gagged.

"Hey!" Theo shook me. "You can't go into shock right now."

I blinked, vision going back to normal. The gray spots floated away. "I'm okay," I answered hoarsely. "What the hell just happened?"

Jenna handed me a paper cup of water. "You just saved all our asses."

I drank, mostly because I didn't know what else to do with myself. "I didn't save Will."

"You saved Chloe," she said quietly.

"And no one could have saved Will," Theo added. He went to Spencer, who was leaning against the wall, eyes glassy and hair damp with sweat.

"He bit you," I said flatly.

Spencer nodded weakly. "I'm okay."

"I've already given him his first antibiotic injection," Theo said, lifting Spencer's eyelids to check his pupils.

"That didn't help Will," I said quietly, trying not feel the panic swelling inside me.

"Will's bite was worse," Theo said. Spencer winced when he applied more pressure on his wound. "He barely grazed him. Still, you're all going to have to get out of here. He needs to be quarantined."

"What? No!" Jenna exclaimed. "You just said he'd be fine."

He hadn't actually said that, but I didn't point it out.

"Procedure," Theo bit out tersely, swinging his shoulder under Spencer's arm to help him to a cot. Chloe started to snore in her chair.

I was really glad Quinn had agreed to help me analyze that pill. Something clearly had to be done. And fast.

I crouched by Spencer, waiting until he looked at me. I made sure there wasn't a single ounce of doubt or worry in my expression. "You are going to be fine."

He nodded jerkily.

"I mean it, Spencer," I insisted. "Don't make me beat you up."

"You can't take me." He tried to grin. "Even like this." He dropped his voice to a whisper. "I never took any pill, Hunter. Not like Will."

"I know." I reached out to touch his dreads but Theo's hand snapped around my wrist.

"No contact," he said. "You know the rules."

I did know the rules. And I had about two minutes before the infirmary was swarming with people and we were hauled bodily away.

"We'll fix this," I told Spencer confidently. Jenna hovered behind me looking grim, even though she tried to smile at Spencer. "I've already got us some help. We'll know something soon."

"You'll beat this thing," Jenna added fiercely just as the first response to the alarm barreled through the front door. We stepped back. If we were all quarantined we'd never get Spencer the help he needed.

There were two security guards and Ms. Dailey behind the first response team. She assessed the situation at a glance, taking in every detail, right down to the dust on my sneakers. She used her cell phone to call for another nurse and the head doctor for Spencer. She sent him and Theo and a guard into one of the back rooms. They'd probably tie him to the bed, like they had with Will. I tried not to think about it.

"What happened?" she asked us. "Hunter?"

"I staked Will," I answered. My voice sounded weird, even to me.

Spencer cried out from the back room and I winced. The guard swore. There was the sound of a scuffle and Spencer moaning. "I'm fine. I'm not *Hel-Blar*. I'm not *Hel-Blar*."

"Hold him down," Theo snapped. "He needs another dose."

Jenna and I swallowed miserably. My eyes burned.

"Hunter staked Will?" Ms. Dailey prodded.

"Will turned," Jenna said dully. "Just like that. Theo was giving him his meds, checking his blood pressure while we tried to get

Chloe to stop licking the tongue depressors like they were lollipop sticks and then he just . . . turned. Ripped the restraints right off the bed frame."

"And he bit Spencer?"

"Kind of," Jenna said. "It happened so fast, we all tried to stop him. I don't know if it's fang damage or the scalpel he grabbed off the counter."

Ms. Dailey's expression was hard but not judging. "And then what happened?"

"Will got free, went for Hunter, then Chloe. Hunter dusted him," Jenna said. "She saved Chloe's life. And whoever else Will might have come across if he'd gotten out of the infirmary."

"I see." Ms. Dailey looked at me for a long moment. "Hunter, you're green. Why don't you go on back to the dorm. We'll look at the security camera footage and then discuss this further in the morning."

I nodded mutely.

"Make sure Hunter has some hot tea," she added to Jenna. "And . . . why is Chloe drooling on herself?"

"She had stitches. Theo gave her something."

"Right. You'll have to get her back to her room then. She can't stay here right now."

Chloe didn't even wake up. Her head just lolled from side to side as we hoisted her up and dragged her out. The last security guard eyed us suspiciously. We didn't speak on the way to the dorm, not until we laid Chloe out on her bed.

Jason knocked on the door and poked his head in. "I had to check on my floor," he said, coming in to sit on my desk chair. "Chloe looks all right . . . ," he trailed off. "But you two don't. What happened?"

"Will turned," I explained. "And Spencer was bitten. Maybe."

He paled. "What?"

"He's in quarantine."

"But he'll be okay." Jason swallowed. "Tell me he'll be okay."

"Damn right he will," Jenna said, low and determined.

"And Will?" Jason asked, looking as stricken as we felt. "What will happen to him?"

"Nothing." I replied. I sat on the edge of my bed, feeling kind of numb but not numb enough. "I staked him."

After a stunned moment, Jason came to sit next to me. "It's not your fault," he said firmly.

"You did what you had to do," Jenna agreed. "Even though it sucks monkeys."

"He was sixteen. And he was nice."

"I know. But he was a student at a Helios-Ra school. He knew what he signed on for."

"He didn't even want to be here."

"And that's not your fault either," Jason pointed out, trying to comfort me. I wasn't entirely convinced I should be comforted. I'd just killed a friend of mine, after all. I should be painfully uncomfortable.

I must have said it out loud because Jenna shook her head. "That *Hel-Blar* woman killed Will. You saved him."

"Hello? I staked him."

"Yeah, and do you think he would have wanted us to let him

become a monster? The same guy who refused to let the maintenance crew kill the squirrels in the attic?"

"I guess not. Still."

"Yeah," Jenna sighed. "Still. You did good, Hunter, even if it doesn't feel like it."

"It feels like ass." I rubbed my eyes hard so the tears wouldn't drop. "School assembly on Monday is going to be a funeral too," I remarked.

"Won't be the first time." Jenna was the color of milk in the faint light of the lamp. "I know what we need."

She went straight to Chloe's secret schnapps in the closet. Jason and I slid down to sit on the floor with Jenna as she opened the bottle and passed it around. I took a sip and the overly sweet peach liqueur ran down my throat.

"Disgusting," Jason spluttered.

"Totally is," Jenna agreed. "Quit hogging it."

"No more for me, you guys." I waved away the bottle and lay on my back, staring up at the ugly beige ceiling. The continuous loop in my head of Will as he crumpled was exactly what I deserved. I shouldn't try to forget it or dull it with alcohol. Or the fact that Spencer might possibly be fighting for his life right now. And it was a battle we couldn't help him with. We didn't have his back. It felt awful. And I should feel awful.

"Hey, eighteen is the legal age in Quebec." Jenna waved the half-empty bottle at me and the liqueur sloshed over the edge. I wiped it off my cheek. She giggled. "Oops. Sorry."

"We're not *in* Quebec." And it was an automatic suspension if you were caught drinking on campus.

"Still. You're gonna make a really good hunter," she added. "Like, really. You know?"

"You will too."

"No, it's different," she insisted. She nudged Jason with her foot. "Isn't it different? It's different."

"Yup." He nodded enthusiastically. "Hunter's a hunter!"

"Ha!" Jenna laughed so loud she startled herself and fell over. Jason and I looked at each other, looked at her, and then laughed so hard we were panting for breath. Chloe groaned.

"What's going—hey," she mumbled groggily. "That's my schnapps."

"Spencer got bitten by Will and then Hunter staked Will," Jenna told her, trying to look serious but just going cross-eyed instead.

Chloe blinked. "Shit." She held her hand out for the bottle. "Gimmee." She fished a pill out of her pocket and swallowed it down with the alcohol.

"Dude, what is that?" Jason gaped at her. "A horse pill?"

"It's a vitamin," she informed him loftily.

"Not you too," he groaned. "All the Niners are suddenly obsessed with vitamins and protein powder. There's some rumor going around that it'll make them strong."

I rolled over to frown at Chloe. "I thought you took one already today. And you shouldn't drink when you're on pain meds."

"I'm doubling up now." She propped herself on her elbow and took another mouthful. "I'm injured. I need my strength."

"Does it make you pee fluorescent yellow?" Jenna asked. "Vitamins always give me Day-Glo pee."

Chloe shook her head and eyed the bottle. "You guys owe me twenty bucks."

"Twenty bucks! No way does that nasty crap cost twenty bucks."

"It's a delivery charge." She grinned and then winced. "Ouch."

"Don't lean on your stitches like that," Jason offered helpfully.

"Duh."

"I hope Spencer's okay." I reached for my cell and texted Kieran and Quinn to tell them what had happened. I hiccuped on a sob that snuck up on me.

Jenna blinked at me. "Nuh-uh," she said, making a grab for the bottle. "Nasty peach booze, stat!"

I made a face. "No way. I'll throw up."

Jason shifted over a foot. "Not on me."

I lay back down. The sound of my friends giggling helped a little.

But not as much as what suddenly occurred to me.

I sat straight up.

"I have a plan," I announced.

CHAPTER 17

◆

Hunter

"Did you hear me?" I repeated louder. "I said I have a plan."

Everybody groaned except for Jason, who was already snoring. I nearly stepped on his head when I stood up. "Let's go!"

He jerked awake. "Mmfwha?"

Jenna helped him up. "Hunter's on a mission."

"It's four o'clock in the morning," he groused.

"Chloe, come on," I insisted from the doorway.

She opened one eye. "I am injured."

"You have stitches," I said, unconvinced. "Come on, already. You'll miss all the fun and then you'll bitch about it for the rest of the year."

"That is true," she agreed, finally getting up. She clutched the bottle to her chest. They moved in an exaggerated slow huddle across the carpet, stopped when they realized we were still in our room, and then burst into muffled giggles. The fact that Jenna sounded like a hyena made us all laugh even harder. My stomach hurt. It was a nice change from my brain.

I just couldn't think about what I'd done or worry about Spencer all night. I'd go mental. This was better. This was a goal. This was action.

Chloe was the last into the hall. She tripped over the threshold as the door slammed shut behind her. "Shhh!" she practically yelled. Jenna slapped her hand over Chloe's mouth to shush her, then pulled away squeaking.

"Did you just *lick* me? Gross."

"Teach you to grab my face."

This was going to be a disaster.

"Cut it out," Jason tossed over his shoulder. "I feel like we're back in kindergarten. Let's go." He stopped in the foyer, under the remnants of the broken chandelier. "Um, Hunter?"

"Yeah?"

"Where are we going exactly?"

"Eleventh-grade floor," I mouthed. "And watch the cameras."

We hurried up the steps, avoiding the creaky stairs, the corner with the camera, the loose floorboard. The common room was empty and all the doors were shut tight. Everyone sane was asleep.

"Anyone know which one's Will's room?" I asked.

Jason stared at me. "Great, you've got a dozen demerits so now you want us to get them too?"

I lifted my chin. "I'm going to find out what's going on. You can go back to bed if you want."

Jenna snorted so loud she coughed. "Forget it," she added. "I want in." She poked Jason hard in the shoulder. "And so do you."

"Yeah, all right," he muttered. He grabbed the bottle from Chloe. "I need to be drunker." He swallowed, crossed his eyes. "Nope. Bad idea." He tripped over nothing. He hadn't even taken a step. "He was in room 209, the one at the end by the back staircase."

"That was obliging of him," I whispered back, cheered.

"Obliging? Who talks like that?" Chloe shook her head. She was right. I'd been reading too many romance novels. But now probably wasn't the time to wonder about it. "You're getting weird, Wild."

"You're already weird, Cheng."

She slung her good arm over my shoulder. "That's why we're such good friends."

After shooting her a grin, I touched the door. "Anyone know if Will's roommate is here yet?"

There were a lot of shrugs.

"You check," Chloe suggested. "You're our fearless leader."

I stuck my tongue out at her, which was terribly leader-like of me. But she was right, though. This was my stupid idea so I should take point. I turned the doorknob slowly but pushed the door open an inch in one quick motion. If you went too slowly, which was the temptation, it actually had more of a squeak. The room was dark. I couldn't hear any snoring but that was hardly conclusive proof.

I took a step inside. The others giggled behind me. I shot them a look over my shoulder. There was a hush and then more giggling. They'd wake up the entire floor if we didn't hurry. I took another step inside and hit the Indiglo light on my watch, cupping my hand over the light. I needed just enough to see if the beds were empty, not so much that it might wake up any roommate.

The beds were empty. I let out a breath I hadn't realized I'd been holding.

"Clear," I whispered. They tiptoed inside with such exaggerated care that I snorted out a laugh. "This isn't a slapstick movie."

Jason shut the door behind him and flicked the light on. We blinked at each other for a moment, waiting for our eyes to adjust. The room looked like any other room—two beds, two desks, two chairs. There was no roommate. There were also no posters on the wall, no books on the shelves, no clothes on the floor.

It was empty.

Will had only just turned. Half the staff wouldn't even know about it yet. None of the students would either.

"Okay, that's weird." Jenna turned a circle on her heel.

"Are you sure this is the right room?" I asked.

Jason frowned. "Yeah. I came down here to give him back a video game I borrowed at the end of last year. He was already unpacked and everything."

"So his roommate hadn't arrived yet?"

"No, not yet."

"All right, so maybe they didn't put anyone in this room because he was in the infirmary and it'd be weird." I looked under the bed, which was swept clean. "But that doesn't explain why they'd get all his stuff out before he was even out of quarantine." I rubbed my arms, suddenly chilled. "Unless they knew he wouldn't recover?"

"Educated guess," Chloe said. "It's possible. We all know *Hel-Blar* venom is nasty stuff."

"So what do we do now?" Jason asked, perplexed. "What were you looking for?"

"I'm not even sure," I admitted. "It's just that the *Hel-Blar* who got him mysteriously turned to ash. And Will mysteriously mentioned something about a vitamin. That's too many mysteries." I wouldn't look at Chloe even when she hissed out a disgruntled breath. I went over to the desk and opened all the drawers. "Nothing."

"Closets are empty," Jenna confirmed.

I did finally look at Chloe.

She narrowed her eyes. "Why are you looking at me like that?"

She was going to be pissed at me for asking. No help for it. "You've been hiding your vitamins, haven't you?"

She frowned. "What?" She backed up a step. "You saw me take one like an hour ago."

Jenna and Jason watched us as if we were a tennis match.

"Why would she hide vitamins?" Jason wondered.

"Because I've been bugging her about them," I said, not glancing away from Chloe. She shifted from foot to foot. It was her nervous tic so I knew my guess had been right. "So if you were Will, where would you hide your vitamins in this room?"

"I don't know." She shrugged.

"Chloe, please. This is important."

She gave a long, suffering sigh. "Okay, but you have to get off my case."

Not a chance.

She surveyed the room thoughtfully. The first place she looked was the desk drawers, feeling for a false bottom. Nothing. We helped her check under the mattress, but there was nothing there but dust.

"This is stupid," she muttered.

But I really felt like we were onto something.

She sat on the edge of the bed and checked under the lip of the night table.

Nothing.

Jenna and Jason were starting to shoot me weird looks.

Chloe lifted the lamp and stuck her finger inside the iron stand. She pulled out a small plastic bag with little white pills.

"Damn," Jason whistled.

Chloe and I met each other's grim gaze.

"These don't look anything like my vitamins," she said quietly.

CHAPTER 18

•

QUINN

I hit the ground just as the stake sliced past me. I grabbed for Nicholas's ankle and he slammed into the dirt, kicking me off before he'd even landed. The second stake landed in a willow tree. The *Hel-Blar* paused. Lucy didn't move.

"Lucy!" Nicholas was back on his feet before I could grab him again. I went for the nearest *Hel-Blar*, cracking my fist across his face, taking care not to get too close to his mouth. His answering punch nearly dislocated my shoulder.

So the *Hel-Blar* from earlier tonight had been tired because Solange had been kicking their asses.

Small consolation.

I broke a kneecap and used my last stake until there was dust on my boots. Nicholas flipped into the air, somersaulting over an attacking *Hel-Blar*, and landed in the river, blood-tinted water

arcing up around him and splashing us. A human wouldn't have
noticed it in the darkness but it had the rest of us distracted,
thirsty. One of the *Hel-Blar* licked his lips, studded with puncture
marks from his fangs.

And then the frenzy hit.

The hissing was nearly loud enough to ripple the surface of the
slow-moving river. Lucy became the focus of such gut-burning
hunger, I wondered why it didn't wake her up. She still wasn't
moving. I didn't know how badly she was hurt. And there wasn't
time to wonder about it. I ran downstream and leaped over the
water, coming back around to block access to Lucy from the other
side. Solange, Nicholas, and I formed a ring around her, like petals
to her blood-soaked center. Then Nicholas fell to his knees, shouting her name. She stirred once, faintly.

"Incoming!" I yelled at him. He knew better than to stay there,
distracted and vulnerable. He finally rose to his feet, his eyes searing hot enough to have one *Hel-Blar* stumbling in his tracks. The
rest just laughed.

"If she's dead, you're dead," he promised darkly. He smiled.
"Wait, you're dead anyway."

I'd worry about that smile later. Right now I had two crazed
siblings to deal with. And no more stakes.

"Shit, give me your pack," I said to Nicholas. He tossed it to me
over Lucy's body. Solange looked at her and bit back a sob. Her
fangs elongated farther until I thought they'd fall right out of
her head. Her flying roundhouse cracked a *Hel-Blar* neck. The
woman fell, snarling, facefirst into the water. Solange turned her

over and staked her in one move. There was blood on her clothes and I wasn't sure how much was hers, Lucy's, or various *Hel-Blars'*.

This was turning into a hell of a night.

To human eyes, the fight probably looked quick, colors smearing with the speed of our movements. Inside the fight, it felt like forever. Lucy needed help and she needed it now.

Try telling that to the *Hel-Blar* currently trying to chew on my face.

"Ow, son of a bitch!" He'd nearly taken a fang off. I hated to admit it but I'd been fighting vampires all night and dawn wasn't far off. It was taking its toll. I kicked, I punched, I staked. The thick *Hel-Blar* ashes resembled a mist on the river. Solange took a blow to the kneecap and stumbled, going down. She flipped to her feet before either Nicholas or I could reach her. The last two *Hel-Blar* ran, scuttling off between the trees. Nicholas scooped Lucy up into his arms, pink water dripping from her hair.

Sunrise trembled on the horizon.

Solange was still snarling, the whites of her eyes now completely red.

She didn't look right.

"Solange," I said, trying to catch her attention. "Solange, focus."

She hissed. The dark sky lightened to a pale gray, glimmering like a pearl. I felt the weariness of the dawn start to tug at my bones. Nicholas's jaw clenched so tight I could see the muscles spasms from here.

"She's still bleeding," he ground out.

Solange licked her lips, stumbled back a step, howled. We both flinched.

"Get Lucy help," I told him. "She can't spend the night in one of the safe houses and you can't wait for me to talk Solange down." The safe houses were actually more like underground bomb shelters hidden throughout the forest in case any of us got caught far from home at sunrise. Some linked to the tunnels connecting our farmhouse to various parts of the area; others locked up tight, impenetrable. We had no way of knowing if Lucy could wait until sunset for medical attention. Nicholas hesitated, glancing at Solange, who was growling low in her throat.

"Just go," I said, approaching Solange as if she were a wild beast. It wasn't far off from the truth. Her internal tethers were new, untested. Fragile. She was strong, already stronger than anyone else so newly turned. But she might not be strong enough to completely control her inner vampire. It wasn't an exact science. I just had to stop her from giving in entirely, and sunlight would do the rest. Assuming I could get her to safety before it dropped her like a stone in a deep pond. We were nothing if not susceptible.

Nicholas looked wrecked, cradling Lucy against his chest. Her arm dropped limply. She'd never done anything limp in her life. Fear for her nibbled at me. Nicholas broke into a run so sudden, the air displaced all around him. Fallen leaves whirled at my feet. Solange took a step, following the scent of blood.

"Stop me," she pleaded, even as she pulled a dagger from her boot. She suddenly looked so much like Mom, I felt disoriented.

"I'm trying," I whispered, holding up one hand. "Solange, you're okay."

She laughed but there was no humor in it. "Quinn, we both know I'm not okay." She swallowed, as if it was the hardest thing she'd ever done. She squinted at the sky. "God, it's burning inside me. Did this happen to you? I don't remember you guys being like this." Her hair was damp. It took a lot to make a vampire sweat. We didn't exactly run hot, temperature-wise.

"You'll be okay," I said soothingly.

"I can still smell the blood," she said softly, as if she was talking about chocolate cake. She inhaled, nostrils flaring. "I have to follow it."

"Wait." I blocked her way. "Just wait a minute."

"No."

She shoved me and then vaulted over my flailing limbs, taking off between the pine trees.

Damn it, I was *not* going to be outdone by my baby sister.

We raced through the forest, the sun burning at our heels. I didn't even know if she was racing to Lucy's blood, to the safety of the farm, or just away from me. I only knew I had to stop her.

There's one sure way to stop a vampire.

Blood.

I had to make myself an easier target than a wounded human.

I reached into my pocket, leaping over a fallen moss-draped tree trunk. I still had the test tubes of blood Hunter had given me. It wasn't much but it might be enough to stop Solange, to give her the strength to find her control again.

I stopped running, acorns and needles crunching under my feet. I popped the lid off one of the glass tubes and flicked a few drops out. Hunter's friend's name was on the label: Chloe.

"Solange," I called out. "Can you smell that? I've got fresh blood here for you."

"What is that?" she asked. I couldn't see her but at least she'd stopped running.

"It's human blood, Sol," I said tauntingly. "It's better than animal blood. Don't you want a sip?" I felt like a freaking drug dealer. This night was not exactly going according to plan. I waved the tube, trying not to react to the scent myself. My fangs elongated a little and saliva filled my mouth. We avoided human blood. It was so easy to become addicted. "Just imagine how it tastes."

She came around an oak, the leaves hanging over her head like a crown. She was as pale and slender as a shaft of moonlight. She moved slowly toward me, feral and predatory.

I waggled the tube. "Come on, Sol. I know you want it."

The sun steadily pushed its way over the horizon. I could see it in the fatigue in Solange's face, under the hunger. And I could feel it in my bones, turning them to water. I struggled against it. This was definitely the worst part of being a young vampire. If we got caught out here we'd be vulnerable. If the sunlight didn't weaken us to the point of death, something else would come along and finish the job. A well-meaning hiker who'd take us to the hospital where lab tests would prove disconcerting, or else an anti-treaty Helios-Ra hunter who knew exactly how to dispatch us. Or even a human loyal to a vampire family who didn't particularly care for the Drakes.

I had to hurry.

I circled around so that I was in the lead and then headed toward the farmhouse.

"Come and get it," I told her grimly.

We were on Drake land when she caught up to me.

"Give it to me!" Her nails scraped into my hand. She grabbed the tube and licked the glass rim, tilting it for a greedy mouthful. There wasn't much in there but she gulped at it like it was water and she'd been lost in the desert for a year.

Then she spat the whole mouthful out without swallowing.

"Gross. What the hell's in there? Tastes like medicine." She grimaced, throwing the tube at my head. I caught it and slipped it back into my pocket. There was just enough blood left to smear the inside of the tube, like stained glass. One thing was for sure—Chloe's vitamins were definitely not vitamins.

"There's blood at the house," I told her. "We're nearly there."

I grabbed her wrist and dragged her toward the squares of lamplight. We reached the house just as the light sent spears of fire between the branches. Solange was asleep on her feet, sliding onto the porch floor like a silk scarf. The lethargy was so sudden, so deep that I was limping when I fell, dragging her through the door.

CHAPTER 19

◆

Hunter

Sunday afternoon

The next day came entirely too soon. Will was still dead, we didn't know if Spencer would get better, and now my head felt like I'd landed on it repeatedly during the night even though I hadn't gotten drunk.

All in all, not exactly an improvement.

Chloe made a weird sound, like a grunt, as she pulled her pillow over her head. "I hate my life," she added.

"I hate your schnapps," I said, squinting at the alarm clock's digital numbers: 2:03 P.M. It felt way earlier. "It makes you snore like a horse."

"Karma," Chloe maintained from the depths of her covers. "That's what you get for stealing."

I snorted. "You steal chocolate from me all the time."

She poked one eye out from her pillow. "You know about that?"

"Well, duh," I said. I shuffled from the hall to the bathroom. It felt as if I hadn't gotten any sleep at all. There were way too many students running around, unpacking and reconnecting with friends they hadn't seen all summer. Someone squealed.

"Can we stake her?" Jenna begged, coming out of one the stalls and wiping her mouth. She stood at the mirror looking miserable. Even her freckles looked miserable. Then she winced at her choice of words. "Sorry." She filled the sink with cold water.

"Any word from Spencer?" I asked.

"None." Jenna shook her head, then moaned at the movement. "But as soon as I'm sure my head won't crack right open, let's go see Theo."

"Okay." I finally caught a glimpse of myself in the mirror. "Gack!"

Never mind the haggard combination of my too-pale complexion and dark smudges of fatigue; there was also a mottled bruise under my cheekbone from last night's fight. I poked it gingerly, hissed out a breath. Jenna toweled her face, finally looked at me, and winced.

"That looks painful."

"I guess I should learn to duck faster." I poked at it again and sighed. "At least he didn't give me a black eye."

"How's Chloe?"

"Same. Seen Jason yet?" Someone let one of the bathroom stall doors slam shut and Jenna clutched her head and whimpered. "Ow! That's it," she said, shuffling down the hall like an old lady—or an asylum patient. "I'm calling Jason. I hope the phone rings right in his ear. He's so not escaping this hangover."

Simon walked past us, eating a sandwich. I didn't know him personally but Jenna had been crushing on him from afar for two full years. She tried to smile at him.

Instead she threw up on his shoes.

"What the hell, man?" He leaped back, crashing into the wall. "Gross."

Jenna turned bright red and ran all the way back to her room.

I felt sure she was never going to drink again. Simon just stood in the hall. "What is wrong with the girls at this school?" he muttered.

I eventually wove my way around suitcases and went back to my room. Chloe was still a lump of disgruntled blankets.

"Are you dead?" I asked.

"Zombie," she answered. "Don't tell my Supernatural Creatures prof. She'll try to decapitate me." She pulled her blanket over her face. "On second thought, decapitation sounds soothing. Hook me up."

"Try aspirin first," I suggested, handing her the bottle after shaking two out for myself. I downed an entire bottle of water and felt marginally more human. Still, I didn't want to do anything but lie there and feel pathetic.

I definitely didn't want to answer the door.

"If that's another one of your Niners . . ." Chloe's threat trailed off menacingly, as if she couldn't think of anything bad enough to inflict on whoever dared knock on our door.

The second knock had us both snarling. I swung the door open, scowling. "What already?"

Ms. Dailey stood on the other side, eyebrow raised drily.

"Oh, um, Ms. Dailey." I flushed. Chloe smothered a snort of laughter.

"Hunter." Ms. Dailey smiled knowingly. "May I come in?"

I stepped aside to let her pass. "Is Spencer okay?" I couldn't think of another reason why she'd be here in our dorm room. My heart fell into stomach.

"Spencer's condition is unchanged," she assured me. "And he is receiving the best care possible. His parents are on their way here to the school today."

"Oh." So he was sick enough that his parents had been called. We'd known that already, of course, but this just made it feel more awful. More final. "Can we see him?"

"You know that's not possible," she told us gently and glanced at Chloe, who finally sat up, her curly hair looking like a bird's nest squashed on one side of her head. "He's in quarantine." She pursed her lips. "Which is why I won't be commenting on your obvious hangover, Chloe. After last night, I suppose you all deserve a break." She speared her with a stern glare that had Chloe squirming. "I won't tell the headmistress about this, but you're on kitchen duty until Christmas break. And if anything like this ever happens again, you'll be expelled. Understand me?"

"Yes, ma'am," Chloe murmured. It was pretty cool of Dailey not to bust her.

"Good." She turned to me. "Now, Hunter, there is something I'd like to discuss with you."

I tried to make my brain work. "Yes?"

"I am starting my own student group. The Guild will recruit the best of the best to help take out the new *Hel-Blar* and other threats. I'd like to formally extend an invitation for you to join us. You've exhibited leadership, team spirit, courage, loyalty, and resourcefulness time and time again and you ought to be rewarded for it. And I'm very proud of you for resisting whatever party was going on here last night. We could use you."

"Thank you!" I finally exclaimed after a stunned silence. This was way better than floor monitor duties. And Grandpa would puff up his chest with pride and brag to all his friends. I grinned.

"We'll expect you every Sunday afternoon for training and Tuesday evenings after supper for weekly orientation." She shook her head at Chloe. "Drink lots of water" was her parting advice before letting the door shut behind her. Loudly.

I tuned to Chloe, beaming. "Can you believe it? Cool."

She did *not* look happy for me.

She swung out of bed, glowering. "Figures."

I narrowed my eyes, some of my happiness congealing in my chest. "And by that you mean, congratulations?"

"I mean, I'm tired of the elitist nepotism of this school."

My mouth dropped open. "What the hell, Chloe? I work my ass off."

"And I don't?"

I was really sick of this argument.

"Well, it's not actually about you for one second," I told her. "It's about me."

"It's *always* about you."

I rolled my eyes. "I'm so over your pity party. Green's not a good color on you."

"Shut up." She stalked toward me, her hands clenched into fists. "You don't know what you're talking about."

I stood my ground. "I know exactly what I'm talking about so back off, Chloe. I mean it." I couldn't believe one of my best friends was all up in my face like that. It was totally surreal. "I really hope that this is a side effect from your dumb-ass vitamins," I told her grimly. "Even so, it's getting tired."

"God, get off my case, already," Chloe shouted, and shoved me. I stumbled back a step, shocked.

"You did not just do that." I shoved her back before I could stop myself.

"So what if I did? Going to tattle on me to your new Guild friends?" She shoved me again, or would have if I hadn't jerked my shoulder back. The momentum tripped her up, which infuriated her all the more. Frankly, I was past caring.

Especially when she hauled off and punched me.

The ensuing silence was cold and sudden, like a bucket of water. I'd managed to duck enough that her fist glanced my chin and shoulder but didn't do too much damage. Still, I felt the throb on my jaw. She stared at me, eyes watering, cheeks red with fury.

I really wanted to punch her back.

Before I could give in to some idiot catfight, I turned on my heel and stormed out of the room.

◆

Sunday night

"Are you telling me Chloe actually punched you?" Jenna stared at me. She whistled through her teeth. "Dude. That is messed up."

"I know," I agreed grimly. We were walking across the quad toward the infirmary. I hadn't seen Chloe all day, not since our fight. Definitely for the best. I shoved my hands in my pockets. "I'm tired of getting punched in the face."

"I can't believe you didn't punch her back. You are a better woman than I am." She shook her head.

"Remind me of that when my jaw goes purple to match the rest of my bruises." At least it was only a dull ache; she hadn't cracked a tooth or bruised the bone. I'd have been mad at myself if she'd managed to get the best of me, even hungover and doped up on those weird vitamins.

"You two weren't the only ones fighting," Jenna told me.

"What? Who else?"

"Two eleventh graders went at it over the last box of cereal in the common room."

"Seriously?"

"Yeah, one of them needed two stitches. And someone got carted off to the infirmary. Some kind of flu."

I hunched my shoulders. "Jenna, we have to figure this out. It doesn't add up."

"We will."

I wished I had her confidence. I felt as if we were going backward; everything was making less sense, not more. And it was starting to piss me off.

The safety lights blazed along the path and we could hear someone beating on the punching bags from the open window of the upstairs gym. Music poured out of the dorm behind us. It was familiar, homey.

Worth protecting.

We went straight to the infirmary, blinking at the bright fluorescent lights. The minute he saw us, Theo jumped up from his chair and blocked us.

"No way, girls."

We both scowled.

"Theo, come on," Jenna finally wheedled when he didn't move. "Be a pal."

"Not a toe past quarantine, kid."

"Kid? You're what, twenty-five?"

"Yeah, old enough to know better."

"We just want to see Spencer," I said.

"I know what you want. Forget it." His expression softened. "Look, I know it's hard. But he's in quarantine for a reason. You won't help him by getting locked up in quarantine yourselves, or getting demerits or expelled. You know the headmistress doesn't mess around with this stuff." He raised an eyebrow. "And you could get me fired as well."

"Guilt trip," Jenna muttered.

"Damn straight."

I knew we wouldn't change his mind, but all the same, I had to try.

"Theo, he shouldn't be alone. He's our friend," I said.

"He's not alone," Theo said just as Spencer's mother came out from behind the curtain blocking the quarantine rooms. Her eyes were red, her cheeks so pale under her tan that they looked paper-thin. The rest of her was the same, from her sun-bleached blond hair to her sandals and silver toe rings. Spencer got his love of surfing and the ocean from his mom and his supernatural obsessions from his dad. She saw me and her lips wobbled. I stared, horrified. If she cried, I didn't know what I'd do. Just because I'm a girl doesn't mean I do public displays of emotion. Luckily she clenched her jaw and tried to smile.

"Oh, Hunter, come here, sweetie." She hugged me hard. She smelled like salt and coconut oil. It was comforting.

"How is he?" I asked when she let go and squeezed Jenna's hand.

"He's strong," she said, her voice breaking. It wasn't really an answer. I shifted from one foot to the other. I felt guilty and I didn't know why. The clock on the wall ticked too loudly. "I have to get back to him."

She wasn't allowed in quarantine either, only on this side of the window. Once a day she was allowed in a full medical suit to go inside and hold his hand and talk to him. We'd studied the procedure in class last year.

The reality was so much worse.

"I miss him already," I said miserably as Jenna and I shuffled back outside. It was Sunday night; everyone was in a frenzy of last-minute unpacking and organizing and pretending school didn't start tomorrow.

"Me too," Jenna said. She kicked at a garbage can. "I wish there was more we could do."

And then it hit me.

"There is."

She turned to eye me. "What? What are you talking about?"

I stopped, nodding slowly. "I bugged the eleventh-grade common room after Will was bitten," I said. "I forgot."

"You forgot you bugged a room?" Jenna goggled. "Dude, you're fierce. And I totally love you right now."

"We might not find anything," I quickly added.

"But at least we'll be doing something. No wonder Dailey tapped you for her Guild."

"Didn't she ask you?"

Jenna shrugged. "No."

"She totally will," I said, utterly convinced. "No one handles a crossbow like you do."

"Thanks." She tugged on my hand, dragging me after her as if we were heading for a giant mountain of Ed Westwick–shaped chocolate. "Now let's go! I want to listen to those recordings of yours."

"Slow down." I tugged back. "If we go in there like a stampeding herd, people will notice. We're going for subtle right now." I scowled. "And everyone's staring at me as it is."

"I know," Jenna said, slowing her pace and relaxing her shoulders, as if we were just hanging out, strolling back to our rooms. "Everyone's heard about Will by now."

I nodded, my throat clenching. The dorm was buzzing with activity as students tried to put off going to bed. Morning meant school had officially started. We climbed the stairs and hung around the eleventh-grade common room but it was packed. If we stayed any longer people would start to wonder. There was no way to get in and get the microphones without giving ourselves away.

"Damn it," Jenna muttered. "It's like eleven o'clock. Don't they sleep?"

"Apparently not." We turned away, going back down to our own floor. "I'll sneak up tonight after everyone's in bed," I assured her.

She looked deflated. "Okay."

We couldn't stop from pausing outside of Spencer's room. The door was open a crack and we could see his roommate's desk, piled with books and hand-whittled stakes. There was already clothes on the floor and an Angelina Jolie poster on the wall.

But Spencer's side of the room was bare.

His surfing posters were gone, along with the old surfboard he usually hung over the bed. I kicked the door open, Jenna crowding in behind me.

"What the hell?" His roommate, John, jerked back. When he recognized us, his face went red. "Oh. Sorry."

"Where's Spencer's stuff?" I demanded. His bookcase was cleared of his supernatural encyclopedias and boxes of charms and spell bags. Even his jar of sea salt was gone, which he always kept on his nightstand because every protective spell he researched called for it. I marched over to his dresser and yanked it open.

Empty. Not even a single turquoise bead to prove Spencer had ever been here. Fury and something darker, more debilitating gnawed at me, fraying my temper. "John, where's his stuff?" I barely recognized my own voice.

John stood up, pity making him shuffle awkwardly. "They packed it up today. Didn't they tell you?"

"No. They did not."

"Who packed it?" Jenna snapped. She was vibrating with anger as well. Between the two of us we could have powered a nuclear reactor. John wisely took a step backward.

"A couple of the guards." He held up his hands beseechingly. "Look, I don't know."

"Well, they can damn well unpack it," I seethed. "Because he's going to be fine."

"Yeah? I mean, yeah, of course," he hastened to add. "Of course, he is."

I had to turn away from the bare mattress. It was making my eyes burn. It should have been heaped with Spencer's Mexican blankets.

"Don't let anyone move in here," I told John, whirling to glare at him. He swallowed, his Adam's apple bobbing.

"I don't really—" He swallowed again when Jenna added her glare to mine. "Of course. I won't."

Out in the hall, Jenna and I exchanged bleak glances. I knew she was remembering Will's room, stripped of his belongings long before I'd had to stake him. I shivered. Jenna looked like she wanted to throw up.

"We're going to fix this," I told her grimly. She nodded just as grimly.

"Damn right we are."

◆

I waited until I was sure everyone was asleep. I paused in my doorway to listen, and again at the bottom of the stairs, and once more on the landing outside the eleventh-grade common room. I didn't hear anything and saw no one except Chloe asleep on the couch in our common room, her laptop half open on the floor next to her. I didn't wake her up to go with me. I honestly didn't know if I could trust her. She'd feel the same way about me if she knew I'd gone through her stuff. I wasn't sure how we'd gotten here. It was a long way from counting the days until we could be roommates to punching each other.

But I couldn't worry about that right now.

Spencer was my only concern. He didn't have much time and we didn't have much information. I hadn't been lying to Jenna when I told her there was no guarantee my microphones had recorded anything worth listening to. But I could hope.

I could hope really hard.

The common room was finally deserted, the smell of barbecue potato chips lingering in the air. I crept forward, stepping as softly as I could. I retrieved the microphone from under the couch first, taking care not to stick my finger in the wads of old gum. Next, I plucked the one from the dresser. The one inside the coat rack was going to be decidedly trickier.

I stood in front of it, frowning as I ran through my options. I could tip it over and shake the microphone loose, but those old coat racks weighed a ton. There was a good chance the bottom would slide out and hit the floor. I didn't have a magnet to lure it up the pole either. If Chloe and I were still talking to each other, she probably could have rigged up something. She was good at that sort of thing. I unscrewed the top and stood on my tiptoes to look down the length of it. Darkness and dust. I took the small penlight from my pocket and switched it on, keeping the light angled down the pole. If it flashed into a window, one of the guards outside might see it and come to investigate. It didn't do me much good anyway. It only served to glint off the microphone pen casing and prove that it was far out of my reach.

I shook it once, rattling it. I'd have to abandon it until I had a better plan and hope the other ones had recorded something useful. I hated to do it. It galled my stubborn streak.

But I had bigger problems.

Such as the cool pale hand that suddenly clamped over my mouth, jerking my body backward against a hard chest.

CHAPTER 20

◆

Hunter

I jabbed my elbow back as quick as I could but he was already dancing away. My heel caught his instep hard enough for him to make a sound. And then he tugged and whirled me around, backing me into the wall. His hand was still over my mouth. I hooked my foot around his ankle and shoved. He staggered back and went down, slipping on the area rug. He took me with him, yanking so that I landed on top of him. He sprawled with uncanny silence, not even rattling the furniture when he landed. Blue eyes laughed at me.

"Quinn," I snapped, finally recognizing him. I whacked him. Hard. "What the hell are you doing? I could have staked you, you idiot."

He grinned. "I'm quicker than you are."

"Shut up, you are not." Okay, so he was. But only because he had supernatural abilities. If he'd been a normal human guy, I could have taken him. I could still take him. I just needed a few more weapons to do it.

"I didn't think you lived on this floor."

"How do you know where my room is?" I asked. "And what are you even doing here? You do realize this is a school for vampire hunters, right? Why do I have to keep reminding you of that?"

He smirked. "I have a pass." He was telling the truth. I hadn't noticed it yet but there was a discreet metal button, like the ones you get at museums, pinned to the collar of his T-shirt. The shirt was almost the exact blue of his eyes. The pin was contraband. It allowed the bearer to be on campus without a mess of security coming down on his or her head. It almost certainly had never been worn by a vampire before.

"Where did you get that?" I demanded.

"Off Kieran."

"Kieran gave you a campus free-access pass?" I repeated dubiously.

"Not so much 'gave' as left his knapsack out while he was kissing my sister."

"So you stole it."

"Did I mention he was kissing my *baby* sister?"

All the talk about kissing was making it hard not to look at his mouth. Or to pretend I didn't know exactly how his lips felt on mine.

He frowned suddenly, his fingers on my chin, his expression going hard as steel. "What happened to your face this time?"

I wrinkled my nose. Great. I'd forgotten I was bruised and

probably looked like a mottled grape. "Chloe punched me. Well, she tried to."

"*Chloe* punched you?"

"Yes," I grumbled.

"Well, I can't punch her back." He sounded disgruntled. "She's a girl."

I blinked. "I didn't ask you to."

"That's what guys do," he muttered. "When someone hurts a girl. Especially you."

I wasn't sure what he meant by that but I felt kind of warm and jittery inside, like I'd had too much hot chocolate.

And then I realized I was still lying on top of him.

We were pressed together, close enough that my breath ruffled his long hair. He had the kind of beauty that almost burns, as if he belonged in a Pre-Raphaelite painting of a poet or a mythic doomed lover. He was that gorgeous.

He raised his eyebrow, the trademark smirk getting more pronounced.

And he was a vampire. Which meant he could hear the sound of my heartbeat accelerating while I stared at him and thought about how pretty he was.

Crap.

Totally unfair advantage.

I pushed up on my palms to launch myself off him before I embarrassed myself completely and irrevocably.

"Hey." He watched me back away as if he was dangerous. He looked entirely too pleased with himself. "Where are you going?"

"To bed." Double crap. What if he thought that was an

invitation? Was it an invitation? And when, exactly, had I lost my mind? "Uh, I meant to my room. Where my bed is. And—shit." I forced myself to stop babbling.

He rose into a crouch, looking feral and predatory. "Do I make you nervous, Hunter?"

I stopped, glaring at him. "Excuse me, I know seventeen painful ways to kill you. You don't make me nervous."

"I know seventeen different ways to kiss you."

I ignored the flare of heat in my chest and focused on the fact that it was clearly a line. I tossed my hair off my shoulder. "I'm not one of your groupies."

"Good," he said, suddenly serious. He didn't bother denying that he had groupies. That made me like him even more.

I was in so much trouble.

"Look, Quinn, what are you really doing here? Do you have info on that pill I gave you?"

"Not yet. But I got your text about Will," he replied, straightening. He only towered over me a little. "And I thought you could use some company."

"You came for me?" Yup. So much trouble.

He nodded, touching my hair and tangling his long fingers in the ends, as if it was a fire and he was as cold as he was winter-pale. "What are you doing up here?"

"Retrieving personal property," I explained, mesmerized by the feel of his hand as he tugged me a little closer, winding my hair around his wrist like a golden rope.

"From the coat rack?" he whispered, puzzled. He must have seen me staring at it.

I nodded, wondering why my voice felt like it had faded away completely. I cleared my throat. "Yes, but it's stuck in the bottom."

"Allow me." He let me go so abruptly I stumbled back a little. He lifted the coat rack and turned it upside down, as if it weighed no more than a broom. The microphone tumbled out and I caught it before it hit the ground. He grinned, shaking his head. "Your personal property is surveillance equipment?"

I shrugged, slipping it into my pocket. "Thanks."

"You're welcome."

I peered out of the doorway, making sure it was clear before I started to creep back down the stairs. I paused on the landing. Quinn was right behind me.

"Where are you going?" I asked.

"I'm going with you."

"I don't remember inviting you," I said drily.

"That's a vampire myth," he shot back just as drily. "I don't need to be invited. I would have thought they taught you that here." He winked. I rolled my eyes. He followed me and I let him. Gladly. The truth was, I didn't think I wanted to be alone just yet. I was wired and exhausted and worried.

And I liked having him around. He was distracting. In a good way.

He paused, nodding to Chloe, who was still sound asleep on the common room sofa. "Want me to pull her hair?"

I grinned, shaking my head. He took a step forward.

"What are you doing?" I grabbed his arm.

"I'm going to sniff her."

I blinked. "I'm sorry, what?"

"You're worried about those vitamins, right? I might be able to smell them in her blood and I *might* be able to tell if they're messing her up."

"They're definitely messing her up," I muttered, touching the bruise on my jaw. "But go ahead. That could help. Just don't wake her up."

"Hello? Give me a little credit. Vampire stealth, remember?"

"Vampire arrogance, you mean."

"That too."

It went against a lifetime of training to crush on a vampire and, worse, to watch him skulk toward one of my friends. My hands actually twitched. But I stayed where I was. I trusted Quinn Drake, despite the fact that I was the latest in a long line of vampire hunters.

He was graceful as moonlight, fluid and pale as he draped over Chloe. She slept on peacefully, utterly unaware. Not exactly proof of the effectiveness of our education. Then again, right now, neither was I. Quinn was a dark silhouette out of any standard vampire horror movie, leaning over, teeth gleaming. And I just waited trustingly, patiently, hopefully.

Grandpa would pop a blood vessel if he could see me now.

I pushed that out of my mind and watched as Quinn's nose hovered along the line of Chloe's neck, sniffing as if she was a fine wine. His fangs lengthened. I tensed, took a step, stopped. He inhaled, or whatever passed as a smell-seeking inhalation for the undead, and then recoiled sharply.

He didn't speak as he approached, just jerked his head down the hall toward my room. Later, I'd have to ask him how he knew that was my room. Right now, I just wanted to know why he was wiping his nose as if he'd snorted pepper. I shut the door quietly behind him. The single lamp lit on my desk cast his face into shadows.

"Well?" I demanded.

"Those aren't vitamins," he said.

"I *knew* it!" I winced nervously. "What are they?"

"I don't know," he admitted. "There are vitamins in there—they have a very distinctive smell. But there's something else too."

I wiped my damp palms on my pants. "She'll never believe me. When can you get the lab results from your brother?"

"Maybe tomorrow. I'll make him hurry."

"God, her *mom* gave her those." I rubbed my arms, suddenly cold. "And she's hidden a whole stash of them somewhere so I can't even flush them. Well, maybe something here will convince her."

"Is that why you bugged that room upstairs?"

I nodded. "I thought Will was going to get better. And that whatever he was into, some of his friends might know about it. I don't know. But students keep getting this weird flu that doesn't get better. Something's just off."

I fumbled the microphones out of my pocket and switched the first one on. The quality wasn't very good; the scratchiness of the background was louder than the voices, but it was better than nothing. I'd set the motion sensor recorder to switch on and off throughout the evenings and late at night. I figured there was less chance of people whispering in the common room at lunchtime when anyone might hear them. It was mostly complaints about classes and people leaving milk out of the fridge in the kitchenette. I listened for about a half hour, fast-forwarding where I could.

Quinn leaned against my door, patient in a way I hadn't thought he was capable of being. He was usually teasing or taunting or eager for a fight. I was seeing another part of his personality, quiet and thoughtful but just as intense.

"Nothing," I said, dejected. "I guess it was a stupid idea."

"Wait." He pushed away from the wall. "Let me hear that one again." I handed it to him, showing him how to rewind. He held it up to his ear. "It's faint but . . ." He listened harder and I suddenly envied him his supernatural senses. I'd never envied a vampire before. I was too fond of sunlight and spaghetti and ice cream.

"Got it," he said, his eyes flaring triumphantly. He rewound again and repeated what he heard for my benefit. *"Are you sure this stuff works? Shut up, you moron, someone will hear you. It's pretty steep for a bunch of vitamins. I told you, they're better than vitamins—watch it. Leave it, we'll never get behind that TV. It weighs a ton."*

I shot to my feet. "They dropped some!"

He nodded smugly but stopped me from reaching for the doorknob. "Let me go."

"What? Why?"

"For one thing, I can move an ancient TV that weighs a ton without making much noise."

"Oh. Good point." Use the tools you've got. It was a hunter motto. And it made sense, even if my tool, in this case, was a vampire.

He was only gone long enough for me to notice the flashing light on my answering machine and to press play. Grandpa's gravelly whiskey-and-cigar-smoke voice rumbled out of the speaker. For some reason it made me feel like crying. I missed his confidence and certainty. It was in short supply right now. Even if I cringed at the actual words he was saying.

"Hunter, honey, I got a call from the school. Heard you did good. I know it's hard, but you did what you had to do. That's what hunters do and that's what Wilds do. And you saved your friend's life, the way I hear it. Your headmistress was making noise about seeing the school psychologist but I told her you don't need that quackery. You be strong. You're a good girl. I don't want you going soft over a *Hel-Blar*. Vampires need killing, you know that."

My bedroom door shut with a soft click. Quinn raised an eyebrow at me. I winced, knowing he'd heard every word of my grandpa's message.

"He means well," I said defensively.

"Okay," Quinn replied with deceptive nonchalance.

"He raised me the only way he knew how."

"Okay," he said again.

I frowned. I didn't know why I was justifying Grandpa. He was a good man. So was Quinn. One wasn't mutually exclusive of the other.

My head was starting to hurt.

"Did you find it?" I asked, changing the subject.

He nodded, sitting next to me and holding out his hand, palm up. The white pill looked innocuous. Hard to imagine that something so small was making such a big mess.

"It doesn't look like Chloe's vitamins," I said, confused. "Hers are huge and yellow."

"I know," he said grimly. "These aren't vitamins."

I blinked. "Wait. So there's *two* kinds of pills making the rounds now? What the hell is *wrong* with people?" I sat back, disgusted. "It does explain why we keep running in circles."

Quinn was staring at the pill as if it were a coiled cobra that might strike at any time. His nostrils twitched, his jaw clenched.

"Okay, what?" I asked uncertainly.

"This thing's poison," he answered through his teeth.

"Seriously? Is that what made Will sick? Not just *Hel-Blar?*"

"It's toxic to humans," Quinn explained. "But it's absolutely fatal to vampires."

The silence felt charged, like a battery about to explode. I grabbed the pill off his hand, as if it might start leaking acid. He shook his head once. "It's only fatal if ingested."

"So people are taking vampire drugs now? Along with some weird vitamin? That doesn't make any sense." I wrapped the pill inside a tissue. "Can you get your brother to analyze this too?"

"Hell, yes," he said, putting the little package in his pocket. "I want to know what this is. I've smelled it before."

"Where?"

"That's the thing, I don't know. I can't remember." He sounded annoyed with himself.

I scooted back to lean against the wall, the blankets twisting under my legs. "Spencer wasn't taking drugs or vitamins or any of that stuff. He barely takes aspirin."

"Spencer was bitten by a *Hel-Blar*," Quinn said, also moving back to sit next to me. "He's not a mystery."

"Then why is his stuff all gone from his room?"

"It is?" Quinn looked surprised. "Is he that sick?"

"Theo says Spencer's badly off, but stable. The meds are helping him more than they helped Will. But his room's empty, just like Will's was. And there's that flu everyone's worried about."

Quinn whistled through his teeth. "Look, obviously I've never really trusted the Helios-Ra, and maybe I've lived in Violet Hill too long, but this has 'conspiracy' written all over it."

"I know. And I won't let what happened to Will happen to Spencer." My throat burned. "I had to stake him," I added in a very small voice. "I *had* to."

"I know," he said softly, sliding his arm around my waist and tucking me into his side as if he was trying to protect me. It was kind of sweet. I let myself lean into him. "He was *Hel-Blar*," he added. "He wasn't Will anymore."

"Everyone keeps saying that."

"Because it's true." His hand stroked my back up and down, softly, soothingly.

"It doesn't feel like that. It feels like a betrayal. I couldn't help him, Quinn. I've never felt so helpless."

"Hunter, the last thing you are is helpless." He sounded so sure. I couldn't stop the first tear from falling.

"I don't want Spencer to die."

"He won't die." His lips were in my hair.

"You don't know that."

"I know about bloodchanges, Hunter. And Spencer is strong and healthy. He has a better chance than most."

I wanted to trust the little bubble of hope in my stomach, but I couldn't.

"Will didn't even recognize me," I said brokenly. "And it happened so fast. Why did he have to attack Chloe? Why did I have to be the one to stake him?" More tears fell and I didn't try to stop them this time. I cried because I couldn't not cry anymore. Quinn just held me, not saying a word. His hand cradled the back of my neck, running through my hair. I sobbed and trembled and sobbed some more until I felt weak and dehydrated. And a little bit lighter.

I sat up. Quinn's shirt was wet. "Sorry," I said hoarsely.

"Don't be." He touched my face, lightly skimming over my bruises so that I barely felt his fingertips. I wiped my nose on my sleeve, feeling well enough not to want to look like a disgusting mess.

"Thanks," I murmured.

He leaned in, closing the distance between us. His eyes stayed on mine. I didn't think, I just leaned in too. I kissed him first and his hands closed around my shoulders, pulling me closer. I slid my tongue along his, feeling warmth tingle throughout my body, melting the ice that had been creeping inside of me. He kissed me so thoroughly I felt naked, even though not a single button was undone. We were fully clothed and I had blades in the soles of my shoes and a stake in a harness in the small of my back but I'd never felt more exposed, or vulnerable. Still, I wasn't scared. I wanted more.

It became a kind of duel fought with lips and tongues to see who could make the other feel more, need more. I made small noises in the back of my throat. His arms were lean and strong under my hands and his hair fell to curtain our faces, smelling like mint shampoo. We tried to get closer to each other but it wasn't physically possible. We didn't care. We were so determined, nothing else mattered.

Until we tumbled right off the bed and landed in a lump on the floor.

"Ow," Quinn muttered. He rubbed his elbow. My shoulder shook. "Hunter. It's okay. Are you hurt? Hunter?" He sounded horrified.

I was laughing too hard to answer. He tipped my face up, saw the soundless chortle, heard the wheeze as I tried to haul in a breath. His answering grin was quick, followed a chuckle of his own. And another.

And then we were laughing so hard we had to hold on to each other. I wheezed. It felt nearly as good as Quinn's very wicked kisses. I'd been afraid it would feel like a betrayal of my friend who was lying in a hospital bed or my friend who was about to lie under the earth, but instead it felt like breathing again after being underwater for too long. Keeping the ability to laugh might be the only thing that would get my balance back. I couldn't fight for them, couldn't find out what was really going on, if I was crushed under sorrow and guilt and misery, which I could easily give in to if I let myself. But I couldn't risk that. I had to kick ass. All sorts of ass.

Starting now.

I eased back, holding my aching stomach. I tasted copper in my mouth. "Ouch, I think I bit my tongue," I said, wiping the tip of my tongue on my hand and seeing blood. "Yup. Gross."

Quinn went very still.

I was an idiot.

I'd let myself forget what Quinn really was.

I think, maybe, he'd forgotten a little too.

And now I was kneeling on the floor with blood in my mouth and there was no forgetting for either of us.

"Quinn?" I said softly. I didn't move.

It was just my luck that I finally got what I thought might be a real boyfriend, and now I might have to stake him.

Quinn was even paler than usual, crouched in front of me, his lips lifting off his fangs, which protruded as far as they could. I barely breathed. There were so many conflicting emotions chasing across his features, I hardly knew how to read them all. Most prominently I saw fear, violent restraint, desire, hunger. He swallowed and the movement rippled his throat. He looked like he was in pain.

And then he smiled.

And I knew real fear for the first time.

There was nothing more unpredictable than a young vampire. Nothing stronger or faster either. Or more hypnotizing. Speaking of hypnotizing, my vial of Hypnos was sitting on top of my pack at the other end of the room, where it did me no good at all.

I looked away from Quinn's burning eyes, from the flash of fang.

"Quinn," I repeated, sternly this time, like a cross librarian.

He flinched. Agony sharpened his smile into a humorless smirk.

"Hunter, run," he begged.

I lifted my chin. "No," I said, even though adrenaline was pumping through me like a sudden monsoon in the jungle of my insides. I was flooded with biological chemicals that made me want to bare my teeth back at Quinn like some caged panther.

"Please run," he pleaded again, but even as I shifted my weight, barely moving, he was on me.

His hand clamped around my wrist and he jerked me up as he surged to his feet. I was practically plastered to his chest, even as I leaned back as far as I could. Only my head and neck and shoulders had any freedom of movement, and I felt like one of those half-swooning pale girls in a Victorian novel.

Not a particularly nice feeling, as it turns out.

Quinn struggled but the animal inside him was at the surface, scenting blood and prey. No one knew what beast slept inside the vampire; all we knew was that it had sharp teeth and an insatiable appetite.

And I had no intention of being someone's supper, no matter how well they kissed.

Quinn lifted my hand to his mouth, closing his lips over the side of my thumb. His tongue moved over my skin, licking at the smear of blood. I would never admit this to anyone at any time, but it made my knees weak. It should have grossed me out. I was sure my heart was pounding because I was afraid. Not because of the way he was looking up at me, his eyes the blue of the hottest part of a flame, the part that burns the most.

"You taste like . . . raspberries."

I swallowed. "No, I don't."

"You do." He was staring at my mouth now. I clamped my lips together. The tiny cut on my tongue throbbed. It felt like a beacon, only it was calling the ship toward the rocky shoreline instead of safely away. I ran my tongue over my teeth, trying to get rid of the blood.

"I can get that for you," he purred.

I jerked back but I was still trapped in the cage of his arms. I narrowed my eyes. "Quinn Drake, stop it right now."

"But I don't want to," he drawled. "I want more."

"I don't want to dust you."

"I just want a little taste."

"You've had one," I pointed out.

"Not nearly enough. I'm greedy for you."

I didn't say anything, only stomped down suddenly, aiming for his instep. He easily spread his feet just as suddenly and leaned back against the wall, securing me between his legs.

"Damn it, Quinn."

"When you get mad like that, your blood smells even sweeter."

"Then you're about to go into sugar shock."

"Let's see, shall we?"

He kissed me, crowding out all the alarm bells ringing in my head. I kissed him back, hoping to distract him from his thirst. His mouth was gentle when I expected it to be predatory. He was dangerous like water, soft and smooth, even as it filled up your lungs, relentlessly stealing your breath away.

My head tilted and I wasn't sure if it was the pressure of his mouth on my jaw or my own movement. My throat was exposed and his fangs scraped the tender skin there, but he never pierced my neck. He didn't drink from me until I collapsed, didn't drain me until I was too weak to fight back, didn't let the beast win. He went against everything I was ever taught.

The longer we kissed, the more his hold loosened. He finally let me go, shoving himself farther against the wall.

"You should have staked me," he said. He looked as if he'd been in a battle, as if he should be carrying a stained sword and a battered shield. "I have to get out of here." He yanked the door open like it was rope and he was dangling from a cliff top.

"Wait."

"I have to go!" He snarled and the door slammed shut behind him.

CHAPTER 21

◆

QUINN

Later Sunday night

When I got home, Lucy was lying on the couch saying the same thing she'd been saying when I left.

"I'm *fine*."

Solange was wearing sunglasses and sitting on a chair as far away as she could and still be in the same room, looking like she was about to throw up.

"Stop it." Lucy threw a pillow at her. Solange didn't move, and it hit her in the chest. Lucy snorted. "Nice vampire reflexes you got there."

Nicholas came in holding a painted tray with a steaming mug. Lucy sat up, glaring at him.

"No way."

He blinked at her. "What?"

"I am not drinking one more cup of chamomile tea. You can't make me." She folded her arms over her chest.

"You have a head wound."

"Yeah, and it hasn't affected my taste buds." She rolled her eyes. "Anyway, I have three tiny stitches. That's hardly a real head wound. They always look worse than they really are. Your uncle said so."

"You didn't see yourself passed out in the river," he said stubbornly. "We thought . . ." He trailed off.

Lucy's expression gentled slightly. "I'm okay, Nicholas. Promise. A little headache now, that's all."

"Are you sure?"

"For the hundredth time, yes." She looked sheepish. "I passed out when I saw the blood. It just took me by surprise."

I leaned in the doorway, feeling as if I couldn't catch my breath. I could still taste Hunter's blood on my tongue, like candy. I shuddered.

Lucy looked at me, then at Nicholas, who was hovering with a worried scowl, and then at Solange, who was sitting with her knees up to her chest. She let out a disgruntled sigh. "What is *wrong* with you guys?"

Nicholas and Solange exploded at the same time.

"You nearly died!" Nicholas shouted.

"I could have eaten you!" Solange added.

Silence throbbed for a long moment before Lucy rubbed her face. "You're both dumb. And way overdramatic." They just stared at her, clearly expecting a different reaction. There were smudges under her eyes but otherwise she looked fine. Uncle G. had checked her out. He had a couple of medical degrees stashed away, another benefit of a long life span. "Nicholas, stop worrying. I've been hurt worse in gym class. Solange, you like blood. Duh." She pushed three layers of afghans off her lap. "Hello? Vampire."

"You don't understand."

Lucy glowered. "Don't you dare pull that crap on me, Solange Drake. You might be a vampire but I've known you practically our whole lives. I totally understand. Give me some credit." She turned suddenly, jabbing a finger in my direction. "And you look weird."

I felt weird. Hunter just did that to me. But even she would understand the danger in being the only human in a room full of monsters. Lucy was stubbornly oblivious.

"I'm fine," I said with a dry smile. "Drink your chamomile tea."

"Only if it magically turns into hot chocolate." Lucy smirked suddenly. "You're all dressed up."

"Am not. I just naturally look good."

She grinned. "You went to see Hunter Wild, didn't you? That is so much more fun to talk about than my stupid stitches and Solange's meltdown."

"I did not have a meltdown," Solange protested.

"Please, you totally did." Lucy smiled briefly. "And I love you for it. But cut it out already." She waggled her eyebrows at me. The light reflected off her dark-rimmed glasses. "Did you kiss her?" She stopped. "Of *course* you kissed her. How was it?"

"I'm not a girl, Lucy. I don't want to braid your hair and talk about kissing."

Solange stared at me, sniffing the air delicately. She looked confused. "Did you bite her?"

"No, I didn't bite her," I answered, a little more roughly than I'd intended. "Instead of talking about me, why don't we talk about what the hell were you doing out in the woods in the first place?"

"Yeah," Nicholas agreed silkily. "Let's talk about that." He nudged Lucy into a chair. When he reached for the teacup, she narrowed her eyes at him.

"I will pour that on your head."

He didn't look particularly worried. "I'll tell Mom you're not resting."

Her mouth gaped open. "Dirty pool."

"Hell, yeah."

At least no one was talking about my love life anymore. "Solange, seriously," I said. "What the hell?"

"I just needed to get out," she said quietly. "With the abductions and the assassination attempts and the bloodchange, forgive me for feeling a little overwhelmed." She lifted her sunglasses. "And look at my eyes." Her pupils were still ringed in red, the whites bloodshot. They hadn't changed back.

"Ouch," Lucy winced. "Do they have vampire Visine for that?"

Solange didn't smile. "Anyway, you guys patrol all the time," she told Nicholas and me.

"Not alone!" he shot back.

"She wasn't alone," Lucy interrupted. "I was with her." She smiled sheepishly. "I followed her," she admitted.

"Why?" I asked.

"I don't know. I guess I was worried. But I knew she needed

some time alone so I didn't want to bug her." She shrugged one shoulder. "Montmartre's dead. And so's Greyhaven, and he was Montmartre's lieutenant or whatever, so I figured we were okay. It's not like the Host could have regrouped that fast."

"Did you conveniently forget about all the *Hel-Blar*?" Nicholas asked them with disgust. They both shrugged. He looked like his head was going to explode. My little brother had his hands full with those two. I just wanted to lie in a dark room and try not to replay every moment of that kiss.

You know, before I fanged out on the girl.

The *vampire hunter* girl.

I groaned, turning to stomp up the stairs. I didn't need super-sensitive vampire senses to know Lucy was chasing me.

"Oh no way, Quinn. No headache is going to keep me from getting the dirt."

She was as unshakable as a gnat. I couldn't help but shoot a grin at her over my shoulder. "I had no idea you were so kinky."

She flicked me. "If you want to save your brother's and your sister's undead lives, you will distract me right now."

"What, calling you a perv isn't distracting enough?"

She tilted her head. "I have photos of your superhero phase. I'm sure Hunter would love to see the one of you in the Batman tights and cape from that Halloween when you were ten."

"Remind me never to piss you off," I said.

"It's a basic life skill," she agreed cheerfully. "But an important one." She perched on the edge of my bed. "So spill, Casanova."

"Dream on."

She pouted. "I'm injured, remember?"

"Oh, so *now* you play the injured card."

She grinned unrepentantly, popping back to her feet. She'd never been any good at sitting still. "Why are you still all fangy?"

I ran my tongue over my fangs, being careful not to slice it open. I had no intention of telling her I'd had the urge to turn Hunter into a wineglass and drink her down like red wine. "Only you would reduce centuries of the mythical undead to 'fangy.'"

"I call 'em like I see 'em, fangboy." She paused at the window, frowning slightly. "There she goes," she said quietly.

"Who, Solange?"

She nodded. "She's going to hide in her pottery shed. I'm worried about her, Quinn."

"Why?"

She gnawed on her lower lip. "Because she's being weird. She told Kieran not to come over tonight."

"That's not weird."

"No, it's the way she said it." She sighed. "And my parents are coming back home the day after tomorrow, and I'm worried you guys are going to try and freeze me out. You know," she made sarcastic air quotes, "for my own good."

"We wouldn't," I lied. We totally would. We were a dangerous family to know right now. In fact, kissing Hunter and then actually tasting her blood had stirred my inner vampire closer to the surface. Even Lucy smelled good right now, and I was as used to her scent as to any of my siblings'. It rarely bothered me.

It was bothering me now.

"Lucy, I'm glad you're okay. If you do something stupid like that again, I'll kill you myself." I smiled to soften the scold. "Now go away. I'm tired."

She glowered at me. "You're not tired. You're trying to get rid of me."

I shoved her gently toward the door. Her neck was bare, washed clean with antiseptic, but I thought I could still smell very faint blood from the stitches under her bandage. "Well, then take a hint."

She turned and shoved her foot against the bottom of the door. "Right there, Quinn. That's what I mean. You guys are all fretting like old ladies. It's like you're more afraid of vampires than I am."

"That's cause we're smarter than you are," I pointed out. "And worried."

"Well, suck it up," she said crossly. "Because you're not getting rid of me that easily."

CHAPTER 22

◆

Hunter

Monday afternoon

I didn't hear from him for the rest of the night. Not a single text or phone message. Even so, I'd released some of the toxic knot of fear and worry clutching my insides, and I felt better prepared to do whatever I might need to do.

Which was convenient, since the first assembly of the school year was just as bad as I'd thought it would be.

It was after lunch and we were all gathered in the auditorium, which was in actuality an old wooden schoolhouse from the turn of the century, outfitted with salvaged church pews, also wooden. Hunters have always preferred everything to be made of wood—it's easier to splinter off a piece to use as a makeshift weapon that way. The first thing my grandfather did when he bought his house was rip off the aluminum siding and replace everything with board-and-batten.

There were rows and rows of windows and the thick, rippled glass diffused the sunlight into every corner of the building. It followed me into the room. There was no hope of hiding. Students whirled in their seats, staring at me as I passed, whispering loudly to each other. Luckily Jenna and Jason were close enough to the back that I wasn't on display for very long. I could see Chloe off to one side but she turned back to stare at the front, ignoring me.

I slid onto a polished pew to sit next to Jenna. She leaned forward and flicked the ear of a girl who wasn't even pretending not to stare.

"Ow," she squealed. She added a glare before shifting to sit properly.

Jenna folded her arms smugly. I sat with a straight back, my boots polished, my cargo pockets filled with regulation weapons and supplies. I couldn't avoid looking at the table near the first pew with Will's class picture from last year and a candle burning on either side. He was smiling earnestly. I tried not to remember him baring his fangs at me, trying to rip through my throat for my jugular. Or the feel of his skin and flesh and heart under the impact of my stake.

Jason leaned over from Jenna's other side. "Any word on Spencer?"

I shook my head. "I went over this morning but Theo said nothing's changed."

"That's not necessarily a bad thing," he pointed out.

"Chloe's still not talking to you?" Jenna asked.

"Guess not."

When Headmistress Bellwood strode across the stage, the heels of her sensible shoes clacking like gunshots, we all sat up straighter. The chatter died instantly. Even the first-year students knew enough to be afraid of her. The rest of the teachers filed in behind her. Mr. York was last, his whistle around his neck as always. I swore he slept with it on. He once blew it in Chloe's ear so loudly she was deaf for three days.

Headmistress Bellwood didn't need a microphone; her stern, crisp voice found you wherever you were. "Welcome to a new year at the Helios-Ra High School. You are embarking on a new journey and creating bonds with fellow hunters that will last a lifetime. Some of you will be discovering new talents and eventually choosing a department of the League in which to serve. The departments include standard Hunting, Paranormal Studies, Science, and Technology. What we do here is prepare you to hunt vampires and join the Academy college for further study in your chosen field."

I was only half listening. We'd heard variations of this speech several times over the years. And I was too busy talking myself out of checking for text messages from Quinn. He was unconscious in his bed; he could hardly have sent me a message.

Every time I thought about that kiss, my lips tingled, my belly grew warm, my knees went soft.

He was dangerous on so many levels.

"You will all be expected to model the virtues of this fine school: Diligence, Duty, and Daring," Headmistress Bellwood continued.

"I will not tolerate rebellion, recklessness, or arrogance. All of those qualities will get you killed and are, therefore, unacceptable. Those of you joining us for the first time will refer to the handbook for rules and regulations. Those of you returning are expected to remember those rules and follow them. I am certain you will all have an educational and enjoyable year. I look forwarding to meeting each and every one of our new students." Each and every one of those new students shuddered. "I am sure you've all noticed the memorial to one of our eleventh-grade students, Will Stevenson. I am saddened to report that he was infected with the *Hel-Blar* virus and did not survive." Everyone but Chloe was sneaking me glances. I lifted my chin, my expression blank. "Please pay your respects to his memory and take from this tragedy the necessity of always being on your guard."

Ms. Kali, one of the Paranormal Studies professors, descended the steps leading off the stage and went to stand behind the memorial. We all stood. The Niners exchanged confused glances before scrambling to follow suit. They'd never attended a student memorial before, but this would almost certainly not be their last. Ms. Kali's voice would have done an opera singer proud. She sang the traditional Helios-Ra mourning song, passed down through the centuries. Fallen hunters were usually buried with rose thorns, salt, and a mouthful of dried garlic. Garlic didn't actually have an effect on vampires, but the custom had started long before anyone realized that. Hunters who weren't cremated had a whitethorn stake driven through their dead hearts, another ancient precaution. Will had crumbled to ashes, so no one would be burying him in the local hunter graveyard. But the song was sung and a marker with his name would be added to the memorial garden behind the race track on the other side of the pond.

I was glad I'd shed my tears last night. It made it easier to get through the rest of the assembly with the weeping girls who'd had crushes on Will, the solemn faces of the teachers, the song raising goose bumps on our arms, the sunlight hitting Will's framed photo.

"Ninth graders will go to orientation on the south lawn," Headmistress Bellwood announced when the memorial was over. "The rest of you will pick up your schedules and get to your classes. On a final note, you've heard of the particularly virulent flu making the rounds. Two more students were hospitalized today, so I urge you to wash your hands and take extra care."

Students filed out, whispering respectfully at first, then chattering loudly and shouting to each other as they poured through the double doors onto the pebbled lane.

"Flu, my ass," Jenna murmured out of the corner of her mouth.

"Well, it's not like the school is ever big on full disclosure," Jason pointed out. "We're supposed to shut up and follow the rules."

"Yeah," I agreed. "Anyone else starting to find that really irritating?"

"I'm not loving it," Jenna confirmed. "Look, I gotta get to archery practice. I'm assisting in a demo for the Niners."

"See you at dinner," Jason called out after her. He frowned at me for a long moment. "When was the last time you actually slept?"

I shrugged. "I got a few hours last night."

"You look like hell."

I had to smile. "You know, if you ever decide to date girls, I have to tell you that's no way to compliment us."

"I'm serious, Hunter."

"So am I." I nudged him. "I'm fine, honest." I didn't tell him that making out with Quinn after sobbing through his shirt had done me a world of good. Quinn was hot enough that Jason would want details, and I wasn't the detail-sharing type. "I promise I'll grab a nap before dinner, okay?"

"Okay," he grudgingly agreed. "I'll see you later."

Classes went the way they always did on the first day. It was mostly roll call and a brief description of what we'd be expected to learn over the year. Ms. Dailey sent us away early; York made us run laps. I slept a little, mostly because I'd promised Jason, and then we had dinner and went to our respective rooms to start on assigned reading. Chloe wasn't around but there were clothes on her bed. I couldn't concentrate, so I went outside to sit on one of the stone walls around the decorative gardens by the front of the main buildings to watch the sun set.

The sky went sapphire, then indigo, and flared orange along the tree line. The stars came out one by one, clustered overhead in patterns I could never remember. I'd made up my own when I was ten: Dracula, a stake, a heart, a crossbow, a sun. I found them now as the crickets began their evening choir in the long grass at the edge of the woods. The harvest moon rose like a fat pumpkin growing in the fertile field of the sky.

Lights went on in the gym and the dormitory. I could hear the muffled sound of music from behind thick windows, the wind in the oak tree behind me, and the spit of gravel as a van roared up the path, lights out, hidden in the long weeds at the edge of the woods.

"Hunter," Kieran called grimly. "We found something."

CHAPTER 23

◆

Hunter

Monday evening

I crossed over to the driver's side, trampling wild chicory flowers under my boots. Kieran's face was solemn and tense, fingers tight around the steering wheel.

"What's going on?" I frowned up at him.

"We've got trouble," he answered, tone clipped. "And we can't talk about it here."

"Is it about the vit—"

"Not here," he cut me off, eyes widening in warning. He was right. There were cameras and microphones all over the place. We were probably being overly cautious since we were in the middle of a field, but something about his expression had me double-checking my pockets for stakes. "Get Chloe."

My stomach dropped. Clearly this was bad news. "Chloe and I aren't exactly talking right now."

I could read the desperation in Kieran's face. "Do whatever you have to do," he said tightly. "Knock her over the head and hog-tie her if you have to."

Gee, I can't imagine why one of my oldest friends wasn't talking to me.

"Does campus security know you're here?"

He nodded. "I told them it was covert ops and to ignore anything I do."

My eyebrows rose. "Seriously? Hart's in on this?" He was the only one with the kind of power to order that kind of covert op.

"No."

I paused, turned back. "No?"

"So we have to get out of here before I get busted."

"Shit, Kieran."

"I know. So hurry up."

I was so going to get expelled on the first day of classes. And then Grandpa would kill me.

I fished my cell phone out of my pocket and dialed Chloe's number. She answered on the third ring. "Hello?"

"Chloe, I have to talk to you."

"I'm busy."

"It's important." There was a long pause. I could hear her breathing, labored and short. She must be working out again. I started walking toward the gym, pointing at it so Kieran would know where to meet us. "Chloe?" I tried to think about what would get her outside with minimal yelling and fighting. I didn't think we could afford to attract that kind of attention, covert ops pass or not. "Look, Dailey wanted me to talk to you about her guild. We can't be overheard."

"Really?" She sounded startled and then pleased. I might have felt guilty if my jaw wasn't still bruised from her sloppy punch. "I'm at the gym. I'll be right down."

"Meet you there. Side door." I clicked off and cut across the lawn to the entrance tucked behind a wall and a copse of birch trees. It was dark and deserted enough that we might not get caught. She must have run down the stairs. She was still in her shorts and T-shirt, her hair in a ponytail. Her face was damp with sweat. She pushed the door open and looked at me warily.

"So?" she asked. "Does she want me to join the guild or what?" Kieran edged the van around the corner, blocking us from any passersby. She frowned. "What's going on?"

"I'm not sure yet," I admitted. "But Kieran has big news. He wants us to go with him."

"Where? And why me—" She cut herself off with a huff of impatience. "Is this about the vitamins? God, Hunter, you're, like, totally obsessed."

"Just get in," Kieran muttered, leaning out slightly. "We don't have all night."

"I'm not going anywhere with you psychos," she said, sneering.

I glanced at Kieran. "How serious is this?"

"*Very* serious," he assured me, hitting the button so the van door slid open. "'Spider-Man' serious." "Spider-Man" had been our code word since we were eight, used only in times of great danger. Chloe was turning away, disgusted. I didn't have a lot of options.

I did the only thing I could think of. I grabbed her shoulder and swung her back around toward us.

And then I punched her.

She staggered back, screeching. Not exactly covert ops. "Shit," she clutched her face. "Shit, are you nuts?"

I hadn't punched her hard enough to actually knock her out. She did look a little dazed though, so I took advantage of her momentary disorientation and shoved her into the van. She cursed as I slammed the door shut and Kieran locked it. I ran around the other side and got into the passenger side.

"I hope to hell you know what you're doing," I told him darkly, rubbing my sore knuckles.

"Oh, I'm sorry," Chloe snapped from the backseat. "Did I hurt your knuckles with *my face?*"

"No more than I hurt yours with mine," I shot back.

"Is that what this is? Revenge?"

"Chloe, don't be stupid," I said as Kieran shot the van into drive. We rumbled down the lane and out onto the road.

"Let me out!" Chloe was yanking at the handle and screaming at the top of her lungs. If she got any louder my ears would bleed. She kept yelling, a wordless high-pitched sound meant to make our eyeballs explode.

When we were far enough away from the school, Kieran slammed on the brakes. Chloe hurtled forward, nearly breaking her nose on the back of his seat. She swallowed another shriek.

"Put your seatbelt on," he demanded sharply, using the tone of an agent used to being obeyed. It was actually something he'd learned from his father. It wasn't common knowledge, but Kieran was only a graduate and not actually a full-fledged agent. He needed to do two years at the college for that, but he'd decided to take the year off to find his father's murderer. The profs had thought he was wasting his talents, that grief was warping him. But he'd been right. His father *had* been murdered—and by one of our own, no less. Hope was out of the picture now, but the damage was done. Still, Kieran had grown up a lot in the last few months. He wasn't the same guy who'd poured corn syrup dyed with red food coloring all over the cafeteria floor to freak the new students out. People still talked about that prank. Especially since a notorious bully fainted at the sight of it.

Chloe snapped her seatbelt into place, sulking. "Where are we going?"

"To the Drakes'."

We both stared at him, then at each other.

"Are you serious?" I asked. "We're going to Quinn's?"

"I get to see the famous Drake compound?" Chloe looked impressed despite herself. "I think you're both messed up, but it's totally worth it if I get to see that house." She kicked the back of his seat. Hard. "But I'm still telling Bellwood."

"Fine," he replied, unconcerned. "But first you'll shut up and listen to what we have to say to you."

I half turned in my seat to face him. "What *do* we have to say to her?" I still didn't know why exactly we'd just kidnapped Chloe.

"Marcus analyzed the vitamin you gave Quinn," he shot me a dry glance. "The vitamin you should have given *me*, I might add."

"He was right there, it was easier."

"Yeah, about that."

Chloe leaned forward. "Hello? Kidnap victim here. Focus." She scowled at me. "And you totally stole from me."

"Yup." I wasn't the least bit sorry about it anymore either.

"It's not a vitamin, Chloe," Kieran told her seriously.

She rolled her eyes. "Whatever. My mom gave them to me, Einstein. I think she'd know."

"Chloe, your mom's a biochemist," I said quietly.

"And a doctor, so shut up."

"She helped create Hypnos."

"So?"

"So," Kieran interjected, "it's not a vitamin, not completely. It's an anabolic steroid."

"I *knew* it," I muttered.

Chloe gaped at both of us. "You don't know what you're talking about."

"Here's proof." Kieran tossed her a folder with printed biological breakdown of her pills. "I need you to read that. When we get to the Drakes', you can go online on a safe computer shielded from the League and do your own research."

"Like the League can crack my computer security."

"All the same."

She ignored him and started flipping violently through the pages. I could tell the exact moment she really began to read and process the information. She went pale. When she looked up again, fear and anger and denial battled over her features. "Well, so what?" she snapped, as if either Kieran or I had spoken. "So she gave me steroids. They've made me stronger and faster. How is that a bad thing?"

I plucked the paper out of her hands and skimmed it until I had answer for her. "Have you grown a mustache yet?"

She blinked at me horrified. "*What?*"

"It says here that's one of the side effects. So's going bald."

She patted her hair a little frantically. It was one of her vanities. "I'm fine."

"You'll get acne too," I continued ruthlessly. I wanted my friend back. "And aggression and mood swings." I angled my head so she'd see the bruise on my jaw. "I think we can safely say you have both of those."

She winced. "I . . ."

"High blood pressure, liver damage, heart attacks, sterility, stunting your growth . . . do you want me to read on?"

She shook her head mutely. "But they were helping me," she finally said in a small voice. "I feel stronger."

"Chloe, they're bad for you."

"But . . ."

"Mustache," I repeated.

She swallowed. "Nothing's worth that."

She sat back and stared blankly out of the window. I didn't know what else to say, so I put the folder away. The trees and fields were dark, broken occasionally by the glint of moonlight or a cluster of stars through the leaves. The mountains loomed in the distance. Kieran drove for over half an hour before he turned into what looked like a field. There were tire marks in the grass but nothing else to mark it as anything but another field. Guards were discreet shadows. I caught the faint glimmer of light on a walkie-talkie. Kieran drove for another ten minutes before the tracks turned into a real lane leading to an old farmhouse.

It was impressive in its size. The logs looked like entire trees; the porch was wide and wrapped all the way around one side. The house itself was comfortably worn, like an antique. There were cedar hedges and oak trees and lamplight at the windows. Chloe let out an excited breath, briefly distracted from her own predicament.

"Wow," she said.

I slid out of the van and just stared for a moment. This was where countless vampires had been made, where blood was sipped like wine, where humans walked a dangerous path, where hunters had no doubt died.

This was where Quinn had grown up.

I thought I saw a shadow move in one of the upstairs dormer windows but I couldn't be sure. Even though I knew I was technically safe here, that there were treaties and friendships protecting me, I was still glad to have pockets full of stakes and Hypnos powder secured under my sleeve.

The front door swung open. I recognized Solange as she came down the porch steps, pale as a birch sapling, graceful as a white bird. The last time I'd seen her she'd been dressed for the Drake coronation. Now she wore old jeans and sunglasses. She smiled softly at Kieran.

He smiled back, taking her hand. "Thanks for letting us do this here."

"Mom and Dad are at the caves, so we should have most of the night." She turned to us. "Hunter, hi. And you're Chloe?"

Chloe nodded meekly. I'd never seen her so demure.

"What's the matter with you?" I hissed at her as we followed Kieran and Solange inside.

"She's royalty!"

"And a vampire, remember?"

"Oh yeah." Chloe paused. "Nope, princess trumps vampire."

"Does not."

"*So* does."

This was the real Chloe. The glimpse was enough to make me feel hopeful and confident. Even the foyer had her ogling again. I'd never been inside a vampire's house before either. The marble floors and crystal chandeliers were impressive, but I preferred the fire snapping in the hearth in the living room off to the right, and the worn sofas.

Somewhere, Grandpa was having a seizure.

I wouldn't have expected it to be so comfortable and, well, normal. I knew better than to rely on stereotypes, but thought I'd see at least one red satin dressing gown and maybe a coffin or two.

All I saw were shaggy gray bears barreling at us from all directions.

"Jesus." I stumbled back, fumbling for a stake. Kieran stopped my hand.

"Dogs," he murmured.

My heart leaped uncomfortably. I let out a nervous giggle. "I really thought those were bears."

"Bouviers," Solange explained, snapping her fingers once.

"Friends," she said, and the enormous dogs sat obediently, tongues lolling. A wolfhound puppy with legs like stilts slid across the hardwood floor leading from the kitchen, nearly kneecapping me. I grinned and crouched down to pat his head.

Lucy laughed, following him at a more sedate pace, a bandage under her hair. There was a peach in her hand. "Hey, Hunter."

"Hey." It was still startling to see a human girl so very comfortable in a vampire's house. She dropped down into a chair, throwing her legs over the arm and swinging her feet. Nicholas Drake sat across from her, watching her bite into the peach. It seemed intimate somehow, private. I looked away, wondering why I felt like blushing.

"I need to call my mom," Chloe said.

"Kitchen's free," Solange offered.

"Thanks." She paused in the doorway, cell phone in her hand. "Hunter, come with me?"

I followed, joining her at a harvest table with ladderback chairs. The kitchen was spotless. I couldn't help but look for a jug of blood. Chloe's foot tapped nervously as she waited for her mom to pick up.

"Mom?" she said. "I know you're in the lab, this will only take a minute." She paused. "Those vitamins you gave me are making me feel funny." She met my gaze bitterly. "Yes, I'm sure. Yes, I'm taking the right dose. I don't want to." She listened for a long moment. She was going to tap her foot right off her leg at this rate. "But . . . I know . . . but . . . Mom? *Mom?* Hello? Damn it!"

She turned off her phone and put it back into her pocket. "She's hiding something," she said with grim certainty. Her chair scraped the floor when she stood up. "Kieran," she called out. He came to the door, Solange at his side.

"Is there a computer I can use?"

He looked at Solange and she nodded. "Connor's got a few in his room," she answered. "I'll show you."

She led us up a wide staircase. "What are you going to do?" I asked Chloe.

"I'm going to break into my mom's files and find out exactly what's going on."

"Good," I said earnestly. "About time."

Solange took us up to the third floor, which had a sitting room and rows and rows of doors. With seven brothers all living up here, it kind of looked like a floor on our dorm. Solange knocked on a door and pushed inside. Quinn looked up from his computer.

"Quinn, where have you—" I stopped, confused. "You're not Quinn." He had the same features, but his hair was short and he didn't have that lazy smirk.

"His room's next door." Connor smiled. "And he'd tell you he's prettier, but I'm smarter."

I shook my head. "Twins," I finally clued in. "Sorry, I'd forgotten."

Chloe let out a reverent sigh. "Nice system," she said. She took inventory and spat out a bunch of technological jargon that had no resemblance to English as far as I could tell. "Sweet." She finally came back to words I understood. She cracked her knuckles. "Which one can I use?"

As she made herself comfortable in front of a computer on a desk made of a wooden door on blocks, I looked around.

"Where's Quinn?" I asked when I couldn't pretend not to care for a second longer. I did *not* like the look Kieran and Connor exchanged. "What?"

They both winced but wouldn't answer me. Dread was a ball in my belly.

Solange was the one to answer. I tried not to react to the tips of her fangs poking out under her top lip. "Quinn's hiding."

I blinked. "He's *hiding*? From what?"

"From you."

My mouth dropped open. Then my eyes narrowed, remembering the way he'd begged me to run away last night, the way he'd licked a drop of blood off my hand, the way he'd ignored my text message.

"Well, that's just stupid."

CHAPTER 24

◆

QUINN

I knew Hunter was in the house even before she started pounding on my bedroom door. I could smell her, taste her.

"Quinn Drake, I know you're in there." She knocked again, harder this time.

"Hunter, go away," I said darkly.

"Like hell. I know what you're doing. So just stop it."

Silence.

I could feel her anger radiating through the door. She turned the knob but it only opened a couple of inches. The chain lock went taut at the top.

She craned her neck, glared at me through the small opening, and took a step back.

And then she kicked my door in.

Was it any wonder I was falling for her?

The chain ripped out of the wall, the snap of wood reverberating down the hall. She stepped through the doorway, glowering.

I shook my head, refusing to let her see how happy I was to see her. "I can't believe you just did that."

"*I* can't believe you're hiding from me."

"Hunter, you're not Wonder Woman, for Christ's sake. You're a good hunter, no doubt about it, but you're human. You're fragile."

"If you call me fragile again, I will personally break off your fangs and wear them as earrings."

I stalked toward her. "But you *are* fragile," I insisted, my hands closing around her shoulders before she could even see me move. I knew that to her I was a blur of pale skin and long dark hair and the glow of unnatural blue eyes. I pressed her against the wall, slamming the door with my boot at the same time. We were alone.

And I was just as pissed off as she was.

I had to make her understand. Even if she hated me for it. "You don't like to admit it, but I'm stronger than you are, and faster." I was so close that her legs, her hips, and her chest touched mine. Every time she took a ragged breath, it pushed her closer to me. "And I've tasted you now." I leaned in, lips moving over her throat, aching to taste her again. She might have been the canary to my smug cat. She'd hate that. "And I can never forget your blood on my tongue."

"I know what you're doing." Her voice was endearingly breathy. She swallowed.

"I'm just making my point." I said.

"You're being an ass." But she tilted her head so I could

continue nibbling. Centuries of her hunter ancestors rolled over in their graves.

"I could kill you, Hunter."

"Mmm-hmmm. I could kill you right back."

"This isn't a joke."

I seized her mouth, and for a long, hot moment there were no more words, no more warnings. Just tongues and tastes and lips seeking lips. I fisted my hand in her hair and hers hooked into my belt loops. And, as usual, it was over far too soon.

I pulled back abruptly, violent need and control twisting inside me. "I won't risk you."

Her eyes narrowed into slits. "You're trying to protect me," she seethed.

"And that's a bad thing?" I just didn't get her sometimes.

She drilled her finger into my chest. "When you make decisions for me, yeah, you're damn right it is."

"I'm just trying to do the right thing. I'm a vampire."

"Duh."

"And you're not."

"Again: duh."

"I could hurt you. I could lose control." I claimed her finger, my grip cool and utterly unbreakable. She'd have better luck snapping her own wrist in half than breaking my hold.

"If you were anyone else, I'd have kneecapped you by now." She poked me hard. "So give me break," she said. "You make out with girls all the time."

"They're not you," I replied quietly.

"Kieran's human," she pointed out. "And Solange is even

younger than you. She turned barely two weeks ago. Should I be worried about him?"

"I don't know."

"And Lucy?"

"I don't know."

She pulled back just enough to meet my troubled gaze. "Do you like me, Quinn?"

"It's not that simple."

"Yes it is. Answer the question." She looked horrified. "Shit. Unless this isn't about protecting me but about not wanting to see me again. Am I just another girl to you? Shit," she said again, going red. "I have to get out of here."

"Yes," I finally said, so softly it was a wonder she heard me at all. "Yes, Hunter, I like you." She released the breath she'd been holding. "I like you a lot."

I heard her heart lurch back into a proper rhythm.

And then she smacked me really hard in the shoulder.

"Ouch, way to ruin the moment," I muttered.

"You . . . ," she sputtered.

I tipped her chin up. "You didn't really doubt me, did you?"

"Hello? You locked yourself in your room to get away from me."

"Only to protect you," I defended myself. "I'm sorry."

"Don't you ever do that to me again."

"It won't be easy, you know. Despite how Solange and Kieran and Nicholas and Lucy make it look, this isn't simple. It might even be dangerous."

"You know I can look after myself."

"I know."

"And I'm way more terrified of my grandfather's reaction than your puny fangs."

"You're hard on the ego," I complained, but I was smiling again for the first time since I'd run out of her dorm room. "Your grandfather's an old man."

"Who could kick your ass."

"I've got moves, Buffy."

"I've seen your moves, Lestat," she teased, kissing me. I gathered her closer, hands roaming down her back and over her hips.

"You're not just a vampire, you know," she whispered. "You're the guy who let me cry all over you, when I never cry. Nothing makes sense right now—people at school are dying, my roommate's on some kind of hunter steroid—but you make sense. Somehow, you make sense."

Yup. I was totally, completely, and irrevocably into this girl.

A thump on the door had us both jumping.

"Hey, get off my sister," Kieran barked from the other side.

"Get lost, Black," I called out. "And she's not your sister."

"May as well be."

"Well, you stop kissing Solange and I'll stop kissing Hunter."

Silence. I smirked. Hunter pulled away, rolling her eyes.

"Hey, where are you going?" I murmured. "We're not done making up."

"We're in crisis mode out there," she answered, reluctantly taking another step back.

"It's always crisis mode in this house," I said with disgust.

"Still. We should go help."

I huffed a mock melodramatic sigh. "This is that Helios-Ra duty thing, isn't it?"

"Afraid so."

CHAPTER 25

◆

Hunter

Monday night

In the room next door, Chloe looked exhausted. She'd pulled her hair out of its ponytail and it was a mess of tangled curls. Solange and Kieran were sitting on the edge of Connor's bed and Connor was at his desk, tapping away at another computer. It was amazing how much he and Quinn looked alike. Quinn nudged me as if he knew what I was thinking.

"I'm cuter," he informed me loftily.

Connor shot me a knowing grin over his shoulder. Chloe scrubbed her face.

"Find anything?" I asked her.

She leaned back in her chair. "I don't really know. I mean, I got into my mom's files. Her passwords have always been pathetic."

"And?"

"And it's definitely a steroid, but that's it. There's nothing else sinister about it." She shook her head. "Except, why in the world would she slip me steroids? It's just weird."

"She didn't make lab notes or anything?"

"Nothing remotely helpful. Although she referred to a 'Trojan Horse' a couple of times. Nearly gave Connor and me a heart attack. I so don't need some hacker computer virus right now. But it's not that—we scanned all the machines to check. So it must be code for something else. I'll figure it out." She grimaced. "Maybe not tonight, but I'll definitely figure it out."

I glanced at my watch. "Yeah, we should head back. Just in case Kieran got busted. I really can't take any more demerits and detention this year. If York sneers at me one more time I might just lose it."

"What about the second pill we found," Quinn asked. "Did Marcus figure out what it is?"

"Should know by tomorrow night." Connor shrugged. "The Academy is basically a high school, you know. It could just be an upper or caffeine pill."

"Maybe," I said doubtfully. There were just too many coincidences and variables.

And secrets. Definitely too many secrets.

At the front door, Kieran kissed Solange good-bye. I cleared my throat at him obnoxiously until he glowered at me, but if I didn't set a precedent right now, he'd be interrupting all of my makeout sessions.

"I'll call you," he whispered to her before heading out to the van. He pulled my hair as he passed me. Chloe was already in the backseat, her knees pulled up to her chest. Quinn grabbed my arm as I was reaching for the front door handle. He twirled me backward into his arms and dipped me, like they do in those old-fashioned black-and-white movies. And then he kissed me cross-eyed.

"See you soon." Even his whisper felt like a kiss. I somehow managed to get into the van and buckle myself in. Quinn slapped the side of the van and Kieran pulled away, spitting gravel.

"Wow," Chloe murmured. "That was some kiss. I need a vampire boyfriend."

I grinned. "He has a lot of brothers."

"And every single one of them is yummy," Chloe agreed.

After that, we rode back mostly in silence, trying to process what we'd found out tonight. It wasn't dawn yet but the sky looked more gray than black, like ashes covering a red ember. The memory of Quinn's kiss kept interfering with my concentration.

Kieran groaned. "I don't trust that smile."

"Yup," Chloe reiterated as Kieran pulled up onto campus. "I definitely need a Drake brother of my very own."

Chloe might be making jokes but I knew she was freaked out. I'd have been freaking out too, if I'd just confirmed my own mother was drugging me. But it was late and we were tired and we both just wanted to fall into bed.

Hard to do that when the mattresses were half off their frames and most of our stuff was strewn about as if a mini hurricane had come in through the window.

We both stood and stared.

"Someone tossed our room!" Chloe shouted, incensed. She ran straight to her computers, running her hands over the wires and checking the plugs like a mother checking a small child for broken bones. "I'll kill them," she muttered. "I'll kill them."

The closet doors were open, spilling cargo pants and school sweatshirts and all my pretty dresses. A tube of toothpaste was on the floor by my foot. My books were everywhere, my organized stakes and daggers were scattered. My jewelry box was upside down and silver chains, turquoise pendants, and bracelets spilled out in a tangle.

"Whoever did this wasn't robbing us," I said flatly, untangling a necklace from the nearby lampshade. "They were looking for something."

Chloe finally looked up from her computers, reassured that no one had tampered with them. She scowled.

"Who the hell would do that? And what the hell were they looking for?" She nearly choked on her own words, staring horrified at the open bottles of aspirin and cold tablets spilling out like confetti. We looked at each other grimly. "Someone was looking for my vitamins," she stated dully, as if she couldn't quite believe it. She held up her Xena action figure, arm bent and marked with a footprint. "Someone who is going to die horribly when I find them."

I shoved my mattress back into position and then dropped on top of it. I was suddenly so tired I could barely stand up. "Who else knew you were taking vitamins?"

Chloe shrugged, wincing. "Anyone who heard us fighting or me bitching about it afterward. A few people asked me for some when they saw me finally do a good roundhouse kick at the gym. I guess they figured it was a magic pill. With the flu and *Hel-Blar* attacks and everything, everyone wants an edge."

"Steroids don't make you finally get a roundhouse," I told her. "Practice does that."

"Yeah, but the steroids made me stronger." She rubbed her palms on her legs, as if they were sweating. "And I'm really suddenly wanting another vitamin right now." She swallowed. "Does that make me an addict?" She stared at me frantically.

"No," I assured her sternly. Chloe's flare for dramatics could create a whole problem where there was none. Sometimes you had to cut her off at the pass. "It makes you a person who got used to taking vitamins, so try taking actual vitamins."

"Huh. That actually makes sense."

"And you might want to go talk to Theo. He'd know what to do."

"Okay." She took a deep breath, then another one. "Okay." She picked one of her bras off the floor. "I'm still killing whoever did this. And I'm doing it before the steroid strength wears off."

"Deal. I'll help you." My trunk poked out from under the bed, bursting with romance novels. I shoved it back under.

"Hunter?"

"Yeah?"

"Thanks for the whole steroid thing." She picked up the compact mirror left on her pillow and stared at her upper lip.

"You don't have a mustache," I assured her.

"I could kill my mom for that. She nearly gave me a beard and a bald spot."

I snorted a laugh, then tried to cover it up with a cough. She shot me a look but I could tell she was trying not to laugh too.

"It's not funny," she insisted.

"Of course not," I squeaked, choking on a giggle.

"I could have looked like the wolfman!" she added. "Or my grandma!"

We laughed until we were crying. Fatigue and relief and tension made us slightly hysterical. We finally wheezed ourselves out and calmed down.

"We should get some sleep," I croaked. "We have class in a few hours."

"God," Chloe groaned. "I have to face York. How fast am I going to get all weak and puny, do you think?"

"You were never puny." I yanked my blanket over me. I couldn't be bothered to change into my pajamas or to clean up the clothes piled messily around me. One of my boots was stuck under my pillow. I tossed it aside. "You're just better with tech than with your fists. It's no big deal."

I was almost asleep when there was a timid scratching at the door.

"Are you kidding?" Chloe mumbled. "Do we have mice? I can't deal with mice right now." The scratch turned into a hesitant knock. I groaned and stumbled out of bed. "What now?"

Lia stood on the other side in pajamas with pink lollipops all over them. Her eyes were red and watery.

"Lia, what's the matter?" I looked over her shoulder and down the hall, half expecting a *Hel-Blar* to jump out of the shadows. It was just that kind of night.

"It's my roommate," she sobbed. "She's really sick. I don't know what to do."

I blinked blearily. "Did you tell Courtney?"

Lia shook her head, biting her lip.

"Why not? That's her job. She'll get one of the nurses."

"No, *you* have to come. You can't tell anyone."

"What? Why?"

Chloe pushed in behind me. "Do you know what time it is?" she barked.

I grabbed Lia's arm because she looked like she was going to run away. "Lia, what's really going on?"

"Savannah's sick."

"And?"

She swallowed. I waited, refusing to let go. "Lia, if you want my help you have to be honest with me."

Her lower lip quivered and I felt like a monster, but I stood my ground. When Lia finally spoke, it all came out in a rush of words that took a moment to sift through. "I don't want to get in trouble and I promised her I wouldn't tell but her lips are going blue and she's breathing funny and I just don't know what to do."

"Okay, calm down," I said softly, as if she were a wild bird and I had a handful of bread crumbs. "What's the big secret?"

Lia reached into her pocket and took out three little white pills. "She's been taking these."

It was the same white pill Quinn and I had found in the common room.

I plucked one from her hand, growing cold all over. It was like an arctic wind was pushing through me, filling my lungs and freezing the blood in my veins.

"Chloe," I croaked. "Look."

Two letters were stamped in the center of the pill.

"TH."

Trojan Horse.

◆

Chloe and I bolted up the stairs, Lia hurrying after us. I called Theo from my cell and by the time we got up to Lia's room, three of Savannah's friends were hovering outside the door, worrying. Too many students had gotten sick already and too many of those had died for anyone to dismiss this as a simple flu, like the teachers were trying to tell us. The last thing we needed right now, though, was more attention and panic. Especially if Chloe and I had just discovered some sort of conspiracy, like I thought we had. We'd need witnesses eventually if we blew this thing wide open, but not right now.

"Is she going to die?" one of Niners asked bluntly.

"No," I answered and pushed inside the room, shutting the door firmly.

Savannah lay in her bed, moaning. Her skin was clammy and damp with perspiration. She was hot to the touch and her eyes, when she pried them open, were bloodshot. Chloe hissed out a breath. We exchanged a bleak glance.

"Savannah." I lowered my voice when she jerked at the sound. "It's okay, we're here to help. Savannah, this is very important. Can you tell me where you got those pills?"

"I don't want to get anyone in trouble," Savannah mumbled through dry, cracked lips.

"You won't," I assured her. "We just need to know where you got them."

"I bought them," she coughed. "I was only supposed to take one a day but I took three. They were supposed to make me stronger."

Chloe frowned. "Like steroids?"

Savannah nodded weakly. Chloe stared at me. "Hunter, these aren't the pills I was taking. Mine were yellow and huge."

"I know," I answered, frowning back. "People don't know there's two different pills, I guess. Who told you they'd make you stronger?" I asked Savannah.

She glanced away, coughed again. I handed her the glass of water on her nightstand. "You won't get in trouble," I told her.

"Some guy was selling them out of the eleventh-grade common room," she answered finally. She swallowed the water but her throat constricted violently, as if she was sipping from a glass of razor blades. She whimpered. "I don't feel good."

"There's a nurse on the way. He'll make you better."

"I'm scared." She clutched my hand. Her grip was pathetically weak and damp.

I didn't know what to say. Chloe didn't know either because she just sat there. "You'll be okay." I said it again for lack of something more convincing. "You'll be okay."

She closed her eyes, lips wobbling.

"I mean it, Savannah," I snapped, terrified she was about to slip into a coma. She had to stay awake. She half opened her eyes. I smiled encouragingly. "Just stay with me. Okay? Stay with me."

"I'll try."

Courtney and Lia rushed into the room. I'd never been so glad to see Courtney as I was right then. She had pillow creases on her cheek and she was blinking furiously as if she couldn't focus. When she finally did, she gasped. She looked scared.

"Not again."

I nodded gloomily. "Theo's on his way."

Lia shifted from one foot to the other. "She's going to be okay, isn't she?"

"Of course she is."

"She looks kind of gray."

Courtney took a deep breath and forced herself to stop staring at Savannah. She touched Lia's shoulder. "Lia, why don't you get her a cold wet cloth? And tell everyone else to go to their rooms and stay there."

"Okay."

We sat around Savannah's bed in a silent vigil, listening to the harsh rattle of her breath. I couldn't help but think of Spencer lying in quarantine. Chloe squeezed my hand, her eyes wet with tears.

"I know," she said quietly. "But Spencer's strong. And he didn't . . . you know."

She was right, Spencer was an accident of time and place. He wasn't the type to take pills. He was going to be fine.

The three of us leaped to our feet when Theo came through the door. He looked capable and confident and I could have kissed him. He lifted Savannah's wrist to feel her pulse.

"Is she lucid?" he asked.

"She was," I confirmed.

"How long has she been like this?"

"I don't know. Not too long, I don't think. Her roommate came to get me just before I called you."

"Okay." He lifted her eyelids, felt her forehead. "We're taking her to the infirmary."

Another nurse wheeled a stretcher into the room. One of the doctors and a security guard pushed in behind her. The doctor's mouth thinned when she saw Savannah.

"Let's move quickly," she ordered.

The room emptied in minutes and the guard stood in front of the door, arms folded. Lia blinked at him.

"But my stuff's in there," she said.

"The doctor said she wanted the room sealed off now, just to make sure it's not contagious," Courtney explained. "Come on, we'll find another bed for you."

Courtney led her away as Chloe and I hurried after the others. Students in pajamas gathered on each floor, craning their heads to see what was going on. Floor monitors tried to shoo them back. York barreled into the building and marched past us, blowing his whistle, practically right in my ear. "Everyone back to bed! NOW!"

The sound of scurrying feet echoed on every floor.

By the front door, I grabbed Theo's arm. "Wait," I said. "She took these." I handed him one of the white pills. He scowled at it. "What are they?"

"I don't know yet."

He shook his head, slipping them into his pocket. "This year just sucks."

(HAPTER 26

•

Hunter

Tuesday night

Most of Tuesday went by in a blur. I slept through all my early classes, but none of my teachers said anything. Everyone was subdued and solemn. Campus felt as if it were covered in ashes.

I loved this place and I loved the League. I'd been raised to think the League was better than Christmas and Halloween candy and birthday presents. And now I suddenly felt like a six-year-old finding out there was no such thing as Santa Claus. I didn't know what to think; I just knew it felt awful.

I went to the infirmary after dinner with Chloe and Jenna, even though Jason had already been and told us they weren't letting anyone in the door, especially with Savannah sick as well. Theo wasn't there so we were stopped at the threshold. The doctor shook her head sternly at us. We might have tried to argue with her, but we could hear Spencer's mom sobbing from behind the curtain so we slunk away. We kept to our schedule because there wasn't anything else to do.

Then I went to the gym that Dailey had reserved for her first Guild meeting. I wasn't really sure what to expect, but I was looking forward to being distracted, to have something else to fill up my brain. There wasn't the usual chatter as we waited for her to arrive. It was mostly twelfth-grade students with a sprinkling of others from the eleventh and tenth grades. There were no Niners at all. We all smiled questioningly at each other, but no one had any answers.

"Good, you're all here." Ms. Dailey strode in with a welcoming nod. "We have a lot of work to do, so let's get started."

One of the students raised his hand. "Um, Ms. Dailey?"

"Yes, Justin?"

"What exactly are we starting?"

She chuckled. "I've handpicked you all as the best this school has to offer. You're all honor students or well on your way to becoming such. And now, you'll be even better." She smiled at us. "We'll cover fighting, of course, and weaponry and tactics, but also stealth and technology and other, newer ways to win the fight. It's no secret that recently *Hel-Blar* have been crawling all over campus, Violet Hill, and even surrounding villages. If we're to contain this new threat, the League will need more help. And my Guild will be first on call, before any other student group. I'm excited to get started."

She gave us a list of books we needed to take out from the

library and the password for the private Web site she was putting together for us. I left feeling better than I had all day. I had a purpose again, and options. And confidence in the Helios-Ra, despite recent evidence to the contrary. I waited until everyone else had cleared out.

"Yes, Hunter, what is it?" Ms. Dailey asked when she noticed I was still hovering nearby.

"Could I talk to you for a minute?" I asked awkwardly. "It's . . . private."

"Certainly." She frowned worriedly. "What's wrong?"

"It's about all the sick students."

"Oh, Hunter, that's not for you to worry about. You're a strong, healthy girl."

"It's not that. It's . . ." I hoped I was doing the right thing. I was pretty sure Ms. Dailey would hear me out and not drag me to the headmistress or the school shrink. "There's some kind of pill going around," I told her. "I think it's making people sick."

She looked startled. "Drugs? Already?"

I blinked. "What do you mean already?"

"It's only the first week of school. Usually the pills don't start circulating until mid-terms." She shook her head.

I smiled uneasily. "I don't think this is that kind of pill."

"Oh?"

"I don't have the chemical breakdown yet, but this one's dangerous. Really dangerous. And . . . vampires don't like it."

"Vampires?" she sighed. "Hunter, what have gotten yourself into?"

"Nothing good," I admitted. "Will you help me?"

"After the speech I just gave everyone? Of course I will."

Relief flooded through me and I had to swallow a nervous giggle. "Thank you, Ms. Dailey! The pills are little and white and have 'TH' stamped on them. Savannah was taking them just before she got sick and I think Will was too."

White lines bracketed her mouth. "We'll get to the bottom of this, Hunter." She flicked the gym lights off. "Now let's not say another word about it until I can do some research of my own. The walls have ears."

I nearly skipped down the stairs. She winked at me before turning down the lane toward the teachers' residence, heels clacking. Teachers like Ms. Dailey were rare. I hadn't forgotten how she'd stood up for me when York busted me at the first drill. If it came to it, at least we now had someone on the faculty we could trust.

Bolstered, I was grinning when Quinn popped out of the edge of the woods and scared the breath right out me. I leaped into the air, shrieking.

So much for Dailey's training.

Quinn laughed so hard he bent right over. I laughed too and pulled his ponytail. "Shut up."

"Hunter, you're adorable."

"Excuse me, I am fierce and kick-ass."

"That too." He took my hand, his thumb rubbing over my palm. "And you're cute in your workout shorts."

I was suddenly aware of all my bare leg. I absolutely refused to blush. His grin widened.

"What are you doing here?" I asked him.

His hand moved comfortingly over my wrist and up my arm. "I'm here to take you on a date."

I blinked. "A date?" I repeated as if it was a foreign word I'd never heard before.

"You know, where we go out, hold hands, cast longing glances at each other? It's tradition. You might have heard of it."

"But I have class."

"Class?" Now he was looking at me as if I was speaking a different language. "But it's ten o'clock at night."

"We have classes until midnight." I smiled pointedly. "The thing about vampires is that they kind of like the night. It's tradition. You might have heard of it?"

"Oh, smart mouth." He grinned back. "Sexy."

He prowled forward, maneuvering me against the trunk of a tall pine tree. The branches started dozens of feet above us, spreading out branches like a green parasol. The ground was soft, carpeted in rust-colored needles.

"Can you ditch?" Quinn asked temptingly. "I've been up to my eyeballs in prep for the Blood Moon. All very political and hush-hush. You'd love it."

I shook my head. "I'm sorry, I can't."

"Can you be late?" he pressed.

"Well, I am interested in compromise between our people."

"My people are grateful." He captured my mouth with his. The kiss started slowly, turning deep and hot within moments. I was in a cocoon of feeling, of warm tingles, pale skin, and tree bark. Electricity ran between us. I half believed that if I opened my eyes I'd see sparks and forks of lightning licking at us.

Further in the woods, ferns shifted. There were stars, crickets singing, an early autumn breeze, and a handsome young vampire kissing me.

It would have been perfect if my grandfather hadn't interrupted us.

"Hunter Agnes Wild!"

Quinn, oblivious to the danger, pulled back, laughing. "Your middle name's Agnes?"

"After her great-grandmother," Grandpa roared. I winced, stepping around Quinn to shield him.

"Hi, Grandpa. What are you doing here?"

"I'm a guest lecturer," he barked. "And what exactly are you doing, missy?" He glared at Quinn. I counted under my breath, one, two— Grandpa choked on another roar. "Vampire!"

Three. He must be really flustered at finding me making out to have needed three full seconds to register the unnatural stillness and paleness of Quinn. Not to mention his fangs, delicately dimpling his lips, brought out by our kissing. I shifted another step in front of him.

"Grandpa—"

"Hunter, stake him and let's get to class," he said impatiently.

I swallowed. "I'm not staking him."

He raised an eyebrow disapprovingly. "Not prepared? Here, take one of mine." He tossed me one of his stakes. I caught it out of instinct.

"Grandpa."

"What are you waiting for?" He glared at Quinn. "And what's wrong with this one that he's just standing there?"

"Grandpa." I sighed. "This is Quinn Drake. Quinn, my grand-father, Caleb Wild."

"Vampire," Grandpa spat again.

Quinn smirked. "Old man."

I closed my eyes. This was going well. My boyfriend was an idiot and my grandfather was going to rip him into bloody pieces. Grandpa was built like a bull. And the only reason he hadn't staked Quinn yet was because I was standing directly in the way. I was also pressing my shoulder back into Quinn, forcing him to stay where he was. Who knew dating was so dangerous?

"Hunter Wild, you get away from him right now."

"No." He goggled, turning so red so fast I thought he might be having a heart attack. "No, sir," I added to appease him.

"I would never hurt her," Quinn said, his smirk fading. "You have my word on that."

"The word of a vampire? Pah."

"The word of a Drake."

Grandpa spit. Quinn growled. I slapped a hand on his chest.

"You can't bite my grandpa." I tossed a look over my shoulder. "And you can't stake my boyfriend."

Grandpa went gray. "Boyfriend?"

I cringed. "Quinn, you should go."

"I'm not leaving you alone," he protested.

"Please." I pushed at his chest. "Please just go. I'll call you when I can."

He searched my face for a long moment before touching my hair briefly. "Fine. I won't be far."

"I know," I said, relieved he wasn't going to fight me on this. I had my hands full as it was. When I turned back to Grandpa, Quinn was already gone, leaving behind shifting leaves and the fleeting touch of his lips on mine.

"Please just listen," I started as my grandfather struggled not to explode.

"I don't want to hear it," he ground out. "You'll stop all contact with that boy, with all of the enemy, and we'll pretend this never happened. Let's go."

"Grandpa, no."

"You're trying my patience, girl."

"I'm sorry," I said miserably. "But I have to do what I think is right. Quinn's not the bad guy here. He might be cocky, but he's also honorable and brave and loyal. He saved my life."

"He's one of *them*." He looked older suddenly, as if all his years pressed down on him at once. "You're my little hunter. Even when you were small you could hit a target with your stakes at thirty paces. You're gifted."

"I'm still a hunter," I insisted. "Nothing's changed, not really."

"Everything's changed!" he shouted. "You're part of the Helios-Ra! The Wilds have been members for as long as I can remember. We kill vampires. It's what we do."

"I'm still Helios-Ra."

"But you're not a Wild," he snapped. "Not if you behave like this."

It felt as if he'd slapped me. "What? Grandpa, don't. I know you're upset but don't."

He pointed a finger at me. "You owe the League your loyalty."

"It has my loyalty, but not my blind obedience. And anyway,

the League has a treaty with the Drakes, remember? Plus, someone's drugging students, Grandpa, someone in our precious League."

"Don't be ridiculous."

"I have proof. Students are getting sick all over. Chloe's own mother was giving her steroids. Have you heard about some operation called the Trojan Horse?"

I was so relieved at his honest bewilderment that I could have wept.

"What are you going on about?" he demanded. "Hunter, leave League business alone. Leave it to the adults."

"I can't."

"And stop seeing that . . . thing."

"I can't do that either."

"Your mother would be ashamed."

"I'm ashamed too."

"As you should be."

"Of your bigotry, Grandpa," I finished quietly. "You know I love you, but I'm not you. You can't force me to be. I agree with the treaties. I *like* what Hart's doing with the League."

"You're young."

"So? That doesn't make me stupid. You didn't raise me to be stupid. You raised me to be strong and independent and clever. Can't you trust that?"

"I don't even know you anymore, girl. How can I trust someone who willingly fraternizes with monsters?"

I took his big callous hand in mine. "It's not that simple. But it's still me. I'm still *me*."

"I love you, girl," he said gruffly. "You know I do. Now stop this nonsense. We have class."

He'd raised me. He was the only family I had left. And he looked at me as if he couldn't stand the sight of me. The only reason I didn't let the tears fall was because it would have convinced him right then and there that I was no longer his granddaughter. I tilted my chin, straightened my shoulders.

And I let him lead me toward the gym where the Niners waited for a demonstration from one of the League's most celebrated hunters.

Kieran was waiting for us outside the main gym. His hair was caught back in a ponytail, his cargos were perfectly regulation. He still wore his cast. Grandpa clapped him on his good shoulder.

"Glad you're here, Black. Maybe you can talk some sense into my granddaughter."

I waited stone-faced. Kieran looked wary.

"What do you mean, Caleb?"

"She's dating a vampire!" he exploded.

Kieran winced. "Oh."

Grandpa's eyes narrowed to slits. "You knew about this?"

"Uh . . . yes, sir."

I sighed. "Grandpa, leave him alone."

"He's supposed to look out for you."

"I do!" Kieran sounded offended. "You should be proud of her. Hart requested her presence personally at the Drake coronation."

I closed my eyes briefly. We were doomed.

"You went to a vampire ceremony?" Grandpa asked evenly.

"He didn't know?" Kieran asked.

"No, he didn't."

"Sorry."

Grandpa vibrated with rage. "I will not tolerate this kind of behavior in my family!"

"It's different now," Kieran tried to assuage him. "I'm dating Solange Drake. They're a good family."

Grandpa went red, then purple. Kieran took a step back. I whacked Grandpa between the shoulder blades.

"Grandpa, breathe!"

His breath was strangled but at least he didn't keel over. Before he could shout the rafters down, the door swung open and York eyed us all with the barest politeness. Grandpa glared at him.

"What?" he barked.

"We're waiting for your demonstration," York barked back.

Grandpa jerked his thumb at Kieran, ordering him inside. I winced sympathetically. Helping Grandpa with fight scenarios when he was in a temper never ended well. I followed, because skipping it would have started another lecture on family responsibility. The Niners looked eager and nervous, chattering among themselves. Lia waved at me.

Grandpa threw a ninja egg at a short boy with glasses before York even blew his whistle.

A pepper cloud had everyone in the immediate vicinity coughing and sneezing.

"First lesson," Grandpa growled. "Be aware of your surroundings."

The boy's face was bright red as he wiped his streaming eyes with the sleeve of his shirt. Everyone else stood at immediate attention, silently cowed. York looked reluctantly impressed.

"This is Caleb Wild," he introduced belatedly. "Mr. Wild has been a hunter for decades. This is his assistant Kieran Black, nephew of Hart Black." Excited glances were exchanged when Kieran's last name was recognized, but the only sound was the pepper victim choking on a cough. Grandpa cut an impressive figure, pacing in front of the cadets, his white hair cut short, his muscled arms scarred. His boots clomped, ringing like an iron bell. Students trembled.

"You've all been given a sacred duty to protect the world against vampires. And every single one of you is capable of winning that fight. You!" The girl next to Lia staggered back a step.

"Yes, sir?"

"What's your skill?"

"I . . . can throw."

"Good. You!"

"Um . . ."

"Figure it out. You!"

"I'm fast."

The students were still terrified, but they started to stand with more pride in themselves as hunters. Grandpa was good at that.

"It doesn't matter how small you are," he continued. "Or whether you're a boy or a girl, or what your last name is. What matters is the League and the amount of fight in you. Even if you're wounded, you can still make a difference. To demonstrate this, Kieran and I are going to spar."

"And I'm going to die," Kieran muttered so only I could hear.

Students broke from their stiff rows and circled the mat in the center of the room. The mirrors surrounding the walls showed their eager faces; the windows showed nothing but shadows.

"The first point I'll make is that if you're wounded, you stay out of the fight. You run the hell away if you can, so you don't endanger the mission or your team. If you can't run away, you damn well win. Understand me?"

"Yes, sir!" The chorus reverberated with enthusiasm.

"And you follow orders, hear me?"

I knew that was for me.

"Yes, sir!"

I didn't say anything. I had no intention of obeying.

"How would you fight me?" he demanded of Kieran.

Kieran already had a stake in his hand.

"Good. But you missed and I have you by the throat. Now what?"

Kieran gurgled since now Grandpa really did have him by the throat. "Another stake."

"And?"

Kieran swept out with his foot, hitting Grandpa's ankles. Grandpa staggered, stumbled. I hissed out a breath when he nearly fell over. Kieran didn't react and I didn't move. If we betrayed a single ounce of concern, Grandpa's pride would be wounded. In fact, he was grinning for the first time that night.

"That's my boy."

Kieran turned his back, glancing at the students. "And then I run," he said, to illustrate the earlier point.

Grandpa leaped to his feet. The floor shook. He grabbed Kieran's ponytail, jerking him to a stop. In his other hand, he held one of the daggers from his belt. I didn't have time to say a word, only to squeak.

The blade cut through Kieran's ponytail.

His hair drifted to the floor and he whirled, bug-eyed with shock. Everyone else gasped. Grandpa looked smug.

"If you have a weakness like a broken arm, you rid yourself of all other weaknesses," he said, sliding his knife back into his scabbard. "If you don't learn anything else, learn this. Weakness is not allowed."

His faded eyes pinned me where I stood.

◆

Grandpa left without saying another word to me. Kieran paused only long enough to squeeze my arm.

"I'll talk to him," he promised severely, holding his ponytail in his fist.

I nodded mutely and stalked back to the dorm, boiling with anger and hurt and guilt. Chloe was sitting cross-legged in the middle of her bed. She looked up when I stormed in.

"Let's figure out this TH thing," I said before she could ask me about my mood. I just didn't want to talk about it. I wouldn't know where to start. "So we know someone's selling the stuff at school and we know it's a recognized Helios-Ra drug. Well, sort of recognized," I amended. "It must be secret or it wouldn't have been hidden so deeply in the files, right?"

"Definitely. We could get your number-one fan Lia to try to score some. See if we flush out the dealer?"

I wrinkled my nose. "I guess. But I'd rather not endanger her like that. And anyway, I'm thinking since the dealer's a student he or she is just a small fish in a big pond."

"Probably."

"Okay, so then let's make a list of the students who have gotten sick. There was that first guy—I don't know his name."

"And then Will. Or was that just a *Hel-Blar* thing?"

"He mentioned he was taking vitamins, so let's add him to the list. Speaking of vitamins, have you talked to your mom yet?"

She grimaced. "No. She's been at the lab and I know she won't talk to me until she's at home. Jeanine after Will," she added. I added her to the list.

"Spencer," I said quietly. "Though I don't actually think he's part of it."

"Me neither. Jonas and James. Those ninth-grade twins, the really short ones?"

"Right. And then Savannah."

"She was short too."

"What, so the drug is for short people?"

She rolled her eyes. "I guess not."

I paused, frowning. "Actually . . ."

She blinked. "What do you mean, actually? You think the school's taking out short people? That's just weird."

"No, listen. What do they all have in common?"

"They're mostly Niners? And short."

"Will was in eleventh grade and tall," I argued. "But gentle." I raised my eyebrows. "All these students would have been considered weaker. Short, skinny, not into fighting." I leaned forward while details fell into place. "And who picks on those kinds of people on a regular basis?"

"Bullies?" Chloe's mouth dropped open. "York." She slapped her bedspread. "That must be why my mom's been feeding me steroids all summer. I would have been one of the weak ones without it! I found the info buried in her files just before you got here. She knew about it. She reads all the lab notes, but she didn't want to pull a society-wide alarm before proper tests were conducted. You know how she is about research. Damn it, Mom."

"So York's been making sure the weaker students get the TH?"

"Looks like."

I met her shocked eyes grimly. "So how do we take him down?"

CHAPTER 27

•

QUINN

Later Tuesday night

I got a text just before dawn. Marcus finally had results from the blood samples Hunter had given me.

He also had Solange sitting on a bench, looking shell-shocked.

Her eyes were red but it was the kind of red you get from too much crying. When I burst through the door of the barn Uncle Geoffrey used for his scientific experiments, she looked away, lower lip wobbling.

Solange's lower lip never wobbled.

Marcus looked like he was about to start running. Crying girls made him nervous, even when it was his little sister. Or maybe especially when it was his little sister.

"Hey, Sol," I said quietly, crouching down in front of her. There were acres of Bunsen burners and glass beakers on the counter behind her. Light sparkled on scrupulously clean equipment that looked like it belonged in a science-fiction movie. If Uncle Geoffrey ever wanted a gig as a mad scientist, he was well on his way.

"Quinn, go away," she said miserably, picking at the dried clay on her pants. She'd probably made a hundred pots on her pottery wheel in the short couple of weeks since she'd turned.

"Not a chance," I said gently. "What's going on?"

"Nothing. I just came to talk to Uncle Geoffrey."

"Okay, so what's the problem?"

She shrugged, keeping her head down and refusing to look at me. I glanced at Marcus. He shrugged too, then patted her shoulder.

"Solange, it's nothing to be embarrassed about," he said. I got the impression he'd said that a few hundred times in the last hour. "It's biological. Like acne."

She made a weird sound in the back of her throat. I closed my eyes briefly. "Nice," I said. "Tell a sixteen-year-old girl everything's fine because it's like pimples. And by the way? What the hell's going on?" I stared at her. "Where's Uncle Geoffrey?"

"He's gone to talk to Mom and Dad."

"Why? Are you sick?" Dread was heavy and metallic in my stomach, like iron.

"Yes!" she exclaimed at the same time Marcus muttered, "No."

Solange pursed her lips. "It's . . ." She finally huffed a sigh and then squared her shoulders. She tilted her chin up. "It's this." She lifted her lips off her teeth. Her fangs were out.

All six of them.

I blinked and counted again. Her regular canine teeth fangs were out, with two more on either side. The second pair were like the original and the third were very small, barely noticeable. Her gums were inflamed and raw.

Drakes didn't grow more than one set of fangs. It was a mark of our ancient blood, of our more civilized form of vampirism. There was some snobbery in the courts—the more fangs you had, the more feral you were. Isabeau had two sets and she flashed them proudly, but she was unique, even among vampires. The *Hel-Blar* had nothing *but* fangs. No wonder Solange was freaked out.

She thought she was turning into a monster.

She swallowed hard, trying not to cry. Marcus patted her shoulder harder.

"Don't cry." He was begging.

"What did Uncle Geoffrey say?" I asked softly.

"That I was special," she snorted, a flash of her regular self. "Special," she repeated. "God."

"Ouch." I winced sympathetically.

She hugged herself, as if she were cold. "Quinn, what if this means I'm not finished with the bloodchange? What . . . what if I turn into a *Hel-Blar* or something?"

I stood up, glowering. "You are *not* turning into a *Hel-Blar*."

"You don't know that."

"I do too. For one thing, you're not blue. And you don't smell like moldy dirt."

"I'm serious."

"So am I."

"Uncle Geoffrey said you'd be fine," Marcus reminded her.

"He said he *thought* I'd be fine. He also said he's never heard of this happening in our family. In any of the old families."

"It's just because you're a girl. You know, the first in hundreds of years and all that. Your change is a little different. That's all."

She poked at her new fangs. "The royal courts are going to have a field day with this, especially at the Blood Moon. The feral princess." She groaned. "Someone's going to write a song."

"Probably. But think of how much harder you can bite them when they do."

Her laugh was watery, but it was a laugh. "True." She stood up. "I'm tired. I'm going home."

"Wait for me," Marcus and I both said together.

Marcus pulled folded computer printouts from his pocket. "Your sample analysis."

I grabbed it, skimming the charts and graphs. I'd skipped the majority of Uncle Geoffrey's science lectures. That was the summer most of the girls my age in town miraculously grew boobs. I had fond memories of that summer. None of them involved anything that might help me decipher the blood analysis. I looked up, disgusted. "What the hell does this say? I don't speak geek."

Marcus snorted. "Careful, little brother, or I won't translate."

"Just tell me what it says."

"That your girlfriend was right." He paused, clearly waiting for me to react to the term "girlfriend." I didn't. I'd take Hunter any way I could get her. If I had to start using words like "girlfriend" and turning down other dates, I'd do it. "It's not vitamins in the blood," Marcus continued. "Those pills are a steroid."

"Yeah, we knew that. Her friend's already off those."

"They're not the real problem," Marcus said.

"This just gets better and better. Hit me."

"The second sample, from that kid who died?"

"Yeah?"

He looked grim. "He was poisoned."

I went cold. Hunter said people at her school were falling sick all over the place.

"And the poison wasn't just meant for him." Marcus's fangs flashed. "It was meant for us."

CHAPTER 28

◆

Hunter

Wednesday night

"Got something!" When Chloe's computer beeped the next night, she dove across the room, elbowing Jason in the gut.

He rubbed his sternum. "The hell, Chloe?"

"I hooked it up to beep when it cracked the TH file password," she said excitedly.

"I thought you didn't want to do that on campus, where they might tamper with the connection?" Jenna asked as we crowded around the back of her chair.

Chloe waved that off. "I put in a few more security shields and a red herring or two. We should be fine. Besides, we're running out of time and I've mostly been concentrating on my mom's files."

"So what've you got?" I pressed, bewildered by the gibberish on the screen. "What did you find?"

"Another file hidden in my mom's notes—labeled TH." Chloe bounced in her chair. I knew that bounce. She was onto something. "I want it." She chewed on her lower lip as the screen flashed. "Different password." She hit a few more keys. "This would be easier if I had my mom's actual computer. I could dust her keyboard." She tapped her foot impatiently. "Come on. Come on, I said!" It took a few more minutes but she finally grinned. "Gotcha, you sneaky bastard."

We all leaned in to read.

"That's some kind of chemical breakdown, isn't it?" Jason frowned. "For medications, or something."

I skimmed the page, nodding. "Looks like. Here's a list of side effects."

"The steroid?" Chloe asked in a small voice.

I shook my head. "No. Just the TH. And . . . holy shit. Holy shit, we were right. It *is* meant for poor fighters. It says right here that it should only be given to weak hunters who aren't expected to survive vampire attacks." I felt sick to my stomach. "It goes through their bloodstream and makes it poisonous to *Hel-Blar*, to any vampires." I remembered the blond *Hel-Blar* who'd disintegrated right in front of me after biting Will. "The League is sabotaging its own hunters to poison *Hel-Blar*." My head was spinning.

No one said anything for a long moment.

"That's just . . ." Jenna shook her head, unable to find a word heinous enough to describe what we'd just discovered.

"There has to be some mistake," Jason said doubtfully.

I marched over to my supplies and started shoving stakes in my pockets and checking microphones and night goggles. They turned slowly, staring at me.

"Hunter?" Chloe asked, as if she was afraid I was about to lose it. "What are you doing?"

"We're taking York down," I said forcefully. "Right now."

"Um, we're going to beat up a teacher? That seems like a really bad idea."

"We're not going to beat him up. Give me a break. We're just going to nail him for passing out that disgusting pill, and then we're going to dismantle the entire League if it comes to it."

Because sometimes you had to betray the League in order to safeguard it. Sometimes you had to break the rules. Sometimes duty was hard and uncomfortable and burned inside your chest. Grandpa taught me that last part well enough.

"How exactly are we going to do that?" Jenna asked. She held up her hands, palms out. "I'm all for a little payback, but I'm hunter enough to know better than to fight a battle I can't win."

"I have every intention of winning."

"I get that, I really do."

I tied my hair back in a braid, tucking it under my collar. "We use the same plan we had before," I explained. "For now. Jason is going to nose around and see if he can't get someone to sell him drugs."

Jason winced. "I feel like I'm in one of those after-school specials. If I get branded a narc, I'm blaming you."

I ignored him. "I'm going to e-mail this file to Kieran and have him give it to Hart. And then Jenna and I are going to switch off shifts staking out York when he's not in class."

"Am I going to need a fake nose and a trench coat?"

"And Chloe's going to ask York for after-school training help and act all clumsy and weak."

She sighed. "I guess I should be used to that."

"Are we ready?" I asked, sounding like a drill sergeant. "We need evidence and we need it soon."

"Sir! Yes, sir!" Chloe shouted with a mock salute.

I made a face at her. "Let's just go. Last class ends in an hour."

◆

I took the first shift, creeping around the pond to perch on a boulder at the edge of the woods, where I had a good view of the teachers' residence. If York left the building for any reason, I'd be able to see him and follow him. I felt a little like a detective in the old movies Grandpa loved so much.

Thinking about Grandpa just made me feel worse.

Helios-Ra and our duty to our hunter ancestors was the glue that had held us together after my parents were killed. I barely remembered them, but I remembered Grandpa dressing up like Van Helsing one Halloween and scaring all the little kids dressed as vampires. He'd taught me how to clean a wound properly, how to look for patterns in the movements of leaves and litter that betrayed a nearby vampire moving too quickly for human eyesight. He gave me my first stake. There'd been tears in his eyes last year when he got my report card. He'd always been proud of me.

Not anymore.

And I'd always been proud of the Helios-Ra.

Not anymore.

The difference was, I intended to do something about it. I wanted to be proud of the League again. And proud of myself. I wanted to make it right.

Making it right was surprisingly boring.

I sat on that rock for two hours, until my legs cramped and I'd nearly staked a chipmunk and a raccoon and traumatized a bunny.

All the rooms in the teachers' hall stayed dark. Even the motion lights stayed dark outside in the garden, where the animals liked to overturn the compost bin. The windows reflected the trees, the moon, the sky. Chloe was long since in bed, and Jenna wouldn't relieve me for another two hours.

I was staring so hard at the residence that when Ms. Dailey spoke softly behind me, I fell right off the rock.

I leaped back to my feet, going red. "Ms. Dailey!"

"At ease." She smiled gently. "Hunter, what are you doing out here?"

"I . . . uh . . . I couldn't sleep." I wondered why she was out here so late.

"Are you worrying about our little problem?"

I nodded. "We found out it's even worse than we thought," I explained in a rush. "It's some kind of weapon against vampires that uses students as carriers. It's sick."

She tilted her head. "Ingenious, actually."

I blinked at her. "Sorry?"

"I had such high hopes for you, dear girl. You've always been particularly talented. A little too clever, clearly, and now, sadly, misguided as well."

"Misguided?" I echoed. "What are you talking about?"

"You didn't think that scene with your grandfather wouldn't be all over school, did you? As well as your unfortunate and disgusting affiliation with that vampire."

I took a step back. Her expression was still pleasant but she didn't sound like the Ms. Dailey I knew at all. The instinct to run vibrated through me.

Before I could take a single step, she pulled a syringe from behind her back.

She stabbed me right in the arm with it.

I swore and jerked back but the needle was stuck in my muscle, pumping its clear liquid into my veins. I scratched at her face, managing to get her blood under my nails before the dizziness assaulted me. I stumbled.

"What did you do to me?" I panicked. My tongue felt swollen; my feet felt as if they were on backward. I stumbled again and fell to my knees. She watched me dispassionately.

"I'm rather grateful you chose to hide yourself away here, where no one will hear you. Very considerate of you."

My fingers shook as I yanked the needle out of my arm. It tumbled into the grass. "What is this stuff?"

"I think you know, a smart girl like you. It's a rather potent overdose of TH. I'm afraid you left me no other choice."

"What? No!" I clawed at my skin. My veins felt as if they were getting warmer, as if all of me was burning up. My breaths became shallow and short. "It was York. *York.*"

She laughed lightly. "He's far too pedantic for this sort of genius."

"But he picks on all the weak students." I was beginning to slur. I felt like I was hit by the worst case of the worst flu ever.

"Caught that, did you? Yes, his temper made my work much easier. I knew exactly who the worst students were, as they made him the angriest. He was so scared for them, you see. He wanted them to get stronger and be able to protect themselves." She circled me, waving her hand to dismiss him. "This is much better. If they are going to die by a vampire's hand, they may as well become weapons in themselves. A sacrifice for the League. And so eager to comply when they think it's a secret pill to make them stronger. It takes a while for them to weaken, and by then—think of the vampires they might infect. Especially if they're like you, Hunter."

"I don't see . . . you . . . sacrificing yourself," I spat. I tried to turn over but I was too heavy. The effort had me gasping.

"There's no use struggling. I gave you quite a high dose. You might survive it. I hope you do, at least for a little while. Then you can take out that Drake brat as well."

She wanted Quinn to drink from me and die.

"Go to hell," I croaked.

Dailey pursed her lips. "To think I picked you for the next Guild leader. I had such hopes after the *Hel-Blar* attack, and after you staked Will."

"You're crazy." I had to call Theo. I fumbled for my cell phone but my hands weren't working properly. I couldn't scream either. I couldn't get enough air into my lungs.

"I'm just doing what must be done. With all these treaties and the *Hel-Blar* infestation, we're losing our focus." She was lecturing me as if we were in class. "I had to test you all, to see who was worthy to be a member of my Guild. I set blood traps for the *Hel-Blar* and they came like rats to cheese."

"You got the *Hel-Blar* to attack the school?" She'd had me totally fooled. York hadn't been the culprit. He was actually the good guy—even though he was a jerk. Dailey was the psycho. I'd had to stake Will because of her. Spencer was sick because of her, at least indirectly. I was drugged and poisoned and crumpled on the ground because of her.

I really, really hated her.

I would have spat at her if I hadn't been so thirsty and dehydrated, burning up with fever.

And I was apparently hallucinating too.

"Get the hell away from her," Quinn snarled, leaping to stand in front of me in a blur of pale skin, long dark hair, and sharp fangs. Dailey took a step back, startled.

"You're too late," she said. "I've already dosed her. It's in her blood."

"What's in her blood?"

I squirmed, as if fire ants crawled under my skin. "Quinn," I panted. "Call Theo and get out of here. She's nuts."

Instead, he punched her. Her nose cracked and she howled. Quinn patted through my pockets.

"What are you doing?"

"I know you must have rope somewhere . . . got it." He turned away for a brief instant, leaving trails of light and color like a smeared oil painting. He tied Dailey up and was kneeling at my side before I took another labored breath. His fangs extended farther, gleaming.

"You can't bite a teacher," I whispered through dry lips.

"I'm not going to," he assured me. "I'm biting you."

CHAPTER 29

•

Hunter

He didn't understand.

If he drank my blood, it would kill him.

I struggled fruitlessly as his mouth descended on my arm, closing around the puncture hole the needle had made.

"No," I moaned. "No."

His fangs bit deep and I cried out. The blood burning my veins rushed toward the sucking of his mouth. I tried to pull away but he anchored me down, holding me still. The grass was cool and prickly under me.

"Don't," I begged, tears stinging my eyes. "It'll kill you."

He lifted his head, eyes blazing.

"It's killing *you*," he said harshly, spitting out a mouthful of my blood. A welt formed at the side of his lip. It looked painful. He went back to the wound, drawing my poisoned blood out of my veins and into his mouth. He spat more into the grass. He kept sucking the poison out and spitting as fast as he could, the way you would a snakebite. The ceiling of stars and cedar branches overhead whirled.

I was fading.

If I closed my eyes the pain would stop, Quinn would stop. He'd be safe.

My eyelids were heavy and I let them close.

EPILOGUE

◆

Hunter

Friday night

When I woke up I was in the infirmary.

The lights were too bright, washing everything out as I blinked furiously, eyes stinging. I was exhausted. I tried to move, moaning when it proved to be too much work. My arm was bruised and burning.

"She's awake!" Quinn was at my side first, holding my hand. He was paler than usual, nearly gray. The blue of his eyes was paler, the shadows underneath darker. "You scared the hell out of me." He kissed my forehead.

"You're alive."

"So to speak."

"Am I . . . am I a vampire?"

"No, you're just a stubborn know-it-all who thinks she can do everything by herself," he answered tenderly. "You didn't drink my blood, remember?"

"Don't hog her," Chloe said, brushing him aside with a grin. He leaned over enough to let her in but didn't let go of my hand. Jenna and Jason and Kieran stood on my other side.

"What happened?" I asked. My throat felt singed. I reached for some water and Quinn grabbed the cup so quickly he spilled half of it down his arm and into my hair. I drank the rest gratefully, greedily.

"You've been out for two days. You had to have blood transfusions," he explained.

"Are you okay?" I asked.

"I was sick as a dog there for a while, but I'm fine."

"Dailey?" I asked.

"Under house arrest until you're well enough to testify against her," Kieran answered. "Don't worry about it now."

"She tried to kill me," I said, affronted. "And Quinn. And she poisoned Will and the others."

"Hart's handling it personally," Kieran assured me.

"Bellwood's furious," Chloe added cheerfully. "It's like the stick up her butt caught fire!"

"Dailey's not going anywhere," Kieran added.

"Damn right she's not," I muttered. I patted myself down, searching for my left cargo pocket but finding only a paper hospital gown. I craned my neck. "Where are my pants?"

"Your stuff's here." Chloe plucked up my pile of clothes from a shelf behind me. She dropped the pants on my lap. I smiled even though it cracked my dry lips. I pulled a microphone out of the pocket.

"I recorded everything she said," I told them smugly. The effort made me cough. "It was meant for York. I guess I owe him an apology."

"He doesn't have to know we ever suspected him," Chloe protested. "He's been a jerk to you. And he yelled at me in class just this morning." She frowned. "He freaked Mom out in my report card last year. He said the usual stuff about me not living up to my potential, but since she'd just heard about the TH, she kind of panicked. She hadn't figured out who was in charge of it, so she snuck me those steroids, just in case. To make sure I was off the TH radar. She was trying to protect me in her own weird way. Mothers."

"Anyway, don't worry about that stuff." Jason patted my hand. "Just get better."

"She'll get better as soon as you all get to class," Theo interrupted, elbowing them aside.

"Wait," Jenna said, eyes glowing. "One more thing."

She and Jason shifted over. Spencer grinned weakly at me from the next bed. His dreads spread out over his pillow.

"Spence!" I squealed. "I would so hug you right now if my head didn't weigh seven hundred pounds."

"Ditto."

"You're better! You're out of quarantine!"

"Also, a vampire."

I tried to sit up. The room wobbled. I lay back down with a thump. "*What?*"

"Turns out your Quinn here accidentally discovered the antidote to TH in humans," Theo said. "Vampire blood."

"Okay, I haven't been in chem or bio class in a while but ... huh?"

"Spencer got a transfusion too," Theo explained. "For one thing, Will transmitted some of the TH poison to Spencer, and we had to get that right out of him. That's what was stumping us—before Quinn's help. If he hadn't sucked it out of your veins, we might not have done enough transfusions with Spencer. Even so, the medications didn't cure his *Hel-Blar* infection. We had to give him even more blood so he wouldn't go feral. The doctor might get an award for that, actually. If she doesn't get kicked out of the League for technically creating a vampire, that is."

"I guess that means I graduate early," Spencer said.

"I'm just glad you're okay."

Theo cleared his throat menacingly. Chloe, Jenna, and Jason left but Quinn and Kieran stayed behind. Theo took my pulse and had me follow his flashlight with my eyes.

"Looking much better. How are you feeling?"

"Like a truck hit me and a bear ate my arm." My stomach growled. "And I think I'm starving."

"That's what I like to hear. I'll get some food sent over." He eyed Quinn and Kieran malevolently. "Five more minutes and you both get lost. Don't make me tell you again." He smiled at me. "Doctor will be in to check on you soon."

"They're talking about giving you a medal." Kieran grinned.

I winced. "No, thanks."

"You'll at least be the valedictorian."

I saw some daisies in a basket on the side table. "Who are those from?"

"Your grandpa," Kieran replied. "He's a stubborn know-it-all too."

"Is he here?"

He shook his head. "He won't come, Hunter."

I swallowed, trying not to let my lips wobble. "He's still mad."

"I'll talk to him," Quinn offered.

"No!" Kieran and I burst out together.

"He'll just try and stake you," I explained apologetically. "You can't rush him."

Theo glowered from the doorway. "Out!"

Quinn kissed me lightly. "I'll be back tomorrow night."

Spencer and I were left alone with the ticking and beeping of the machines and the tubes pushing liquid nutrients and medications into our bodies. There was enough blood being fed into Spencer via those tubes that I wasn't in danger, not the way I would have been if I'd been lying around with any other newly turned vampire. He touched his fangs and then jerked his hand away.

"Vampires are in now," I said quietly. "Don't you read? All the girls will be hot for you."

He tried to smile. "And I don't have to study for any exams this year like the rest of you. I guess I'm officially a dropout now."

"Oh, Spencer. It'll be okay. Things are changing."

"Yeah, I leave you alone for a week and you start making out with vampires."

"I told you," I teased, making my voice bubbly and high. "They're like totally trendy!"

"Dude."

"But you can't hide away and brood and go all melancholy. That's so yesterday. Plus, I'll kick your ass."

After a long moment he spoke again. "I'm going to miss the sun."

"I know." I turned my head. "We'd miss you more if you were dead."

He scrubbed a hand over his face. "Thanks."

"Besides, just think, now you can go hang out with the Hounds and ask them all sorts of magic questions."

He brightened instantly. "True."

I shot him a watery grin when Theo wheeled my supper tray in. "And I don't have to share my chocolate pudding with you ever again."

◆

Spencer was discharged the next night.

I didn't know where he'd gone, but Quinn promised to help him with the transition to his new undead life. I wasn't allowed to leave the infirmary for a full week, and even then it was only after promising that I'd take it easy and wouldn't even look at the gym for at least two more weeks—and then only with a doctor's permission. The doctor whom Grandpa would still talk to since he refused to talk to me. I'd called him twice and each time the conversation was the same.

"Are you still seeing him?

"Yes."

And then he'd hang up on me.

But I wouldn't let that ruin everything else. I was alive. Quinn was alive. Spencer was . . . a vampire but at least he wasn't completely dead. Savannah and the twins were recovering, though slowly. Dailey was being held by the League disciplinary committee pending a full investigation. And Hart had called me personally to invite me to form a Black Lodge of carefully selected students, apparently the first at the school in at least three decades. It was a subgroup within the League that no one knew about except its members and the head of the Helios-Ra. None of the teachers even knew, except for the headmistress. We'd be like a secret roving band of spy-warriors. I couldn't wait.

"Now, that's a dangerous smile," Quinn murmured, his voice tickling my ear. His arms wrapped around my waist and pulled me back against his chest. I leaned into him, my smile turning even more wicked.

"What are we doing out here?" I asked. I'd gotten a text to meet him out by the pond.

"Same thing I'm always doing: trying to get a proper date out of you."

"Who knew you were so traditional?" I turned, teasing.

"Who knew you were such a rebel?" He slid his arm lightly over my bandage and clasped my hand. The stitches from his bite would come out tomorrow. There'd be a scar, but I didn't mind so much. He tugged me through the field, tall grass brushing against my knees.

He led me into a copse of birch saplings. He'd spread a blanket on the ground and lit candles in glass jam jars. He even hung a few lanterns from the branches and they hovered like fireflies. It was beautiful.

"We're having a picnic," he announced.

"But you don't eat."

He shrugged. "But you do."

We sat down and he handed me a thermos of hot chocolate. There were baskets of chocolate chip cookies, a cherry-chocolate cake, sugar-dusted strawberries, and a tower of macaroons.

I grinned. "Finally, real food."

I ate until the sugar buzzed through my veins. Quinn lounged beside me, the candles pouring honey light over his pale cheekbones. He licked chocolate frosting off my finger, grinning darkly. He was everything my grandfather feared: reckless, wild, predatory.

And he was mine.

ALYXANDRA HARVEY studied creative writing and literature at York University and has had her poetry published in magazines. She likes medieval dresses and tattoos and has been accused of being born in the wrong century—except that she really likes running water, women's rights, and ice cream. Alyx lives in an old Victorian farmhouse in Ontario, Canada, with her husband, three dogs, and a few resident ghosts.

www.alyxandraharvey.com
www.thedrakechronicles.com

**Don't miss
the next installment in
The Drake Chronicles,
coming soon!**

by
ALYXANDRA HARVEY